A WEAPON OF MAGICAL DESTRUCTION

AGENTS OF A.S.S.E.T.
BOOK ONE

KATIE SALIDAS

The world is full of magical creatures and artifacts. That's where the A.S.S.E.T. agency comes in: Anonymous Supernatural Security and Elimination Taskforce.

The front line, maintaining the balance of power, ensuring humans remain safely oblivious to the dangerous magic around them.

Acknowledgments

This book was a product of tough love, and I want to thank the team of readers who really put me through my paces. Anne Loshuk, Jacob Devlin, & J.E. Taylor!

Thank you for going over multiple drafts, giving me all of your honest feedback, and really paying attention to the small details. You're honesty and critical eye have shaped this story into something special.

Beyond the critical, thank you as well for the enthusiasm you've had for this book series. You guys jumped on this project the moment I announced it and devoured each section faster than I could produce them. The late night chats, encouragement, & feedback was just the encouragement I needed to keep this project moving, even when I felt it was all for naught.

And last but not least, thank you to my readers!
You are the reason I keep writing!

ONE

"It's not a tattoo, it's a birthmark," Sage Cynwrig insisted as a pair of curious eyes landed on her deformity.

The eyes were always first. Then came the questions. A cycle that repeated with every new person she met. Tattoos were cool, but the hideous way her misshapen veins splayed out in all directions, like broken tree branches, underneath the pale skin of her wrist was far from beautiful, and definitely not intentional. The disfigurement she shared with her mother looked like a toddler had attacked her with a permanent marker.

Why did people have to be so nosy?

"You going to charge me?" Sage waved her credit card to be swiped, hoping the cabbie might find something else to focus on. Discussing her embarrassing deformity ranked alongside jury duty or paying taxes as far as she was concerned, and yet everyone she met seemed to find it a fascination.

"You want a receipt?" The driver's tone held more curiosity than his question deserved. His gaze lingered on her wrist, and she could see the wheels turning in the cabbie's bald head as he silently tried to figure out the strange design.

"No." Sage snatched her card back and exited the cab with her bag.

Outside, the summer winds blasted Sage in the face with the force of a blow dryer on high. Her long hair took to the breeze, attacking her eyes like a cat-o'-nine-tails. She made quick work of taming the whips into a messy bun on top of her head and wiped the tears and grit from her eyes.

Summer, even for desert rats like herself, was a special kind of hell.

It's a dry heat. That's what the locals always say. As if that somehow made it a benefit. Wet or dry, the heat was uncomfortable and anything hitting triple digits was oppressive. Something the city of Phoenix was famous for.

And with that dry heat came sweat, sandblasted in the wind and flash-burned to her skin the instant she stepped outside. It didn't matter that she'd taken a shower that day. She could have taken one in the damn cab for all it was worth. All that effort to make herself clean and presentable was wasted.

Deodorant—no matter how bad the hippies claimed—was a necessity, though Sage doubted it would help her much. L'eau de baked-on toxins was the perfume of the day, and it was leeching from her pores. Clinical strength deodorant didn't stand a chance today.

So much for making a good impression.

A white ten-story building stood before her. Sage had passed through its doors hundreds of times, but now the thought of crossing the threshold caused a lump to form in her throat.

She should have said no when the call came.

A stronger woman would have.

Sage never belonged here. The ASSET Agency was her mother's domain.

Miranda Cynwrig was the epitome of strength and courage, and she never did anything she didn't want to.

Genes she'd failed to pass down to her one and only daughter.

Sage needed her mother more than ever. She looked at her wrist, to the birthmark they shared. Tracing the haphazard pattern with the tip of her finger and remembered her how her mother would tell her to wear it with pride, like a badge of honor.

With a sobering sigh, Sage resigned herself to getting the job done.

Automatic doors parted, welcoming her into a brightly lit reception area. The entire bottom level of the office was bathed in natural light. Glass panels that separated the office walls and conference rooms allowed unobstructed light to flood in from all angles. Architecture aimed at making the place seem as welcoming as it was revealing. It offered a sense of truth to any who came to deal with the agency.

Large LED screens behind the reception desk played silent advertisements for the various security services the company provided.

Anonymous
Strategic
Security
Elimination
Taskforce

The world's leader in specialty security and weapons.

Because of her close ties to Mark Sorenson, Director of Operations of the Phoenix office, Sage had been offered a job numerous times during her high school and college years. She never took him up on it, though. Sage couldn't see herself working with her mom. She was no warrior. Granted, she did count herself among the highest order of Elven Mages, but that was only on game nights. In the real world, dollars made much more sense to her than the intricacies of blades and their balance.

Miranda Cynwrig's image flashed on one of the screens, and eyes like turquoise sea-glass winked at Sage.

The weight of sadness pressed down on her shoulders. Sage choked on her breath, desperate to fill lungs that refused to accept air. The ache in her heart grew with each passing moment, as if a thousand tiny blades were cutting it into ribbons.

Her knees buckled, and she reached out a hand to steady herself against the reception desk.

Try as she might, Sage couldn't tear her eyes away from the image of her mother on the television. Bright red hair woven into a warrior's braid swung around Miranda like a whip as she demonstrated various uses for their latest line of tactical blades, all of which played out with a devastatingly crisp high-definition.

A weapons expert and one of the most gorgeous women Sage had ever known. Her mother was a true superhero who deserved a better fate than had been handed to her.

The news reported nothing of the crash. It had been Mark who'd called and delivered the message when her mother's plane went down in the Atlantic Ocean.

"I'm so sorry, Sage." Mark Sorenson's voice filled the air as he sprang from the glass-enclosed conference room. Surprisingly spry for a man of his age, he crossed the room at a fast clip, making it to the reception desk before Sage could acknowledge him.

"We weren't expecting you yet. The car I sent was supposed to radio in when they picked you up." Dark wavy hair and a full beard masked Mark's expression, but there was no mistaking the sorrow in his voice. He snatched the remote from the reception desk. "We're working on changing these ads. I should have had them taken down as soon as…" His words trailed off as he met Sage's watering eyes.

"Let's just get this over with, please." She forced the words past the burn in her throat and tried to put on a brave face.

"Of course." It was clear from the furrow of Mark's brow that he'd been dealing with his own emotions, though he had much more practice wearing the mask. "I have her personal items boxed up for you. We can have them loaded in your car when we're done."

"I came in a taxi." She hadn't meant to sound so snippy, but the effort it took to hold back her tears left little room for anything else. Mark wasn't her enemy, but he'd been the messenger, forcing her to deal with emotions far beyond her capabilities. Parents weren't supposed to die. Not this early. She wasn't ready for life without her personal superhero.

"Always so stubborn." His demeanor shifted in response to her tone. He'd always been a father figure to her, and he knew exactly how and when to employ the Dad voice to make his point clear. "You're going to let me help you with this. I'll have one of our cars help you back to the house. We've already begun packing things for storage there."

"I shouldn't have come," she whispered under her breath.

"I'm glad you did." He waved a hand toward the conference room. "Missed you, kiddo."

"It's been a while," she replied mechanically as her eyes settled on the two bankers boxes bearing her mother's name.

"I've settled as much of Miranda's affairs as I legally can." Switching hats, he'd taken on a businesslike tone that carried all the emotional weight of a feather, discussing paperwork as if it were simply work rather than the end-of-life arrangements of his longest-term employee. But all it took was a quick glance up to his face, and Sage saw the truth glistening there at the corners of his pale turquoise eyes. "But you're going to have some documents to sign as the next of kin."

"Let's just get this over with." It was all she could say without breaking down.

"I'm so sorry." Mark pulled her into a bear hug, as if he sensed the grief clawing at her insides. "We all miss her. She was the finest agent we've ever had."

Sage wouldn't admit it out loud—not that she was capable of words at that moment—but she needed that human connection. Tears were falling again, trickling down her face one by one. How she could still have so many to shed? Still, they came, and she let them fall. This was infinitely harder than she could have imagined.

"Need a tissue?" He crossed the room, grabbed a box, and pulled one to offer her.

Mark's gaze followed her hand as she took the tissue and brought it up to her nose.

She caught a flicker of something unfamiliar in his gaze. It was as if he saw her birthmark for the first time.

"I... uh... need to step outside for a moment," Mark stumbled backward as he tried to excuse himself. "Need to get the documents for signature." His eyes were wide, but they weren't looking at Sage's face. As Mark backed away, his eyes remained fixed on her wrist. Almost as if what he had seen frightened him. "Be right back."

He slipped from the door and left Sage standing alone in the room, grappling with unanswered questions. He'd seen her birthmark thousands of times. Why did the look in his eyes match that of people seeing her deformity for the first time? What was it about her birthmark that spooked him?

TWO

Two minutes turned into five as she paced around the table, trying to ignore the boxes. The weight of all her tears tugged at her eyes. Headaches always followed a good ugly cry, and she didn't need a mirror to tell her how puffy and swollen her face was.

Ten minutes passed with no word from Mark. He'd been acting so weird as he left. She debated going to find him in his office, but the throbbing pain behind her temples convinced her to stay put.

She collapsed into one of the chairs around the table, closing her eyes as a wave of nausea overtook her. The room blurred around her and the murky despair of ASSET's conference room faded into darkness.

Sage drifted from reality and found herself standing atop a hill as fireworks exploded above, showering her in a rainbow of glittering specks.

This was just like the Fourth of July fireworks shows her mother used to take her to every year. But her mother was gone now, and the realization brought a wave of sadness crashing over Sage once again.

Sage followed the glittering trail of the last explosion as it faded down to the earth, expecting to see families lying on blankets and grills filled with burgers and hotdogs. Instead of children's gleeful expressions, gruesomely disfigured bodies piled up amidst a raging battlefield.

Air escaped from her lungs in a shriek and refused to return. Frozen where she stood, her heart thundered against her ribcage as if it was trying to punch a hole through her chest and escape.

Electricity sparked in the turbulent atmosphere above. Lightning snapped through the cloudless sky and pierced the earth below, blasting a charred crater in its wake.

Her initial shock morphed into fear, as war cries in languages Sage had never heard before rang out around her.

A stranger in an even stranger land, Sage didn't know whether running or hiding were viable options. Fighting armies clashed against each other everywhere she looked. Even if she could run, where could she go?

On a hill to her left, cavalries of beast riders mowed down warriors carrying shields of soft, silvery light. They marched into what might have once been a beautiful meadow ringed with distant mountains. But ravaged by war, the gentle carpet of grass had been burned away, leaving dry, crumbling earth. Once-proud mountains were shattered into skeletons of their former glory, leaving little more than gnarled fingers of rock jutting up from the ground to grasp at the stars. This world looked so much like Earth, but felt primordial.

Stranger still, these armies fought with magic, a thing of fantasy in her world. Sage had to be dreaming. Lucid as she was, this felt too much like her weekly game night raiding party, though far more realistic than role-playing with wooden swords and casting spells with made-up words.

It had to be a dream, and that thought calmed her racing heart. She found her breath and tried to let herself experience the world her imagination summoned.

Sage recognized the mighty centaurs charging into battle. Their enemies were equally familiar creatures from the supernatural realm, werewolves. Men morphed mid-stride into great snarling wolves the size of baby elephants as they met the oncoming charge from the centaurs.

In the distance, cresting the top of a shattered hill, an entire army of grey-skinned foot soldiers marched into view. Each of the giants—or maybe they were trolls—carried weapons she'd never seen before. Guns with numerous gaping barrels. Blasters of corruption, she named them, thinking they'd be handy in her next dungeon raid.

As if conjured from the very air, the giant trolls swung their arms forward, and from the mouths of their oddly shaped artillery sent a volley of glittering death raining down on the cavalry approaching them.

No banners. No sigils. Nothing distinguished the fighting camps from each other. Just magic and death. When a body fell, they tossed aside it to make way for the next soldier as the army continued its march.

Magic and death.

The words formed and took root within her mind moments before a cloaked figure in blue blinked into existence.

Sage shrank backward, shock kicking her heart into overdrive. At this pace, her chest threatened to burst like the magical fireworks still blooming overhead. A moment of silence sent terror trembling up Sage's spine. Anxiety had her strung tight as a bowstring and Sage struggled to get a grip and maintain composure. The cloaked figure exuded a confidence that needed no words. Beyond the darkness of the cloaked figure's hood, there were eyes scrutinizing Sage, assessing whether she was worthy.

Sage opened her mouth, not quite knowing what to say. *Peace? Friendship? Surrender?*

Anything to avoid her body being piled with the rest.

Before any sound could leave Sage's throat, the cloaked figure extended a pair of blue hands. A ball of energetic light flickered between blue palms and grew into an electrified sphere.

Amazement held Sage in stunned silence. Magic. Real. And happening right before her eyes.

The electric sphere glowed blue and then white before the cloaked figure threw it at Sage's feet.

Sage jerked back as the explosive burst singed blades of grass to fine ash.

Why? The question hung in her mind, but her lips trembled too much to ask it.

Blood. Death. Destruction. Sage heard the words form in her mother's voice, as if whispering in her ear. *The result of war fought with magic.*

A raspy laugh emerged from within the cloaked figure's hood, a sound that sent chills down Sage's spine. It pulled back its hood, revealing shimmering eyes. Not red like she expected for all the raw fury they emitted, but a mesmerizing deep blue with subtle shimmers of purple.

How could something so beautiful be so deadly?

Gone were Sage's initial feelings of awe. She'd have given anything to return to her safe and mundane home, where the only crazy things that happened were on game night.

Another sizzling softball-sized charge hit the ground at her feet, making Sage stumble back another step.

The creature was toying with her, prolonging the moment of her death for when it suited the creature best.

Should she run? Live to fight another day? Sage's subconscious screamed for her to do something, but could she outrun magic?

Across the wasteland, another arc of lightning appeared from the cloudless sky, splintering into three branches before striking the ground below.

Miranda Cynwrig appeared, standing underneath the deadly trio of ethereal energy. Long red hair braided over her left shoulder. Sage's personal superhero.

In her mother's hands were twin daggers, held ready to fight. The only thing missing was a cape, flapping in the wind behind her.

No matter how bad things looked, Mom would save her.

In the distance, Miranda opened her mouth, but no sound made its way to Sage's ears.

Another strike caught Sage unawares, pushing her back another step. Four, maybe five more, and she would fall.

"Stop. Please!" Sage screamed. "Why are you doing this?"

Her plea was met with another explosive energy ball aimed at her feet. Sage looked desperately toward her mother, but Miranda had vanished, just like magic.

I'm dreaming. This is only a dream! Wake up!

Sage pinched herself, but that didn't rouse her. She had to escape this world before it ended her. If you die in a dream, you die in real life. That was the story she'd always heard. And damned if she was going to die in fantasyland. Sage tried again, pinching herself hard enough to send her nail through her skin. Her eyes watered, and she squealed from the pain, but it wasn't enough to send her back to the real waking world.

Another strike nearly took out her foot. Sage jumped backward instinctively, without looking where she was heading, and teetered on the edge of the world. Windmilling her hands as fast as she could, she threw her weight forward. Heart racing, she crashed and pawed at the ground. Desperate not to fall, Sage dug her nails into the burnt, black dirt, clinging to the earth for dear life, all the while praying to any gods that might listen to get her out of this.

She allowed herself a peek over the edge. Emptiness ran further down than she could see. Nothing but the blackest of black.

Another strike of energy hit just shy of her fingers, and the sting of its errant electricity tore a cry from her throat.

She had nowhere to go. If she fell, she'd surely die. But if the creature's energy struck her, she'd surely die.

Face your enemy. Show them no fear. Sage's mother whispered the words inside her mind, urging her to be strong.

She looked up, expecting to see the sapphire eyes of her killer. "Do it!"

Miranda's face came into view, bathed in the brightest of white light. Sage could barely make out her features, but intuition filled in the gaps where her sight failed.

A smile. A promise. A flash of that brilliant light enveloped them both. It all happened so quickly. Tingling waves, like tiny pinpricks of static electricity, crawled harmlessly over her skin.

Splayed out on the mangled earth, Sage was conscious of the fact something had struck her, but death hadn't come to claim her. Nor had she returned to reality.

The tiny charges of electricity left their warm fingerprints all over, and her skin drank in the heat. Light wrapped around her with all the physical strength of her mother's arms, lifting and embracing Sage in a loving hug she didn't realize she needed and prayed would never end.

Words echoed in her mind, in her mother's voice. I am with you, always.

Miranda's light flickered, dimming as it merged with Sage. She couldn't stop it or break free from her mother's fading embrace. Drinking it all in, Sage's body pulled in the essence of her mother's fading spirit, giving it permanent residence within her heart.

Miranda had gone, leaving only a small ember of white light floating in midair.

Magic and death. The words echoed again as tears streamed down Sage's face.

She reached a hand toward the tiny speck, not wanting to let go of her mom. She couldn't reason why, but this meeting felt like a true goodbye.

The ember touched down on her wrist with a kiss that burned like wildfire. Sage hissed as her skin singed, and the ember branded a tree into the spot where it landed. Magically twisting branches expanded into a glorious canopy on top, and then below, straggling roots dug deeply into her veins, tapping into the red of her blood to color the mark.

Sage's scream pierced the air, but it was not her own voice that echoed back at her. Instead, a man's chilling call of her name reverberated through the desolate landscape. It was a voice she knew, but distorted by distance. Hollow, like a whisper from beyond the grave.

Pain riveted her eyes to the markings that were etching into her skin. Around the canopy of twisting tree branches, leaves appeared in a semi-circle, crowning the great tree. Once all had been formed, the light and heat faded into memory, leaving only the branding of that tree as a reminder.

The man's voice called out again, louder and more urgent this time.

Sage looked up to find herself standing on an empty battlefield, with only the towering tree mirroring the one on her wrist for company. Its size was incomprehensible, making her step back in awe and terror.

Gone were all traces of the previous battles, replaced by a lush valley and a blinding sun shining through the tree's canopy. A part of Sage longed to stay and explore this strange new world, but the relentless cries for her attention on the wind demanded otherwise.

With each repetition of her name, the voice grew louder and more commanding until it became a deafening roar in her mind. "Speak to me, Sage!" it commanded.

"Who are you?" Trembling and disoriented, Sage shout back despite the pain throbbing in her head. But even as she closed her eyes and covered her ears, there was no escape from the booming voice demanding attention in her mind. "Why are you doing this to me?"

THREE

Sage's eyes opened to a bright, white light that stung her vision. Blinking rapidly, she saw Mark's worried face hovering above her.

"What happened?" Sage asked, trying to shake off the grogginess as she pushed herself to sit.

"Looks like you took a little tumble while I was out," Mark said, his expression etched with concern as he helped her up from the floor and back into the chair. "You had me worried there, kiddo."

"I had the worst headache. Must have dozed off." Sage struggled to separate the dream from reality. She rubbed her wrist absentmindedly, feeling the faint ache of the brand that had been seared onto her skin, and noticed Mark watching her closely as she scratched at it. "Could I have some water? Please."

"Sure." His pale turquoise eyes searched hers as he backed out of the room. "I'll be right back."

She looked down at her wrist, which itched like a healing wound. The mangled veins appeared less haphazard now, taking on more of a tree-like appearance, just as in the dream. But now, she noticed something else. A freckle, maybe. Sunspot was probably the proper term.

A quarter of an inch above her birthmark, a speck had appeared. Shaped like an elongated heart, it looked like a leaf at the top of her tree-like branches.

Her mother had had spots surrounding her birthmark as well. Maybe that was why Mark had seemed so interested. Heredity was catching up to her. She was becoming like her mother. At least, as far as the deformity was concerned.

Mark returned quickly this time, carrying bottles and a stack of papers so high Sage's hand cramped at the thought of having to sign them all.

"After you're done signing these, let's grab some dinner." He sounded as if he was delivering an edict, but food was the last thing she could think of.

"Really, I just want to get this over with and go home… to Vegas." She clarified the destination, knowing that at some point he'd ask if she were going to come back and live in her mother's old home.

He sighed with obvious disappointment and took out a handkerchief to mop the sweat on his brow. She'd never noticed before that he wore a large watch on his left arm, the band more a cuff of leather than a traditional strap. Branded into the leather was a tree. Not a mangled or misshapen mess, like the deformity on her wrist. This one looked like an old Irish knot, with a canopy above and a small root system below. A sigil of some great house or maybe part of a clansmen crest, she wondered. But those things belonged in her Thursday-night gaming group, not in the real world. Though it had not escaped her that the symbol was very similar to the markings both she and her mother shared. Perhaps it was his way of paying homage to her family.

"I'll leave you to it, then." He caught her curious gaze and pulled his arm behind his back as he slowly retreated from the room. "If you need anything, you know where to find me."

Mark was acting strange. The suspicious way he kept looking at her birthmark couldn't be ignored. He'd known her since she was a child. She hadn't changed, but the way he looked at her certainly had.

She'd have to get to the bottom of that mystery later. The mountain of papers he'd left her would take hours to work through. She set herself to reading and signing documents she barely understood. Legalese was a language she didn't speak. By the time she'd made it to the end of the stack, she'd stopped trying to make sense of everything. She scrawled her name where the little *sign here* sticker had been placed and moved on.

The sun had long since departed, and her stomach growled with the need for food.

Mark returned to clear away the final papers, looking as if he'd spent the day battling wargs and ogres. He collapsed onto the seat next to her. "Please, let me at least feed you before you disappear again."

The defeated tone in his voice, coupled with the heavy bags weighing down his eyes, said he needed the company a little more than she might. How could she refuse?

"I've got an early flight out tomorrow, so let's make it a quick dinner." As she said the words, Sage saw the light return to his eyes. But knowing where the conversation was going to go, she finished with, "I still haven't been by the house yet, so I can't be tied up all night."

"How about this?" Mark stood and held out a hand. "Pick your favorite takeout, and we'll bring it to the house to eat."

She noticed it again—the strange watch he was wearing with the intricate tree branded into the leather. It was just the kind of thing she could wear to cover her deformity. It was still a strange choice for him to wear, though. "I could go for some Chopsticks." She kept the conversation going as her eyes lingered on his leather cuff. "Might be the last time I ever have their House Chicken."

She hadn't yet taken his offered hand, but before she could, Mark pulled it back. "Your wish is my command. Let me just grab my briefcase." He rushed from the room, as if desperate to escape.

Scurrying off seemed to be the theme of the day. Then again, she was not herself either. Wrestling with the feelings of depression over the loss of her mother made her want to run screaming from the building with every reminder of the woman she'd never see again. She'd taken for granted the notion that Mom was a fixture in her life. Her personal superhero. She might have moved away and begun her own path, but the anchor of home and family had given her security.

That was over now, and each moment amplified the emptiness of being truly on her own.

Through the glass-paneled walls of the conference room, Sage watched the comings and goings in the main lobby. Twenty-four-hour operations ran on layered shifts, and employees were wandering in and out of the front door and attached offices. Some people looked fresh-faced as they headed for the elevator banks, while others dragged their feet, heading toward the exit.

She welcomed the monotony she'd be returning to when she got home. Idleness made the anguish all that much more unbearable.

Out of the corner of her eye, she spotted a child walking alone from the elevator bank behind the receptionist's desk. At first, she thought it might have been an elaborate costume. Large brown ears protruded from the side of his head, and a green nose jutted out sharply like the beak of a bird. His little goblin face, pocked by warts and moles, had dark wiry hairs sticking out in patches around his cheeks and chin. These were details she didn't normally see in store-bought kids' costumes. This was the kind of thing that could win contests at a comic convention or fantasy festival.

What was a kid doing wandering around alone in the lobby? And why the elaborate disguise? It was too early for Halloween. Sage did a double take, blinking away the weariness from her eyes.

On second glance, the child had gone, and in his place stood a man, shorter in stature than most, but definitely not a child. A green ball cap sat on top of his head and balanced on his shoulder was a long poster tube.

She blinked again and tried to shake away the fog of exhaustion as she gave the man one last look. Normal skin. Normal guy.

A mind fed by weekly role-playing games and a steady stream of sci-fi fandom had given her an imagination that could easily conjure up goblins. A dangerous combination when coupled with mental strain and lack of good sleep. Sage allowed herself a moment to laugh, imagining goblin kids wandering the hallways at ASSET.

Mark returned, looking much more at ease than when he'd left. "Sorry. Last-minute schedule change. Got a whole new batch of recruits, and they… ah, well, you don't need details. Let's go."

If he'd arrived a few minutes later, she'd have planned an excuse to leave, but seeing the renewed eagerness in his smile, there would be no escaping dinner. She followed him out to the car.

"I'll have my boys send out your boxes tomorrow. Delivery to your apartment in Vegas, right?" He unlocked the old green Jeep Wrangler.

"Still have the beast?" She smiled at the caked-on mud by the tires and the thin layer of dust coating the body. With a quick swipe of her fingers, she wrote *Wash me* on a rear panel and giggled at her private joke as she climbed into the passenger seat. As far back as she could remember, that beast was always covered in some form of desert. And if Mark ever dared to wash her, a haboob would blow through and give the Jeep in a fresh layer of mud and dust.

"Never getting rid of this beauty." Mark patted the side of his beloved car.

Most high-level executives drove luxury vehicles, but Mark had only ever driven this Jeep, as far as she knew. Being in it again brought back fond memories of learning to drive out in the desert. Nothing like having a roll cage and being set high above everyone else to give you a sense of security when you're a newbie at the wheel, especially when off-roading.

The sweet memories lightened her mood, and she strapped in and patted the car door lovingly.

"You want to drive?"

Sage shook her head. "I'll just enjoy the ride."

"Nostalgia?" He chuckled.

"A bit, yeah. There are still some good memories here."

"Speaking of… you didn't answer. You want those boxes shipped to Vegas?"

He had to sour the moment with reality, didn't he? She grimaced, but kept her voice neutral. "Might as well put them in storage. I'm not ready to look inside."

"Of course. We have a storage unit for all the things you just want to leave." His tone sounded like an attempt at being upbeat, but Mark failed to invoke any enthusiasm.

It was clear that he wanted her to have some reasons to come back, and Sage dreaded the next step in that inevitable conversation.

"Thanks," she sighed.

"And you know… if you want to move back…"

There it was. The offer to stay. The suggestion to work with him would follow. The answer was no, but saying it so bluntly would be like smacking him in the face for all he'd done for her family, and he was still doing to help her through this rough period. "I'm not selling Mom's home, but I just can't consider moving back right now. The pain is too raw."

"You know I think of you as a daughter, right?" Mark nodded, pulling his face into pleasantly neutral expression. "I take it as my personal duty to ensure you're protected."

"I know you do. And I appreciate it." Trapped in the car, there was no way to escape this conversation. She turned, looking into the parking lot for anything to distract her or a reason to change the subject.

"So, should you ever consider it? I have a job waiting for you here at ASSET." Mark started up the old Jeep, and she roared like a monster, ready for the kill. "I'll say no more. Okay?"

Sage spotted the space where her mom had always parked. She hadn't been gone long, but her name had already been wiped from the curb.

A flash of light caught her attention. A group of agents wearing black uniforms walked toward the back entrance of the building. Between them, a wild man in restraints thrashed while speaking in a language she couldn't understand. Flashes of blue light arced out from the wild man's hands as if he were conjuring bolts of lightning from thin air. But none of the men holding him seemed to notice or care. Even when those streams of light struck their bodies, they didn't so much as flinch.

"What the heck is that?" Was her mind playing tricks on her again, like back in the lobby?

"Looks like the boys are bringing in someone for interrogation," Mark replied casually. "Business as usual."

"But did you see the zaps? It was like…" She couldn't finish the sentence without feeling silly.

Mark turned to her. "Streetlights reflecting off the handcuffs, probably."

"That didn't look like streetlights reflecting off of anything. It was…" She wanted to say *magic,* but the word stuck in her throat.

"Like what?" Mark hung on her response with more interest than he'd had in conversation all day. "Magic?"

"I guess." She feigned disbelief with a shrug. "For lack of a better word." Thank goodness he'd said it, and not her. "Or maybe a Taser gun."

"If it was a Taser, someone would be on the floor twitching." Mark joked as he put the car in gear.

The alternative sounded just as laughable. Magic. Maybe in the dreamland she'd visited during her nap. She'd seen some fascinating uses of magic there. But this was the real world, where magic didn't exist.

She looked again, but the group had already disappeared into the building. That was no reflection, nor had it been a Taser. She wasn't buying Mark's casual dismissal of it. He was the director of operations. The kind of guy who knew everything that was going on at ASSET. If she had to venture a guess, ASSET had some pretty neat weaponry that the public had not yet seen. Maybe something so unique and powerful it had rival companies trying to get their hands on it. And that made her wonder if her mother had been caught up in more than just a simple plane crash. Maybe that was why Mark was acting so weird and talking about her protection. Was he guilty of causing Miranda's death in some way?

"You sure I can't convince you to come work for me?" Mark broke the silence with another attempt to make her stay.

The answer was no, but Sage couldn't bring herself to say the words aloud, especially when her mind was still analyzing the possibilities of what might be going on there.

FOUR

"Achievement unlocked!" Sage triumphantly announced as she opened the door to her apartment. "Matty, I have survived my quest to the homeland and return relatively unscathed by the adventure."

"What loot did you bring me?" Matthew Donovan stalked toward the kitchen, stopping a few feet away from the door. His bulky six-foot-three frame blocked her passage further into the apartment. Arms crossed, he glared down, awaiting payment for safe passage.

"I come bearing gifts of tiny foil-packed food items from the sky kingdom." She smirked, holding up a handful of airplane snacks.

He laughed. "You're such a dork." Crossing the small distance between them, Matt pulled her into a bear hug, lifting Sage off the ground as he crushed the air from her lungs. "Seriously, though. How are you holding up?"

"Can't breathe." She feigned, gasping for air. "Dying. Dead." Sage went limp in his arms. "My spirit is leaving this realm."

"Such a drama queen." He set her down and held the door open so she could bring in her luggage. "Seriously. I want to hear everything. Dish!"

Matt was the best kind of roommate Sage could hope for. Strong, nerdy, and—best of all—only interested in men. He was equal parts gossip and guru, and always there to listen and give advice.

"Thank the gods I have a sparring session tomorrow." Sage pulled her suitcase in and let it collapse on the linoleum floor.

"That bad, eh?" Matt's eyebrow arched sharply.

"So bad." Sage walked into the living room and flopped down on the microfiber sofa. "Mark looked like he was having a hard time dealing with Mom's loss, too. And the worst part. He offered me a job."

"Why?" Matt opened up the fridge and grabbed two beers. He twisted the bottle caps off as he walked over.

"We're as close as family, so he wants to make sure I'm taken care of, now that both my parents are…" She let the unspoken words float off into the air as she snatched hold of the beer Matt offered.

"I get that." He nodded thoughtfully. "But why in God's name would you work for the same company that killed your mom?"

"Damn dude! Drive that nail in harder, why don't you?" Sage snarled at him.

"Sorry, Hun. I'll retract the claws."

"Just a bit, please. The wounds are still bleeding." She took a long pull from her beer, but the minute she swallowed, she knew it wouldn't be strong enough to dull the pain. In fact, she'd done a lot of drinking on the plane and in the airport bar before takeoff, and couldn't remember being even slightly buzzed. Something was seriously wrong with her. And it had all started when she'd gotten that first call from Mark with the bad news.

"I'm just saying...he's kind of an idiot for thinking you'd ever take the job." Matt took a sip of his beer.

"But, his heart was in the right place." That point couldn't be argued. No matter what weirdness she'd seen back there in his office, Mark had made sure all the legalities were handled so she didn't have to fumble through them herself. That was one thing she'd been able to count on her entire life. Mark being there to help take care of things. He'd been the father she never had. "He had the house all packed up. He even lined up a storage unit for me to hold on to all of their things until I'm ready." Those last words hung in the air, a reminder of what Mark had said to her in the car. *When you're ready.* As if he expected her to change her mind.

"You should totally keep the house, though." Matt's suggestion brought her back into the conversation.

How long had she been lost in thought? "Rental?" She threw the word out without really giving it any thought.

"Yeah, and a vacation house, for when we want to get away from Sin City."

"It's going to be a very long time before I'm ready to go back." Would she ever be ready? No. If she were smart, she'd just sell the damn house and cut all ties. But those were thoughts she just wasn't ready to entertain at that time. What she needed was a distraction. Matt was normally good at cheering her up. But, like the beer she continued to sip, the conversation with Matt was doing nothing to make her forget her troubles.

"You'll go back, eventually. I'm not letting your mopey ass dwell forever."

"But I at least get a little time to dwell in goth-like darkness?"

"Oh, no, honey, you're never allowed to go Goth. Don't make me raid your closet." He waggled a finger at her before taking another pull from his beer.

That started a smile spreading across her face. "I could totally pull off a Morticia Addams, though, right?"

"Wednesday Addams, maybe." He rolled his eyes. "On a good day."

"Oooh, someone's going full diva today. When was the last time Josh came by? You need a serious dose of happy right about now."

"Says the girl in mourning." He arched an eyebrow at her that was every bit as fierce as the tone in his voice.

"Touché. So. Since we both need a dose of happy, and I don't have anything to punch till tomorrow for stress relief, how about we do the next best thing?"

A wickedly sharp smile stretched across his face. He dove for the television remote before Sage could reach it. "Mad Man with a Blue Box marathon?"

"Only if I get to pick the Doctor." She matched his fierce gaze, daring him to defy her.

"Rock. Paper. Scissors," he said calmly.

"My mother just died," she countered.

"Not fair, playing with emotions."

"When did I ever give you the impression I played fair?" Of the great battles waged throughout the centuries, this one continued to stir trouble between the sexes. It would keep raging on long after they were dead and turned to dust. But today, she would win control of the remote. Or die trying.

"But you always pick Ten," he whined, countering her defiant stare with puppy-dog eyes and a puffy lip.

"You evil little troll! No one can resist those baby blues. Put those away!" She huffed and made a show of turning away with an exaggerated shoulder slump of defeat as she deployed her secret weapon. "Whatever. It's fine."

Every man who's ever been in a relationship with a woman—platonic or not—knew the most deadly word in the female arsenal. *Fine* had a meaning all its own. Not something defined in any dictionary, but its power was undeniable. "Pick Eleven, then. I know you love him more," she added, with an extra dose of passive-aggressive spite.

"Ha! I win!" Matt pumped his fist in the air triumphantly, as if he'd missed what she'd said, or simply didn't care.

Not possible. She was a master of this game. She'd said the magic word. Sage sent a deadly glare back over her shoulder. Perhaps he needed her to repeat herself.

"But, because I'm the best roommate in the whole world," Matt laughed despite her anger, "I'm not going to pick Eleven this time. I will graciously give in to your desperate need of cheering up and watch the first season of Ten."

The most worthy of adversaries. He'd played her well and managed to come out looking like the champion. *Good game!* Matt was her soulmate in every way except physically. And it didn't hurt that he was drop-dead gorgeous, either. Why did all the really good ones have to be gay? All the man-candy she could take, but none of the calories. The ultimate forbidden fruit.

"And that's why I love you so much." She stood and headed for the kitchen, considering their battle of wills a tie. "I'll make the popcorn."

"Grab me another beer too, would ya, honey?"

"Sure thing, baby cakes." She giggled and reached into the fridge to grab one of the amber bottles and stopped short, knocking it onto the shelf as she noticed her wrist. At first, she thought too much sun had given her a freckle to go with the tree-like veins branching out under her skin, but now her eyes were truly playing tricks on her. The leaf-shaped sunspot had multiplied, dotting her wrist in a semi-circle around the top of her birthmark. "What the hell…"

"You okay in there?" Matt asked.

"How long have you known me?" She pulled back her wrist, leaving the bottle on its side in the fridge. Holding it like a wound, she walked back into the living room.

"Years. Why?" Confusion added to the concerned look on Matt's face.

"I swear my eyes are playing tricks on me. What do you see?" She held her wrist out for him to inspect.

"You get some ink done while in Phoenix? I like the whole tree of life thing you're trying to do." He smiled and traced the new semi-circle of leaves with his finger. "How is it healed already, though?"

"Okay, I'm not insane, then. You see it too." She sighed, but not in relief. She might not have been the only one seeing things, but that didn't explain how she'd gotten the new markings.

"That's not ink?" Matt asked.

"Nope." Sage ran to the kitchen again, lathered up her arm with soap, and ran it under the hottest water she could stand. Scrubbing didn't remove the marks either. "What the hell is this?"

"Don't peel your skin off." Matt came to the rescue with a towel and some lotion.

She'd rubbed herself raw, but the marks still remained. Neither raised bumps nor sunken impressions. They were just there, as if her skin had manifested them… like magic.

"It actually looks pretty cool. Makes all your little squiggles look like a real pattern now. Why are you stressing about it?"

"Marks don't just appear out of thin air." Anxiety sharpened her tone.

"Freckles do. Too much sun?"

"What if it's like cancer or something?"

"Wow! Way to jump straight to the worst-case scenario there, lady. How about we take a breath first? Calm down."

There had to be an explanation for this. Magic was something kids believed in. The stuff of fantasy and games. Fun to play at, but in the real world, it didn't exist. All the crap she'd seen—or dreamed—made her feel as if she were on the edge of a complete mental breakdown. That, or something else she couldn't possibly say out loud, because it was equally crazy. "What's the first sign of skin cancer? Strange freckles and moles, right?" Her stress level had already been at twelve, and it was quickly notching higher with each freaky thing that happened. Soon, she'd been in full panic attack mode, and there was no mom around to help ground her in reality.

Mom had always been her rock.

Mom had always had an answer.

Mom was dead!

Her head began to spin. The world blurred as tears flooded her vision. Her heart knocked frantically at the wall of her chest, desperate to be free of the constant pain of its cage. If only. There was no escape. No easy way out of this. Sage had to learn the hardest lesson of all—how to endure. Because her mom would never again be able to make everything better.

"Mom's gone!" She gasped as if her lungs were fighting against the very air she breathed, and her knees buckled. She'd have crashed to the ground if not for the strength of Matt's arms.

"Slowly now." He pulled her into a bear hug and stroked her head. "In and out. Nice, deep breaths. You're fine. You do *not* have cancer."

Where she was panic, he was calm. His soothing voice guided her back from the brink. She'd jumped from panic into full-blown depression, but Matt made the landing as soft as possible.

Thank the gods for him. She opened her mouth, but all that came out were mouse-like squeaks.

"C'mon. The Doctor will see you now." He walked her back into the living room and hit the button on the remote.

Theme music came on, and for a moment paused her downward spiral into madness. "I'm a hot mess right now."

"I know. But you're allowed to be. And I'm here for you. If you're that worried, we'll make an appointment with a dermatologist. I know a decent one."

"You're too good to me." She finally found her breath and sucked in as much air as her lungs could hold before letting it go with a loud sigh.

Matt disappeared into the kitchen and returned with two more beers. "You say that now, but wait until you get my bill."

Her wrist began to itch again, but Sage didn't dare look at it, fearing another spot might appear. Somehow it all tied to her Mom. All the crazy things she'd seen, which had started after Miranda died. Especially her birthmark, which was growing more like her mother's with each day. Sage might have been in mourning, but she wasn't going crazy. Even Matt had seen the change. There was a connection, but Sage doubted a dermatologist would have answers to questions she didn't know how to ask.

FIVE

The alarm blared with ear-piercing intensity. Sage whimpered at the clock, pleading for it to stop without having to get up and hit the button. The damn thing never listened. Instead, it kept screaming at her from across the room, the true master of the morning.

On a whispered curse, Sage lifted herself from the bed and began the ritual of making herself look human for the workday ahead.

Life, under normal circumstances, was a mind-numbing routine of business casual dress, coffee on the run, and microwaved lunch at her cubical workstation—monotony at its finest. But she couldn't complain. Fresh out of college and working in an entry-level position in a large accounting firm was more than many people her age had, and she counted herself lucky for it.

Sage lumbered into the office and tossed her gym bag under the desk. It wasn't even nine in the morning and her inbox looked like Mount St. Helens threatening to erupt at any moment. That was her punishment for daring to take two days of bereavement leave. Cost-to-completes needed to be entered, a pile of charge offs and expense forms that needed to be sorted by job, and if she managed to finish those tasks, there were always the endless stacks of filing.

She mentally prepared for a thrilling day of carpal tunnel and paper-cuts as she booted up her computer.

"Back so soon?" Genevieve called out from behind the cubicle wall. Her quad-desk neighbor was an accounting lifer. Thirty-something with kids and an addiction to caffeine. She had already been working for the company for eight years when Sage was hired on. She was the office gossip guru.

"It's not like I can afford to be off for long. Still have bills to pay, right?" Sage peeked over the top of the cubicle to speak to her.

Her mask must have fallen. Sage thought she had hidden her despair enough to manage the workday, but the pity reflected in Genevieve's hazel eyes said otherwise.

"You doing okay, honey?" She had the mom voice down pat, and just that simple phrase brought Sage back to tears.

She ducked down below the walls of her cubicle, hoping to shield herself from embarrassment. But there too, she found reminders of just how gaping the hole in her heart was. A card had been wedged between her keyboard and monitor, signed by the entire office. A touching note of solidarity. The waterworks were coming. She couldn't break down. Not here. Not now. "I was. I'm…fine." She sniffed back her emotions, hoping to dam them up inside. "Just need to bury myself in work."

"If you need anything, sweetie, just let me know. I've got your back."

"I will." Sage packed the card away in her bag to avoid being sent into another fit of tears. She had to be strong. Her in-box was calling, and there was more than enough work there to keep her busy for the rest of the year. After a few deep breaths, she was able to put the mask back on.

"Oh, and plan for margaritas on Friday. We're putting together a happy hour at the Iguana," Genevieve chirped happily between shuffles of papers. "Don't tell the rest of the girls, but your first drink is on me. Okay?"

Pain relief with a salted rim. Who could say no to that? Even if it did mean socializing with the entire accounts team. Harkening back to the school lunchroom, social hierarchy in the office was well defined. Dealing with each person one-on-one was easy enough when you had deadlines and assigned tasks to complete, but beyond the confines of their cubicles and job titles, navigating the various personalities required skill and finesse that Sage had yet to master. Like on a reality TV show, befriending and allying yourself with the right people could save your job.

Before she could answer, Genevieve warned, "Heads up—Marcy is on the warpath. Someone on the uniform account misplaced a decimal point on a CTC change request, and she fired them on the spot."

"Seriously?" Sage popped her head over the wall again, shocked to hear Genevieve's report.

"Oh, yeah. Word is Marcy is getting a divorce, so stay off her radar until things cool down. But you didn't hear that from me."

"My lips are sealed." She pantomimed zipping her mouth shut and re-took her seat.

Hours dragged on as Sage meticulously went line by line, entering job cost information into a spreadsheet. The numbers began to look the same after a while, and the gentle clack of the keys as she typed became hypnotic in their cadence. She'd fall under their spell if she didn't do something quick. Coffee was the only solution, but as she stood to grab a cup, she bumped into the infamous Marcy.

Sage shrieked, and her heart nearly stopped. Marcy had the reputation of being the troll of the accounting office. Ruthless as she was evil, she was the department head known for cutting costs as well as employees with brutal efficiency. That alone was enough to make Sage fear stepping on her toes. But on first glance, the normally poshly dressed head of accounts had suddenly grown a foot taller. Her skin was a sickly grayish-green that had nothing to do with the fluorescent lights above.

"Follow me please, Miss Cynwrig." Coal-black eyes stared straight through Sage as teeth like razors snapped together after the shrill order.

Staring dumbstruck at her boss, whose face had sprouted moles with thick black hairs jutting from their tops, Sage couldn't bring herself to do more than slap a hand over her mouth to keep it from gaping in surprise. Was this a joke? It had to be. But Marcy wasn't the kind of woman who played around. She was as strict as they came and known for having no personality whatsoever, which had earned her the nickname *troll*. But to see her standing there, looking the part... Marcy even had the long-tipped ears to match. Sage didn't even want to look down at her feet. But searching for somewhere else to look, she did, and nearly shrieked again. They were more claw than foot, with red-painted talons for toenails.

What the hell is happening to me? It wasn't the first time Sage had seen a transformation like this. And seeing her boss now reminded her of the dream she'd had—the army of trolls fighting a magical war.

"Is there a problem?" Marcy growled, after an uncomfortably long period of silence had earned stares from everyone else in viewing range.

Sage blinked and shook her head. By the time she opened her eyes again, her boss had reappeared. Curls of fiery red hair circled a heavily made up, heart-shaped—and very human—face. Dark eyes still glared at her, reminding Sage she was not in a position to cause problems.

"Sorry, ma'am." Sage gulped back her initial revulsion. *Snap out of it!* Her mind had been playing tricks on her lately. Stress and grief playing havoc with her sanity.

"My office. Now!" Marcy demanded.

The Rumor Mill girls were standing up at their desks, looking to see what all the commotion was about. If she still had a job after this meeting with Marcy, she might need to check and see if her insurance benefits included mental health. More and more, it seemed a shrink was in order.

Sage hung her head and slowly made the walk of shame all the way to Marcy's office.

"I'm sorry to hear about the passing of your family member. I hope you were able to settle the affairs during your bereavement leave." Marcy marched through her office, taking a seat behind the large desk.

Sage took a spot opposite the desk but didn't sit. She bit her tongue to avoid scoffing. She'd had all of two days to make it home and back, hardly time for true mourning or settling of anything, but already at strike one, she knew better than to reply with anything less than, "Yes, ma'am."

Cunning eyes scanned her from head to toe, looking for another strike to add to the tally.

"May I remind you, Miss Cynwrig, we have a standard of appearance here?" Instinctively, Sage pulled back her arm, covering it quickly, but it was too late. Marcy whipped a manicured finger out, aiming it straight at her wrist. "Tattoos of any kind may not be visible during working hours."

"It's not a tattoo. It's a birth mark." *Not now. Please, not now!* Just the thought of having to talk about it made her cringe.

Marcy's eyes dilated cruelly and her lips parted in a smile more frightening than anything Sage had seen before. As if she had gift-wrapped a reason to be fired, her boss held out her hand and demanded, "Let me see."

With a defeated sigh, Sage reluctantly showed off her deformity. Embarrassment of the highest caliber. Working in a right-to-work state gave employers carte blanche when it came to firing people. By rights, she shouldn't have had to reveal any part of her body to an employer, but at the risk of losing her job, it was the lesser of two evils.

Marcy snatched her arm, pulling Sage off balance as she brought it closer.

She cringed and closed her eyes, awaiting her boss's verdict, but rather than the sting of the guillotine's blade, she felt the hardwood of the desk as her knuckles crashed down.

Marcy sucked in a breath, dropping Sage's hand as if it had burned her.

When their eyes met across the desk, it was Marcy who looked frightened, but that fleeting emotion quickly disappeared behind her usual mask of self-importance.

"I see. Quite an interesting...birthmark. Is that what you called it?" Marcy averted her eyes, suddenly taking more interest in the papers on her desk.

"Yes, ma'am."

Something about her deformity had struck a chord with Marcy. Most people thought it was ugly or a bad ink job, but no one had ever responded with fear after seeing it.

Still avoiding eye contact, Marcy asked, "Who was it again that passed away?"

"My mother," Sage responded as calmly as she could.

A moment passed in stunned silence before Marcy finally looked up at Sage. Emotions warred for control of her boss's face. Eyes that had been calculating and cruel moments before suddenly softened. Fine lines appeared at her brow as if she was deep in thought, but she didn't speak her mind.

"I'll do my best to keep it covered," Sage offered as a way to break the silence.

"I'm truly sorry, dear. I'm sure this loss has affected you in more ways than you can imagine."

"Yes. Thank you." Her boss's words were too kind. There had to be a trap somewhere in this conversation.

"Perhaps you should take a little more time off to grieve," Marcy continued.

And there it was. Her job was about to be eliminated. Even the cruelest of trolls couldn't let her go directly after a death in the family. But if she played along, maybe she'd get enough paid time off to find another job.

"Okay." Sage hung her head as she turned toward the door.

"Have Genevieve take over your duties for the next week." How could Marcy speak so sweetly while stabbing someone in the back? No wonder she was getting divorced. That woman was pure evil. "Oh, and I'll make sure your paycheck is delivered to your apartment. No need to come down here to pick it up."

"Am I being let go?" Sage decided to go for blunt. What was the worst that could happen? "When do I come back?"

Marcy smiled, but it was far from genuine. "We'll discuss your career later, after you've had proper time to grieve and deal with all the changes."

Cruelty with a dash of crafty on top. *What a bitch! There's got to be a special place in hell for trolls like her.* Sage took her leave and headed back to her desk.

"You okay?" Genevieve popped her head over the cubicle.

"I think I just got fired," Sage replied angrily.

"She fired you?"

"She told me I should take more time to grieve. Those were her exact words." Sage picked up her bag. "Oh, and she'll mail me my check." The reality of being let go from her job hadn't quite settled in, but anger was quickly taking hold.

"Unless she said you're fired, you still have a job." Genevieve offered a weak smile.

Semantics aside, Sage knew her time with the company was over. It might be a week or more before the paperwork was sent to her, but the truth was obvious. Her hands shook with anxiety as the realization hit her. She might have to consider Mark's offer to work at ASSET. Her mom might be dead, but she still had a life to live, and she couldn't without a job.

SIX

When life tries to kick you in the nuts, fight back!

After wallowing in her misery, wondering what she was going to do for work, Sage looked forward to the opportunity to punch something… hard.

She'd only just started a membership at Bulwark Gym. Two days a week. One mixed martial arts class and one personal session comprised exactly the kind of ball-busting workout she needed.

Sweat poured down her forehead as she grappled with the seven-foot-tall steamroller Devon—her personal trainer. Struggling to gain enough leverage, Sage failed time and time again to throw him to the mats.

"You're distracted." Victory glinted in Devon's silvery eyes as he swept her leg, sending Sage crumpling to the padded ground. "I send you away for a few days and look at you."

His taunting, however well meaning, scratched at an itch she didn't want to touch. In less than a week, her life had been turned upside down. How could she not be anything but distracted? She hesitated, and he came down on top of her before she could roll out of the fall.

Straddling her torso, he snatched her arms and pinned them above her head. "Distraction is a weakness. Weakness makes you a victim, Sage. What are you going to do?"

Devon's weight squeezed the air from her lungs. He was easily double her size and had muscles for days. Just the kind of person she was learning to defend against. Small as she was, there would never be a chance for a fair fight. She would always be the underdog. Miranda had made it look easy—her mother had had neither bulk nor size, but she had always overcome those disadvantages. Sage's inspiration to look into self-defense. And with Mom dead, this was even more important—honoring the memory—though Sage might never be as graceful. She certainly wasn't at that moment as she wriggled underneath Devon's massive body like a worm. Leverage. She needed leverage.

"You're going to have to do better than that," he yelled, two inches from her face, those steely silver eyes daring her to make a move.

"You're crushing my ribs," Sage groaned. Devon had demonstrated this hold only a week ago, and she'd been able to get out of it. How had she done it so easily, then?

"If I was some asshole out there in the street, I'd be doing a hell of a lot worse. Now, what are you going to do to stop me?" Cruel in his methods, Devon wasn't a trainer who let you wuss out of things. The only way he was going to get off her was if she figured out how to make him. If only she could remember the right maneuvers.

Other people in the gym had stopped to stare. Embarrassment seared her cheeks. She didn't need to hear their laughter to know they were enjoying the spectacle of her failure.

Devon shook her wrists. "Focus."

His physical cue was just the thing to kick-start her memory. Jerking her arms in different directions, she threw him off guard. As he adjusted his grip, she shifted her hips, finally finding the leverage she needed. She threw all her weight to the side and as she came around on top of him, Sage finished with a mock punch to his jaw.

"Sloppy!" Devon's voice had all the authority of a drill sergeant and the volume to match. "That was a simple hold. I shouldn't have had to remind you how to break it."

Devon Kade wasn't known for his gentle approach. But he was known for strength and expertise in multiple forms of combat. The awards hanging on the wall were proof of that.

"Bad week." Sweat ran in fat drops down her face, and she struggled to maintain her breath as she stood and wiped her brow.

"Reset. We're going again." Devon pointed to the mat. "A bad week is no excuse. Channel that negativity into something useful, like not getting your ass handed to you."

"Sir, yes sir!" She mock saluted, trying to fight aggression with laughter as she caught her breath and prepared to go again.

"Was that supposed to be funny?" Devon's glare darkened.

"Sort of." She shrugged.

"Let me remind you that you are here to learn how to defend yourself. You want to play around and have fun, go take Zumba and giggle with your girlfriends."

"I didn't mean anything by it."

"Don't waste my time if you're not serious. I will happily refund your membership."

She'd wanted to be taught by the best if she ever hoped to be even a shadow of her mother's greatness—and Devon was the best. The sobering reminder that she paid for the privilege of being yelled at and mocked in the name of developing skills to protect herself wiped all emotion from her face. She dropped into a fighting stance. "Let's do this."

He came in hard and fast, stepping into her personal space with a close strike aimed at her chin. She blocked with one arm and countered, throwing her elbow out.

"Good." He backed away before her elbow connected with his chin. "But don't get cocky, kid."

Sage snorted, and was immediately rewarded with a kick aimed at her knees. Pivoting a little late, she narrowly avoided being taken down.

"Don't guess. Anticipate," he barked at her. "Watch me. Watch my muscles. Watch the sway of my stance. There are clues for the observant."

He was as fast as a viper and preyed on her distraction. If she blinked, he'd strike. If she wasn't watching his feet, he'd kick. It was tough love meant to teach her, but frustrating just the same. He expected her to be a mind reader when it came to an attack, and that was magic she simply didn't have.

"You know I'm coming for you. Be ready," Devon growled.

Sage forced herself to focus, breathing slowly as she watched his movements. Her eyes darted from his arms to his legs, catching the shift in his hips.

She blocked the fist that came cross-body toward her face, but missed the foot that followed.

"Don't pretend I'll stop with a single strike. Keep your head in the game." Devon threw another quick jab. "It's your job to make sure I can't hit you again."

There was no point in answering his taunting. She needed all her energy for blocking his attacks.

Focusing on his upper body, she watched for telling twitches or the tightening of muscles. Sweat stung her eyes, but blinking would be the end of her. He'd strike and then kick her while she was down.

Lose hard until you learn how to win—the motto was scrawled out across the doors to the locker room. No doubt, Devon claimed that as his personal quote.

As tiring and frustrating as this session was turning out to be, it had taken her mind off her troubles. For that, she was endlessly thankful, but she remained alert.

His left bicep twitched. Anticipating the strike, she instinctively brought her arm up to block her head. He came in hard, a freight train of muscle bent on crashing through her defenses. Her stance lacked balance, and she knew they'd both end up on the ground, but in a moment of frantic defense, she brought her knee up as he closed in. Somehow, through the blur of motions, she connected with his groin, earning a satisfying groan from Devon. They toppled to the ground, but Sage quickly maneuvered back to her feet to face him.

He clutched his stomach, his eyes narrowing with strain. Sage smiled inwardly, mentally high-fiving herself as she saw his jaw set tight to hide the pain. He'd told her to stop him, and at least for the moment, that done it.

No matter how tough a person is, if you find their soft spot, you can send them to their knees. Her mother had said that to her years before. Sage had always been small, and kids liked to pick on small people. Fighting dirty was sometimes the only way to avoid getting beaten up. That was one bit of self-defense she'd mastered. *When in doubt, kick 'em in the nuts. Or use a knee. Either way, it gets results from most men.*

"Well played." His eyes watered in pain, but his voice remained calm.

"Lucky, I guess."

He reached out and grasped her forearm. "For someone of your stature, that's probably your best move. Flex for me."

She made a muscle, but she had no bulk. Years of going to the gym had given her well-toned arms, but as scrawny as she was, they lacked the definition or thickness that usually translated into strength. Even when she flexed as hard as she could, her arms looked like twigs compared to Devon's. She saw the flicker of doubt in his eyes. Devon dropped her arm and took a step back, scrutinizing her, looking up and down as he took stock of her physical appearance.

"Make a fist," he ordered.

She brought both arms up in a boxer's stance, double-fisted, wondering if he was about to start another round of sparring.

Slowly, he reached out, holding his hands unthreateningly as he took hold of her left hand and corrected her thumb placement. His eyes landed on her deformity, and she held her breath, waiting for the usual round of questions, knowing she couldn't smart off to him no matter how sick she was of hearing people ask about the damn mark.

"I saw your instincts kick in back there. You're not entirely untrainable." She was shocked that Devon didn't mention her mark. And the look on his face. Not even a flicker of surprise. He didn't seem to care at all, save for the way she held her hands, ready to strike. "But if you want to truly be able to defend yourself, you're going to have to put a little meat on those bones."

She smiled at his praise.

"Weights might actually help you. How often do you exercise?"

"Other than classes here?"

"Obviously."

"I try to get in an hour of cardio after work most days."

"Do you have a personal trainer, or access to one?" Devon asked.

"Other than you?" She winced, realizing that losing her job meant she'd soon run out of money to pay her membership fees. "No. I'm too broke for that."

"I want you to add muscle groups to your rotation. Cardio is useless by itself. If you want true strength, you need to work on those muscles."

"I'm not trying to be the Hulk," she chuckled.

Devon didn't even crack a smile. "Tiny as you are, that's never going to be an issue."

"So, like leg day, arm day, core?" She hoped he'd say no. Some families were religious nuts and attended mass, confession, and Bible study multiple times a week. Not hers. The Cynwrigs prayed in the house of pain. She'd been well versed in the teachings of the weight training cycle from an early age, and though she appreciated the way she'd looked and felt because of it, the monotony had bored her to tears. Kickboxing, Krav Maga, and other forms of combat fighting were much more interesting forms of prayer and penance, though she still attended the treadmills with fervent regularity.

"Exactly." A smile finally cracked his stony expression, but she knew better than to take it as approval. "I'm going to give you a routine to work through. Most of these things can be done at home with a few weights. You've got some hidden strength in there. Let's see if we can pull it to the surface."

In other words, she was in for a brutal workout regime. Sage could already hear her muscles screaming in protest. "Sounds fun."

"Like I said—if you're not committed, there's the door. I'm here to make you better than you are now. If that means kicking your ass and tearing you a new one, so be it. But I'm not wasting my time and effort on a quitter."

"I never said I was quitting."

"You didn't have to. It's there in your eyes."

Damn him and his Jedi-like senses. Sage sighed, but before she could defend herself, he continued.

"I see a hundred girls like you come in here every month. You think you're a badass because you're taking a street-fighting class." He waved his hand in the air and planted it on his hip in a diva-like move that would have made Matt drop his jaw. "Ain't no sexual predator gonna mess with me."

Sage stifled a giggle.

"Learning a few moves doesn't make you a badass." Devon speared her with a silencing glare. "Most of those hundred girls a month that come knocking on my door get sent to the black belt farms and McDojos. There are plenty of gyms that will take your money and kiss your ass. You pay them enough and they'll give you a damn medal of honor. Not in my gym. You have potential, Sage. What are you going to do with it?"

After Devon's motivational tirade, Sage disappeared into the locker room.

What was she going to do? Truth be told, if she had lost her job, she might not be able to afford to work out in this gym anymore. And then she'd never realize her dream of reaching the same level of bad-assery as her mom. No. She couldn't let that happen. She'd have to find a way to keep training with Devon, no matter what sacrifices she had to make. Sage owed it to her mother's memory.

SEVEN

Darkness had descended, but Sage wasn't ready to call it a night just yet. Matt was working, so she'd only be going home to an empty apartment if she did. That kind of alone time didn't mesh well with the day she'd had.

After the brutal workout she'd endured, her stomach roared for food. Around the corner from her apartment complex sat a small English-style pub, the next best thing to going home. She'd been in there so often they knew her by name, and she decided to reward herself for surviving the day with some sliders and ale.

Scooting into a back corner booth, she waved at Julie, the waitress, and mouthed the words, "The usual."

Some people hated to eat alone, but not Sage. Sitting back and watching the surrounding people was like a front-row seat to her personal soap opera. The daily drama of date nights, breakups, friendly drunks, and groups celebrating who knows what were always there. The faces might change, but alcohol and people always made for excellent entertainment. Sitting in the farthest corner was the perfect spot to see, but not *be seen*. No one came by her table, except Julie.

Across the room, clinging to the bar like a crutch, sat a familiar barfly. Blatantly drunk, he flailed his arms as he pleaded with the bartender. Though she couldn't hear him, Sage put words to the movement of his lips. "Please sir, may I have another?"

Julie arrived with food in hand. "Bad lip reading again?"

"Can't help myself," she giggled.

Julie pointed to a couple sitting three tables over. "Breakup."

Sage gave the guy a quick once-over. Dressed too nicely to be slumming it in a neighborhood bar, he had the look of a captain in the air force. She cleared her throat before delivering his words. "I have a confession to make. I'm not in the army. I just like wearing uniforms."

Julie snorted and took on the role of the woman arguing and near tears. "I should have known better. There is no Unlimited Security Patrol, is there?"

"Nice." Sage narrowed her eyes and watched the man for an emotional clue to his next words. "Postal workers are an army of sorts."

Julie nearly dropped the tray she was carrying in a fit of laughter. "I could play this game all night. But duty calls." She set down the food and turned to head back toward the kitchens.

Sage giggled to herself, glancing at the fighting couple between bites of her mini-burgers. Her stomach groaned with appreciation as she devoured half the plate in under a minute.

Witnessing someone else's misery wouldn't earn her any karma points, but sitting alone in a pub left her little else to do. She finished her last bite just as the jilted woman stormed away, and she wondered if she'd find another equally entertaining bit of drama.

It was a slow night in the bar, leaving little else for her to watch. She returned her attention to the guy who'd been the dumpee. He remained seated, as if he'd not been bothered at all by the scene that had played out moments before. That piqued Sage's curiosity. She tried to be inconspicuous as she threw glances back in his direction. Maybe he had been the dumper in that relationship. Maybe she'd imagined it all wrong. Her mind concocted a variety of scenarios as she spied on him while picking at her fries. Smearing them one by one in ketchup before popping them into her mouth, she invented a new persona for the strange man across the bar. He was a secret agent, and the woman who'd left was his informant. He was attractive, and the suit he was wearing only added to the appeal. Probably more middle management than secret agent, but he could be under cover.

Julie came by and set down a new beer in front of Sage. "You looking to swoop in now that he's single?"

"Have I been staring that hard?"

"Wipe the drool off your chin, honey."

"I was zoned out, really," she half lied. But as she glanced once more at the guy across the bar, their eyes connected. The bluest of the blue. His eyes reminded her of the dream she'd had with the blue magic creature trying to kill her. "Shit!" Sage ducked, turning her head away.

"Whatever you say." Julie turned to make the rounds at tables, refilling their waters and clearing away plates.

Sage hadn't been interested in him, but Julie's insinuation made her feel guilty of grave robbing. She resigned herself to keeping her head down and studying the exercise routine Devon had given her. Not exactly riveting entertainment, but safer than locking eyes with the guy who'd sent chills down her spine with little more than a look.

"I couldn't help but notice you checking me out."

She could have sworn he was across the room only a moment before, but his voice sounded as if he were right on top of her. Cocky, with just enough amusement to send every alarm bell ringing in her head.

"Sorry, I didn't mean to..." Sage lifted her eyes, shocked to see him up close and personal. She hadn't even heard him walk up. He had the deadly combo of dark hair and blue eyes that were her personal kryptonite. Words refused to move past her lips, though she desperately wanted to explain she hadn't been ogling him.

He flashed a sideways grin, revealing white teeth that looked dangerously sharp. He was everything her mother would have warned her to stay away from. And here he was, trying to chat her up.

Meanwhile, all she could do was stare. Those eyes—there was something so different about them. The color of pure blue. She'd have sworn they were contacts. They reminded her of the creature in her dream that had tried to push her toward death with electric balls.

"Can I sit, or are you expecting someone?" he asked.

She nodded like an idiot and immediately regretted the speed at which she said, "Sure." He was the kind of good-looking that screamed *bad boy* and at the same time silenced the rational part of her brain that recognized the danger.

"I don't normally do this..." He slid onto the bench next to her. "But I just had to come say hi."

Damn. Good looks, gorgeous eyes, and a silver tongue too. He had *lady-killer* written all over him.

"You probably have guys lining up. No wonder you're hiding in the back. Sick of the attention, am I right?"

"I...no...really? Okay, what's your deal?" She stumbled over her tongue, trying to sound cool but realizing too late that she might have veered into bitchy.

"You saw my friend leave, huh?" His smile didn't falter for a minute. "She had an awful week, and I just couldn't console her. Poor thing."

"Didn't mean to pry. Sorry. She just looked..." Sage hadn't paid much attention to the girl who'd left. Had she been angry, sad, or just walking away? She let the words hang in the air until the stranger picked up the thread and ran with it.

"It's okay. I know the girl code." He flashed a toothy grin, and Sage's stomach somersaulted as she caught sight of his unusually sharp teeth. But before she could summon her voice, he continued, "You all stick up for one another. I admire that."

How was he so quick on the draw? He had an answer for everything. No one was *that good* a flirt.

"Yeah." Sage feigned a laugh. "Girl code."

"So, is this your normal bar? I've never been in here before, but I'd heard the food was excellent."

He'd been on a roll up to that point, had her on the hook, ready to reel in, but his mistake was tossing out a cheesy pickup line. That broke the spell. Reworded from the usual, *Come here often?* But even as dense as she could be with guys, the message came through loud and clear. Player, womanizer, and not worth her time.

"Try the sliders."

"Maybe next time. I was planning on heading out tonight. Maybe you'd like to join me." He gave a flirty wink.

Moments earlier, when she'd been under his spell, she might have considered it. But her brain had rebooted, and the reality was a definite no. Sage looked herself over. She'd showered after the gym, but dressed in yoga pants, tank top, and sports bra, the only place she planned to go was home. "Not tonight."

"Oh, c'mon. The night has only just begun. Don't tell me you don't like to get out and party." Those brilliant blue eyes went well beyond gorgeous, with a hypnotic power behind them, trying to draw her in.

Damn, he was hot. But then again, what the hell was he doing trying to pick her up? She could see him trying if she'd been at a club and dressed to impress, but gym wear—as cute and comfy as it was—hardly screamed *Date me.*

"Oh, I party. But, you know, girl code."

His smile faltered for the first time since he'd sauntered over, and confusion narrowed his eyes. "You're batting for the other team?"

She should have said yes. She could have said yes. It might have been a lie, but it would have ended the awkward conversation. "No. I just meant... Uh... I have to be up to code to party. Girl standards and all."

"So how about we swing by your place and I'll wait while you get ready?"

Creeper alert! She grabbed her beer and chugged it down, to give herself time to formulate an appropriate response. Normally, alcohol was liquid courage, but she was two beers in and felt nothing, which wasn't helping. It might as well have been water for all the effect it had on her.

His eyes left her face for a moment and widened as he looked down at her empty beer bottle. No—her wrist. "What an unusual tattoo."

She needed to invest in a leather cuff like the one Mark wore to hide her damn birthmark. It was all people could talk about these days. "It's not a tattoo."

"It's gorgeous. Can I take a closer look?"

She sighed and held out her wrist. He bent his head and inspected, but thankfully did not try to touch her.

"It's really not a tattoo? I've never seen such beautiful artistry." His tone screamed *lie*. She saw that, clear as day, in those icy eyes he'd been trying to hypnotize her with. Marcy had that same look, too. Something about her birthmark was affecting the people around her. Ever since her mother's death, anytime someone asked to look at it, they acted as if they were seeing the mark of the beast or something equally damming. What the hell was so special about it? And for that matter, why didn't she know?

"Nope. I call it a birthmark for lack of a better term," she responded mechanically, having had this conversation so many times she might as well put it on a business card to hand to everyone she met. Might save her time in the long run.

He leaned in and whispered. "Well, that makes you special."

Chills ran the length of her spine and goosebumps erupted all over her body. "You'd be the first to say that. Growing up, most people just called me a freak."

"Children don't appreciate uniqueness."

"And you're definitely not a child." God, could she be more awkward? The moment the words left her lips, heat flushed her cheeks. This had to end before she shoved her foot all the way into her mouth.

"No," he chuckled. "I'm definitely not."

"And on that note, I should probably call it a night." She tried to scoot out of the booth, knocking her knee into the table as she scrambled to get to her feet.

"You sure I can't convince you to come out with me this evening?"

The conversation had turned weird, and alarm bells were going off in her head. She needed an escape, fast. "How about we exchange numbers and try for another night?"

As if by magic, his eyes became an even icier blue, a no-ticeable contrast against the paleness of his skin and dark hair. She felt something, like an invisible presence in her mind, try-ing to persuade her, but her intuition screamed, *no!*

"If you're sure." He reached into a pocket and pulled out a business card. "Here's my number."

She accepted it and slipped it into her bag without even looking at it. "I'll call you."

"Don't I get your number?" His request took her aback, halting her attempt at an escape.

"Sure. Um..." Her heart raced as she tore off a corner of the paper Devon gave her. She scrawled out her name and cell number, and handed it over. "Here."

After taking a quick glance, he folded it and placed it in his shirt pocket. "Thank you, Sage."

Hearing her name roll off his tongue had her tripping over her feet as she bolted for the bar. Slapping down a twenty, she waved to Julie. "See you tomorrow."

The day had gone completely sideways, a roller coaster ride of ups and downs that left her uncertain which direction was which. Sage felt his eyes on her as she walked away and prayed she'd make it home before anything else happened.

As Sage navigated her way through the labyrinthine streets heading toward her apartment, she couldn't shake off the memory of those piercing blue eyes. A part of her was flat-tered by the unwanted attention at the bar, but another part was wary and on edge. The stranger's charm was alluring, but also triggered a warning in her gut. Yet, even with every part of her screaming no, there was a reckless curiosity tempting her to say yes.

How stupid would that have been? Invite a stranger to her home? That could have landed her on the evening news. Another Las Vegas murder statistic.

But she'd had the sense to walk away. Achievement unlocked. If this had been game night, she'd have earned herself a badge of honor. She couldn't wait to share her triumph with Matt.

How many girls could walk away from a dangerous hottie like that? And live to tell the tale?

Patting herself on the back, Sage rounded the corner to her apartment complex, radiating pride and holding her head high. Even better, she hadn't asked his name. She'd toss out his card the minute she got inside. No attachments. No connections.

Though she had given him her number. Damn.

She clutched her keys like a lifeline, their cold metal reassuring against her skin.

Well, she didn't have to answer her phone to unknown callers. Not a complete fail.

Men were a distraction she didn't need at the moment. She had Matt in her life and his awesome boyfriend, Josh. Between the two of them, there was plenty of testosterone to go around.

She unlocked the after-hours security gate to the apartment complex and took the short path to her building. Kids were swimming in the communal pool, laughing and splashing each other. Some of her neighbors were taking their evening strolls now that the brutal heat of the day had cooled. For the first time in all the long day, she could take a deep, cleansing breath. Everything was as it should be.

"Sage Cynwrig?" A deep voice pierced the darkness as a looming figure stepped out of the shadows and onto Sage's front porch.

EIGHT

Her heart kicked into overdrive. For a moment she'd worried the guy from the bar had followed her somehow, but this man was wearing different clothes. With a black fedora cloaking some of his head and a leather duster over a dark shirt and black pants, he was camouflaged within the shadows. The dim lights did little to reveal his features, but there was a glint in his pale turquoise eyes that held a hint of familiarity Sage couldn't quite understand.

"Who's asking?" Sage demanded, trying to keep her voice steady despite the fear coursing through her veins.

"Are you Sage Cynwrig?" The stranger stood at least a head taller than Sage, making her crane her neck to get a better look at him. Not a face she recognized.

How the hell did he know her name and where she lived?

She scanned around for others hiding in the shadows.

"No." She squared her shoulders and readied herself for a fight, summoning all the training Devon had given her. "And this is private property. If you don't leave the premises, I'll call security."

He reached out faster than she could react and took hold of her left hand, flipping it over to reveal her birthmark.

Her instincts kicked in and she twisted her wrist, breaking his flimsy hold and rounded on him, sending her fist flying at his face.

The stranger blocked her strike with ease. "We need to talk." He stepped into the light and held his arms up in surrender.

She'd been ready to hit him again, but caught sight of his wrist. He had the same birthmark. She'd believed that only she and her mother shared this special marking, but now she knew that to be a lie. And suddenly the turquoise eyes made sense too. Was he family? Some distant relation she'd never been told of? He not only shared the same eye color as her mother, he also had the same deformity. All the way down to the crown of leaves above what appeared to be a tree shaped out of broken veins.

"I'm not here to fight with you." He lowered his hands and whispered, "I'm here to help."

"I don't need any help." She relaxed her fighting stance. What the hell was going on? Her instincts should have been telling her to run. She should be screaming for help or calling the police. Normal people didn't skulk in the shadows. But standing in front of this guy, who clearly wanted to look like a dangerous badass—he'd have to lose the fedora if he hoped to achieve that—she felt only curiosity.

"You need more help than you know." He angled his head toward Sage's front door. "Can we go inside and talk? I can explain."

"We can talk out here." She crossed her arms in front of her.

"No. Too many ears listening." He nodded upward. Sage turned to look in the direction he'd indicated and saw someone drawing curtains shut in a second-story apartment window. "You and I share the same symbol. Aren't you the least bit curious what that means?"

Sage opened her mouth to say *yes*, but the word refused to come. That was exactly what he would want her to say.

After a moment of silence, he let out a deep sigh. "Does the word ASSET make a difference?"

That word threatened to bring her to tears. She didn't want to say it out loud, but if he knew about ASSET, then he had to know about her mother. Maybe he was connected to her family.

"Fine," she groaned, hoping she wasn't about to make the stupidest of all mistakes by allowing him inside. "But I swear, if you put a hand on me again..."

He smirked. "I have no interest in putting my hands on you."

Feeling more than a little stupid for allowing a stranger into her home, Sage made a beeline for the kitchen to grab a weapon. The man shared the same mark as she and her mother, and as someone who had been plagued by questions her whole life about her deformity, curiosity had won over common sense. But at least she could arm herself.

"Really? A knife?" The stranger's mocking voice filled her kitchen as Sage pulled a butcher knife from the drawer.

His words bounced off the cold tiles and echoed in her ears, igniting a spark of defiance within her.

"There's a strange guy in my kitchen, who appeared out of the shadows and demanded to be let inside my house." Gripping the knife, Sage stood her ground and faced the intruder with defiance, ready for whatever might come next. "If I had a gun, I'd have grabbed that."

"And yet you just revealed to this stranger that you're weaponless," he taunted. "Not exactly the brightest bulb, are you?"

Sage refused to back down or let the sting of his words shake her resolve. "If you're just going to insult me, then get the hell out."

"You going to make me?" His eyes narrowed in a taunting glare.

She twisted the knife in her hand, one snarky comment away from sheathing it between his ribs. "You want to test me?"

"Okay, truce." His smug expression softened as he held his hands up in surrender. "Can we just relax for a moment and talk?"

"Go ahead. Say what you need to say." She stood firm, one hand on her hip, the other keeping the knife ready. He stepped toward the kitchen table and took one of the open seats before removing his hat. Underneath the dark fedora was a mess of dirty-blond waves that fell around his head. Under better circumstances, she might have thought him cute. There wasn't a woman alive who didn't secretly harbor a thing for bad boys, and he had the look for sure. But as she waited in silence for him to finish making himself at home, his level of attractiveness faded.

"Anytime now." Sage tapped an impatient foot.

"You might want to sit down for this." He pointed to the chair opposite him.

"I'll stand. You talk."

"Fine," he sighed. "Your markings. They've come alive recently?"

"English please."

"The tree-shaped branding on your wrist. It's changed, yes?"

"You mean the spots?" Instinctively, her eyes lowered to her birthmark. "I'm having it checked out by a doctor. What of it?"

"A doctor won't be able to tell you anything," he scoffed.

She'd already come to that realization, but short of any other options, had still held out some hope.

"That's why I'm here, Sage. Your mother just died recently, right?"

Compassion clearly isn't his strong suit. Sage gritted her teeth, biting back the pain that followed from the mere mention of her mother.

"Fine. Don't answer. I don't need to hear you confirm it."

"How much do you know about me?" Her knuckles were turning white from the pressure of her clenched hand around the knife's handle.

"Your wrist bears the mark. That's all I need to know. You're a Terra."

Not at all what she'd expected him to say. *What the hell is a Terra, anyway?* "Yeah… you're going to have to start making some serious sense soon."

He lifted a hand and pinched the bridge of his nose, at the same time letting out a sigh that registered as pure annoyance. "You're special, Sage. Part of an ancient race of people as old as time itself."

"Who put you up to this? Was it Matt?" She laughed nervously and looked around for her roommate to jump out and surprise her. This was the kind of comic book insanity he might come up with to cheer her up. "Wait. No. Keep going. Am I blessed with some kind of supernatural ability?"

"This isn't a joke," he groaned.

"Right. Of course it isn't." Snickering under her breath, she scrunched her face in a strained attempt to look serious, at the same time loosening the grip on her knife. "I'm sorry.

Quick question. Can I fly?" She barely got the words out before bursting into a fit of laughter.

"Okay, good chat." He stood abruptly and picked up his hat. "I'm going to go. Have fun being converted to a Darkling. Or if you're lucky, maybe a vampire will just kill you instead."

NINE

"Hold on." Sage cleared her throat and wiped the smirk from her lips as she looked around the kitchen for hidden cameras. The strange man was playing his part so well, even the anger seemed real. This ruse her roommate Matt had set up probably took a lot of trouble to put together. The least she could do was play along.

"Don't go just yet." She patted the table, hoping the stranger would sit down. "What is it you're trying to tell me?"

"Are you going to take me seriously?" He glared at her. "Or continue with fantasy land bullshit?"

What is Lord of the Shire for 500, Alex? Sage fought to hide her laughter. "Sorry... I don't even know who you are. Maybe start with that."

"My name is Grey." He held out his arm, showing her the tree-like marking on his wrist. "This is the sign of our people. The Terras."

Sage made a show of inspecting his markings and comparing them to hers. The leaves around the tree seemed to grow more defined each day. And in the center of what would be the trunk, a figure eight symbol had taken form, though it was only a shadow. Whoever was in on the joke had gotten the tree bit pretty close, but the ring around Grey's was much more defined. And in the trunk of his tree, there was a symbol she didn't recognize. Still, though, A for effort.

"We're bound to the earth by the gods who made and marked us. And we pass on our gifts through our lifelines." He pulled back his hand. "I'm guessing that since losing your mother, you've noticed some strange things happening around you, right?"

Sage's jaw hung open in stunned silence. She hadn't told Matt about the strange things she'd seen.

"When your mother's light was extinguished," Grey's voice filled the silence. "Her strength passed down to the next person in her line… you."

"Okay." A chill ran down her spine. He was describing the dream she'd had. Sage set the knife on the table and took the seat she'd originally rejected. "So what exactly does that mean?"

"Our people were created by the gods to—"

"Hold on," she cut him off. "Gods. Like… Are we talking big G or little g?" Being raised pagan and hearing someone else talk of gods in the plural piqued her interest, regardless of whether she believed his story.

"Creation was the responsibility of the big G gods." Grey smirked and his tone softened. "Then they kind of sat back and enjoyed the show when they were done, leaving lots of little g's to screw everything up."

"So which little g created us?"

"Good question. Our people are older than humanity, so we came before various cultures gave names to the gods that you'd recognize."

"So does that mean our people worship some god we can't pronounce?" Sage tried hard to stifle her giggling. The way he spoke about the gods sounded suspiciously like mythology from her Dragon Raiders game.

"Pray to whomever you like. The gods aren't here to solve any of our problems," he shot back at her with a cynicism that hinted at his own disbelief. "We're like reality TV. Interesting to watch, but forgotten just as quickly."

"So the gods don't care about us?" That felt wrong on so many levels. Weren't gods supposed to be like celestial parents, disciplining their children as much as they nurtured them?

"They only care when it affects them. And that is why our race was created. We were an answer to a problem. Our Mother Earth goddess took abuse from the first beings that were created. The race of Terras… *us*… were brought into existence to stop that abuse. We belong to Mother Earth herself and are extensions of her great tree of life. As such, it's our duty to maintain the order among other creations so that none might overthrow the balance and risk damage to our world."

Rehearsed as his words sounded, Sage couldn't shake the feeling that he was speaking some truth. And that scared her more than she wanted to admit. Mundane life sucked at times, but she couldn't complain. It was at least safe. Being part of some secret society that did who knows what didn't sound appealing at all. Especially if they were the reason for her mother's death. ASSET. All those working trips she'd gone on through the years. How many of those had really been trade shows? And how many of those trips were Miranda fighting to maintain some cosmic balance, or whatever it was this guy said they did?

"Let's say I believe you." She looked down at her wrist. The tree of life was there. If the stranger's word were true. He wore it. Her mother wore it. Now that hers was becoming more defined, did that mean she was destined for the same fate? "Why wouldn't my mother have told me about this?"

"Terras have a unique lineage." Grey shrugged. "There are only so many of us awakened at a time. We are creatures of balance by nature. Your connection awakens when another of our kind loses their inner light."

"But what about my father?" She had no memory of the man. Her mother had never been one to take pictures, and the few that Sage had seen of her father were old. Even now, she couldn't recall his face. Did he have the same turquoise eyes? Had he borne the mark too? "He died when I was little. Why wasn't I awakened then?"

"Your father wasn't one of us," Grey answered, as if it should have been obvious. "Your mother had the mark, and so do you. Any children you have would bear the same."

"She should have said something," Sage grumbled. A secret like that was too big to be kept. How could anyone prepare for a destiny they didn't know about, and then be expected to roll with it after it's been dumped in their lap? "Assuming this is all true, how could my mother have hidden this from me all these years?"

"It is true!" He growled. "Look. We don't age like humans. She could have lived for centuries before her light was extinguished. And had you lived out a normal human life and continued the line through children of your own, they would have been awakened when the time came. Why burden you with knowledge that might never have affected you?"

"But it does..." Sage argued before the meaning of his words struck her. "Wait. Are you telling me that since I'm *awakened*, I'm... immortal?"

"Catching on, are we?" He smiled slyly. "Effectively. Yes. But you can still be killed."

"You're one-hundred percent serious, aren't you?" Crazy as it all seemed, part of her wanted to believe him. Who wouldn't want to be part of a magical destiny? The chosen one. It was fantasy come alive. But the other half still felt that, at any moment, someone was going to jump out with a camera and scream, *You got scammed*!

"Serious as death. Which is what you'll be if you don't listen. Being Terra isn't just a marking, it's a birthright and duty to our people." The small glimmer of personality he'd shown moments earlier faded into the abyss as Mr. Doom, Gloom, and All Things Were Deathly Important returned. "And because we have a duty, we also have enemies—"

"Look, I'm listening." She cut him off before he could go full apocalypse. "This sounds really superhero-y and cool, with an added dash of danger. Magical destinies and special powers are great. I'm totally into that kind of thing, but even I have to admit that it sounds like a really well put together prank." She spoke loud enough for anyone in an adjoining room to hear her. "And I kind of hope my roommate is listening because I'm not falling for any more of his pranks."

"Can't say I didn't try," Grey whispered under his breath as he shook his head. "I don't have time to force-feed you until you believe. This isn't a joke or a prank. No one is listening in on our conversation." His jaw tightened, and he gave himself a second to breathe before continuing. "My job is to bring you safely to headquarters. If you want proof and answers, they'll give 'em to you."

"I don't care what your job is." His aggressive tone had her hackles up. How dare he come at her with this and expect her to just take him at face value? Who would? And then get all offended when she wanted proof. Hell no! "This is a lot of crazy you just dumped into my lap after an already insane day."

"You want answers? Then grab your shit. We're going on a trip."

"Ah. No." She'd hit her quota of stupid mistakes for the day. Letting him and his crazy talk into her apartment definitely ranked at the top of that list. "Convincing as you think you are, I'm not following some strange man to some base for mythical people."

"Suit yourself." He raked his fingers through his hair before putting his fedora back on. "I'll let my superiors at ASSET know you declined."

Without another word, he left Sage to ponder the utter lunacy of her day. Truth and fantasy blurred into one another until she couldn't decide what was real. So much of what he'd said made sense. And ASSET was a company that dealt with secrets. Could that have been why Mark was always so eager to have her work for them?

TEN

Time distorted. Hours passed like minutes while Sage struggled to find threads of truth to cling to. She barely registered the heavy sound of her roommate pushing open the front door as he came home from his shift at the bar.

"What are you still doing up?" Matt's tone held more caution than surprise. He'd been walking on eggshells, given her recent breakdown. Or had he orchestrated that elaborate scene with Grey? She had to know. If for nothing else, her own sanity. She listened for any hint of humor in his voice, some small clue to give away his ruse. Asking him outright wouldn't work.

Matt tossed his gym bag at the foot of the kitchen table and gave her a quick kiss on top of her head before turning to the fridge. "Bad day at work?"

"Too much on my mind." She traced the branches of the tree-like markings on her wrist. It had grown even more defined. The tree canopy above had widened, with the branches twisting in a beautiful rope-like pattern. Below, the roots shriveled into nothing as they slithered down her wrist.

"I called my dermatologist. She can see you next week. Don't stress about it, okay?" Matt gave her shoulder a squeeze as he walked past to the coffeemaker. "Planning on an all-nighter, or would you rather have some chamomile for sleep?"

Sleep wasn't in the cards—too much crazy and not enough time to digest it all. It was going to be a red-eye kind of day. "Make me Irish."

"Damn, honey, are you stressing out that bad?"

She listened as he filled the coffeepot with water. The clink of ceramic mugs being set out on the counter suggested he was planning on joining her. Good—she needed company. Matt was her rock. He could ground her back in reality. "Just a really weird day… and night. I should be tired, but I can't shut my brain down. How about you? Not seeing Josh?"

"He's away at a conference this week." She didn't see his face, but the pout was clear in his voice. "So, what happened to you today?"

"You ever feel like you're stuck in a dream, and you know you're dreaming but can't wake up?"

"You need me to pinch you?" He chuckled.

"I'm serious."

"I know, honey. I'm sorry." He came over and hugged her from behind. His arms were her security blanket. She felt safe with him. But even he didn't have the kind of strength that could protect her from the destiny Grey said she was born into. "I can't imagine what you're going through, losing your mom and all. And I'm not trying to downplay your situation. Just trying to lighten your mood."

"How? By making me a superhero?"

"What?" Matt's voice confirmed he hadn't played a practical joke on her by sending Grey. He'd have admitted that straight away if he thought anything he'd done had caused her more pain.

"Nothing… Not sure my mood can be lifted right now." She sighed, weighed down by all the information Grey had dumped on her. If what he said was true, then so was the danger he'd hinted at. Danger she couldn't possibly fathom.

"Didn't you have karate tonight?" Matt's voice broke through her thoughts. "I thought punching things would help you blow off steam."

"Something like that." Her muscles had gone stiff, sitting at the table for so long. They protested even the slightest movement now as she turned to face her roommate. More pain would follow tomorrow. If she hadn't been so worked up, she'd have remembered to stretch. "You should see what Devon wants me to do now." Sage welcomed the distraction. Talking about anything ordinary felt good. She pulled out her shoulder bag and grabbed the paper listing her new workout regime.

Coffee percolated, flooding the air with the rich aroma of roasted beans and just a hint of bitter chocolate. Such a simple thing, easily taken for granted, but after the day she'd had, Sage allowed herself time to breathe it in, appreciate it, grasp at normalcy. There had been so little of that today.

Matt took the page, snickering as he ran his finger down the days and assignments. "If nothing else, you'll be too tired to be mopey after this workout. And he still wants you to come in twice a week for sessions with him?"

As if she'd absorbed the caffeine from the air, Sage roused from the doldrums. "One personal class and one group session, yeah."

"Damn, killer." Matt threw a faux punch at her upper arm. "You're going to be the Terminator after all this training." He pulled back into a boxer's stance, bobbing and weaving as if ready to take her on.

As amusing as that idea was, Sage didn't engage, but managed a giggle at her roommate's attempt to make her smile. "Assuming I survive."

"That's the can-do attitude I've come to expect from you." Matt playfully brought up his fists, ready for a strike that would never come. "What's it going to take to perk your ass up?"

"I just need time." She shrugged. "That's all."

With a frustrated sigh, he stood and turned back to the counter to prep the coffees. "Well, while you're taking your time, you can go through the boxes that arrived today."

Those words hit her harder than any punch he could have thrown. She'd sworn she'd never open them. Even after Mark had pleaded with her, she'd instructed him to put them in storage. Of course he wouldn't listen. She needed them to properly mourn the loss of her mother—his words. Mark doing his best impression of a father. Damn him. He would overnight the boxes just to rub salt in the wounds. "That was fast," Sage swore under her breath.

"I left them in your room. It's just two."

Matt couldn't understand how frightening the contents of those boxes were. He still had both his parents living in the same city. "I'm not sure I'm ready to open them."

"Your mom was awesome. Ignoring her memory won't make you heal any faster." Matt poured a generous shot of Irish crème into the mug before sliding it over to her. "Take this. We can go through the boxes together if it helps. You can have an ugly cry with me tonight."

"Marry me, will you?" Tears were already beginning to form. And he was not only giving her permission, he'd offered to put up with her at her worst. She couldn't ask for a better friend.

"I would, honey." He winked as he held up his mug and took the first sip. "But you're just not my type."

"I'm good with an open relationship. I just want to lock this down." She waved a hand between them. "You know. Because no guy will ever measure up to you."

"Next time Josh is over, I need you to repeat that." He pointed to the hall. "Now, go get those boxes, and let's have a pity party."

Looking just as ominous as the last time she'd laid eyes on them, the two banker's boxes with Miranda's name written on them taunted her, daring her to open them and reveal the cursed treasure inside. She set them down on the kitchen table and took a chug from her coffee for strength. "Where's a 'disarm traps' spell when you needed one?"

"No games. This is the real world. Now, rip that band aid off!" Matt cheered.

Hands shaking, she sliced the tape around the edges of the first box. Dust poofed out as she lifted the lid, and her eyes settled straight away on an item she recognized. Right on top, folded neatly, was her mother's leather jacket. Tears could not be held in check as she pulled it out and caught a whiff of perfume. The notes of bergamot and tangerine had always been the essence of happy, bringing up her mood no matter how dark, but for the first time, they failed to elicit that response.

"That's a sick jacket. Put it on."

She held it close, caressing the supple leather worn buttery soft through years of use. The inner lining had a few small tears and odd seams where hasty repairs had been made. But none of that rendered the jacket unwearable. Sage slipped one hand into the sleeve. The satin lining caressed her arms, inviting her to be its new owner. The other arm slipped in just as easily. She shrugged the jacket up over her shoulders, feeling it mold to her body as if it had been meant for her all along. She'd often asked to borrow the jacket, but mother had never let her. Wearing it now almost felt naughty. She told herself if she didn't, the jacket would never see the light of day. And that would be a betrayal of her mother's memory.

The approval in Matt's eyes said he agreed. He cleared his throat and twirled his finger.

Happy to play model, she spun for him.

More coat than jacket. It draped below her hips, ending just above her knees. A wide notched collar with buttons that started below her breast and a slight taper at the waist gave the coat a feminine look.

No need for a mirror. She knew how awesome the jacket looked.

Loops left wanting for a strap of leather said there had once been a belt, but that had been lost years ago. After a round of applause from her roommate, she dug further into the box, hoping to find the missing piece.

Envelopes filled with documents, multiple passports from various countries, and a handful of pictures made up the next layer of her mother's things. Each new artifact stung as she pulled them out to examine, but Matt was there with a nod of solidarity and a fresh shot of Irish crème for her coffee. Liquid courage to continue, though she had yet to feel even the slightest bit buzzed.

Tucked into the side of the box was an impressive-looking knife and leather utility belt.

"Damn. Mommy was a badass." Matt whistled as he pulled out the belt before Sage could. He held it up, fiddling with the fasteners and opening the small compartments. "Shit. She's got throwing knives in here." He opened a pocket and pulled out two slim knives with a ring on the end.

"She was a weapons expert. One of ASSET's best." Sage remembered her mother in demonstration fights with her effortless grace and form, as if she were dancing rather than engaging in battle. Miranda had the reputation of being able to take down opponents larger than herself and disarm them without breaking so much as a nail.

Below the belt lay a soft velvet cloth. Sage unfolded it and revealed more weapons. Daggers—most likely meant to fit into the pocket of the weapons belt Matt had laid claim to—and some very odd-looking needles that were clearly not for knitting.

"Do you have dark pants?" he asked. "Maybe leather?"

Sage narrowed her eyes at her roommate. She could see the wheels turning in his devious little brain. "Why?"

Matt waggled his eyebrows at her and held up the weapons belt. "You could totally pull off this outfit."

"No!"

"C'mon. Give a guy his fantasy."

All those years spent together—all the times she'd made passes at him when she was too drunk to know better—he'd been her rock. Never taking advantage. Never judging. Matt was safe. He was gay. How could he now suggest this as a turn on? "Dude, seriously?"

"Eye candy, honey. A badass in leather is sexy no matter what the gender."

Sage let out a very unladylike snort. "Well, in that case!" She'd deny it if asked, but part of her wanted to play dress up, to become that image of the dangerously hot chick in leather, if only for a moment.

Matt squealed like a girl and clapped his hands, offering to refresh their drinks while she changed.

Some leather pants, her best push-up bra, and a tight-fitting shirt under her newly acquired jacket gave her the look she was hoping for. She stepped into the thigh loops of the utility belt and clipped it around her waist.

"Something is missing." Matt scrutinized her look. "Boots. You need kickass boots. You still have those black ones with all the belt buckles on them? Killer heels?"

Matt treated her like his personal doll, dressing her and pulling her hair into a severe ponytail. Smoky eyes and the reddest of red lipstick finished the ensemble. By the end of it, even Sage had to admit she felt the part.

Hours passed as Irish coffee turned into full-blown shots. As much as Sage had drunk, it might as well have been water for all the numbing effect it was having on her. But the simple act of playing the part had been just the therapy she needed.

Matt succumbed to the long hours and alcohol and passed out, draped across the living room couch.

Still unable to sleep, Sage continued to rummage through the photos and memories her mother had saved.

By the time she broke into the second box, all apprehension had faded, and she dove in with an eagerness to explore.

Buried at the bottom was a small sealed jewelry box. She opened it, and a handwritten letter bloomed from within, falling to the floor as it unfolded in the open air. Sage set aside the box and bent to retrieve the last words her mother might have written.

Sage,

I am so sorry for leaving you alone in this world. There is so much I wish I could have told you, so much I wanted to prepare you for, but it is not our way. You are not ready for the darkness in this world, but you must find strength in the days to come.

Our family is special. We all share an inner light that is passed down from generation to generation. Find the light within yourself and allow it to illuminate your future.

Remember that true strength comes from determination. Like your birthmark, you must find new avenues when one becomes blocked. There is always another way. Defeat is not an option.

When the time comes, you'll understand why I had to remain silent. But know that I have never once left you vulnerable, and even in my absence, I thought of your protection.

Enclosed is my final gift to you. Wear it close to your heart and you will never be far from the light we share.

Love always. Until the end of time.

Mom

"Way to be cryptic there, Mom." For all the alcohol she'd drunk, her mind remained sharp, but her mother's message felt like a riddle that she couldn't answer.

She retrieved the box that the letter had come with and found a necklace inside. The pendant matched the pattern of her birthmark down to the roots, but circling around it were symbols in a language she couldn't read. Not the kind of jewelry she normally wore, but because it came from her mother, she immediately put it on. It hung from a simple silver chain, long enough to be worn under a shirt with the pendant to sitting close to her heart. Just as her mother had requested.

ELEVEN

The hangover she expected from drinking so much the night before never came, a small win that Sage didn't dare to question as she popped out of bed and had a look at the clock. The day had passed her by in dreamless sleep, and her stomach ached for food.

Matt had long since departed, leaving a note on the kitchen table next to a bottle of pills.

Drink some OJ and take two of these. Doctor's orders.

He really was the perfect man. She smiled to herself, thanking her lucky stars for having him in her corner. But juice and pills wouldn't sustain her, and cooking wasn't something mommy had ever had time to teach her. Her hunger demanded something much more substantial than a microwave dinner.

Sage popped down to her favorite neighborhood pub and claimed her regular back corner booth.

"Is lover boy meeting you here tonight?" Julie came up to the table with a beer and a bowl of chips.

"What… No! Why would you…" Before Sage could finish her sentence, Mr. Blue Eyes himself strolled into the bar. "Shit!" Sage ducked behind a menu.

"You need me to run interference?" Julie asked with restrained laughter. "Or is that just nerves talking?"

Sage thought about it for a minute. Her eyes drifted over to his tight fitting grey shirt. A black canvas jacket and loose cargo pants were a far cry from the secret agent disguise he'd had the last time they met, but he still walked in with a cocky swagger. Even his hair had casually slept-in waves, giving him a devil-may-care vibe that screamed bad boy!

Mr. Blue Eyes scanned the room, possibly looking for her. Damn. She was a glutton for punishment. Intuition said no. Do. Not. Engage! But the part of her still wearing leather pants and a push-up bra—showing maximum cleavage desperately wanted a win. Just minor flirting over dinner was exactly the kind of ego boost she needed. "How about I give you a signal if he crosses a line?"

"Just order a white wine spritzer and I'll know you're in trouble." Julie set down the mug of beer and dropped a bowl of chips on the table.

"What if I order a tequila sunset?" Sage joked.

"You're on your own, babe." Julie snickered and headed back to the bar.

Sage buried her head in the menu again, more to cover embarrassment than anything else. She stuffed chips into her mouth to stave off the growling in her belly, all the while trying to rein in her nerves.

"Found you." Mr. Blue Eyes appeared above the menu. "Looks like you're up to girl code tonight."

His eager enthusiasm took her aback. She'd several men before, some worth remembering, others regrettable. But this man elicited a reaction she hadn't experienced before. His presence alone sent her stomach into an ecstatic frenzy. Despite having barely eaten anything, her hunger inexplicably subsided.

"Stalking me now?" The words flew out before she could restrain them, followed by a rush of embarrassment that painted a delicate shade of pink onto her cheeks.

"Would you blame me if I said yes?" He slid into the bar as smoothly as he'd delivered the line, and her mouth fell open in stunned silence. "But something tells me you're just as happy to see me as I am to have found you here tonight. And let me just say..." He waved a hand at her while his eyes devoured every curve her expensive bra highlighted. "Damn!"

"Your...name?" Words swirled above her head like fireflies, but she was too overwhelmed to catch any and weave them into a coherent response.

"I was hoping you'd ask. You left in such a hurry yesterday I thought I might have spooked you."

"You did."

"I get that," He admitted readily. "I was here with a girl, then came and chatted you up. Looks pretty shady, huh?"

"You said it, not me." She cracked a smile, and the pressure in her chest released. Nerves were bastards like that, tying her tongue while choking the connection to her brain, making real conversation damn near impossible. But playful snarkiness always came out with ease.

"Zack." He trained those hypnotic blue eyes on her.

"Sage," she answered a tad too quickly.

"I know," he chuckled, amusement dancing in his eyes.

"Did it again, didn't I?"

He cocked his head to the side in an adorable little move that made him look like a confused puppy.

"Open mouth. Insert foot." She added with a chuckle. There was no denying the attraction simmering between them. An exciting promise of what could be.

"Nah, you're just bolstering my ego a bit. I'll enjoy the compliment."

Julie wandered up. "Can I get you two something?"

"Yeah, maybe another beer," Sage responded, hoping at some point alcohol might effectively shut down the nerves. If not, she was doomed to sound like the village idiot all night.

"And for you?" Julie looked at Zack.

He waved away the question like a buzzing fly. "Nothing for me now."

"Not thirsty?" Sage asked.

"Maybe later," he replied slyly.

Julie met Sage's gaze for a moment, silently questioning whether she was okay. Always looking out. Sage set down the menu, butterflies filling the space where hunger had once been, and answered Julie's concern with a nod.

Zack's eyes followed the movement of her hands, and she caught the familiar light in his eyes as they landed on her wrist. Not wanting to have that conversation again, she sent her hands to rest in her lap, under the table.

"So, tell me about you," he asked after a moment of uneasy silence.

Small talk. She cringed at the thought. Inane conversation meant to fill empty space. That was the worst. She would almost rather discuss how much her birthmark looked like a tattoo over topics like the weather or where she saw herself in five years. But, as she met his eager expression, she knew he was just doing the awkward first date type thing, fishing for something to start an actual conversation with, so she tossed him some bait. "I'm a time-traveling alien from the planet Gallifrey."

"Where's your big blue box then?" he replied, without missing a beat.

Geekery was something she could talk about for hours. His speedy response gave her hope. Maybe he was just as much of a nerd as she was. Good looks and good taste might even knock Matt out of his place as Mr. Perfect. "You passed the first test with flying colors, but how do I know you're not an imperial spy or something?" she shot back at him, silently daring him to answer incorrectly.

"I am one with the Force." He smiled back at her. "And among my other affiliations, I'm a Browncoat, as well as part of the rebel alliance."

"You sound like a proper nerd." She laughed, feeling more at ease than she had all evening.

"I aim to misbehave." He waggled an eyebrow at her.

"Before I entrust you with my secrets, answer me this." Sage paused, reaching back into her databanks of nerdy trivia and catchphrases for something truly obscure. "What comes after second breakfast?"

"Elevensies, of course."

She caught sight of his sharp and unusually white teeth as he laughed. Clearly a man who took care of himself. "Then luncheon and afternoon tea."

"You don't need to know much more about me than that." Sage took a sip from her beer, feeling the cool liquid slide down her throat. "I'm a total nerd."

"I don't know a man alive who doesn't appreciate a woman who knows her sci-fi or fantasy."

"Oh really?" She snorted in disbelief. "Should I bring up the Princess Bride then?"

"As you wish. But only if I can counter with Labyrinth."

"Marry me." She snorted and immediately realized how bad that was to say in a first date situation. She said it to Matt all the time, knowing it could never be misconstrued, but the awkward pause that followed slammed her right back into reality. "I mean, you're like the perfect guy. Who knows the classics, am I right?" Her backpedaling didn't stop Zack from looking like a deer in headlights.

"You have to have some appreciation for the fantasies of man." His wording caught her a bit off guard. "Truth is stranger than fiction, they say, so where do people come up with the Goblin King, for example, or trolls or vampires, for that matter?"

Sage shrugged, having never given much thought to it. Fantasy was just make-believe. "Reality is kind of harsh, I guess. We need some kind of escape." The idea of trolls being real had never been a consideration before, but then she had just witnessed her boss turn into one the day before. What if all the stories she loved had a basis in reality? What if they'd been written by people who could actually see them? What had that guy, Grey, called himself? A Terra? If she had any writing ability, she'd put her story on paper and see if it was worth selling. For that matter, if all of it was true, where was the Doctor? Because she could definitely use a timey-wimey, wibbly wobbly big blue box to help her escape the awkwardness that had developed during their silent pause. "Escape is such a perfect word." His tone sharpened. She'd probably scared him off. "Feel free to head out if you need to."

"If I go, you're coming with me. I was hoping I could sway you into giving me a shot. No need for the club scene, maybe just a stroll? There's a park just around the corner."

Sage eyed him warily, feeling her suspicion creep back in, setting off warning bells in her mind. Less than five minutes together and he was already pushing for a change of scenery.

"Your bodyguard hasn't stopped staring daggers at me." Zack gestured subtly toward the bar.

Julie's vigilant gaze hadn't wavered since Zack's arrival. She was on standby for any cue to usher in reinforcements and whisk Sage away to safety.

"She's just looking out for me," Sage admitted, her fingers absentmindedly twirling her new necklace while she thought of something to say that might turn the conversation back to the lighter topic of fantasy. "Can't be too careful. You know how the story goes…"

"Truth is so much stranger than fiction."

Across the room, Julie held up a bottle of white wine for Sage to see.

"That won't help your case." Sage stifled a giggle and shook her head dismissively at Julie's silent offering.

"I guess not. But not everything is a horror story." He winked. "Cool necklace. Tree of life?"

"I think so."

"C'mon, fantasy nerd," he teased. "You're wearing a mythical symbol around your neck."

"It is? I mean. Yeah. It is!" Her nervous laughter did little to mask her discomfort. "It was a gift, actually, from my mom."

"Can I see?" he reached out, but as the tips of his fingers grazed the metal, he pulled back as if it had stung him.

"You okay?"

"Just caught myself on something sharp," he assured her with a grin that didn't quite reach his eyes as he withdrew his hand below the table. "It's lovely though. Definitely the Tree of Life."

Sage bowed her head playfully in defeat. "Might as well turn in my geek card, eh?"

"I'm disappointed." He chuckled. "You just aren't the woman I thought you'd be."

"Story of my life." She lifted her gaze and met his eyes. Kryptonite, for sure. Those things should come with a warning label.

"C'mon. Let's get out of here. I know how you can find redemption."

He was trying so hard to get her to leave. Was Julie's mad-dogging really that intimidating?

"I know this awesome little café bookstore not far from here." His smile sharpened suddenly. A fleeting glimpse of something predatory. "They have an entire section of occult and mythology. Let's go look up that symbol. The more you know."

The prospect of a fact-finding mission in a café bookshop was more than tempting. And it was a public place, which minimized the danger enough to tip the scales.

"Walking distance?"

"About a block or two." He stood and extended an open hand to help her up.

"Why not?" Sage stood without accepting his assistance. "Lead the way." She motioned to Julie, asking to have the beers put on her tab. Sage ate almost all her meals there, so she was more than good for it.

Though Julie didn't question the charge, the unease creasing her brow as Sage followed Zack out was impossible to miss.

The sun had set only a few hours before, but already the night had cooled into double digits. Still hot, but much more manageable than triple digits. They walked a little way down the road, heading to the quieter residential streets just off the main road. Sage lived around here and tried to remember any bookstore close to her apartment, but came up blank.

Doubt swirled in Sage's mind, but before she could voice her concerns, she felt a sudden emptiness beside her. Panic shot through her as she spun around, searching for any sign of Zack.

He'd been right there only a moment ago.

"Zack?" Her voice sliced through the stillness. No response came save for the distant shuffle of fabric against the breeze, and then pain shattered across her skull and darkness dragged her down into a suffocating void of unconsciousness.

TWELVE

The edges of Sage's vision blurred and twisted. The world shifted and morphed until she finally regained consciousness in a strange bed. Panic shot through her as she sat up, and she immediately regretted the sudden movement as it triggered an intense throbbing, like a sledgehammer repeatedly slamming against her skull it making it nearly impossible for her to focus or think clearly.

The air she breathed was stale and cold, reeking of cigarettes and disinfectant. The room itself was sparsely furnished with old, worn-out furniture. The only source of light came from a dim lamp on the nightstand and an outdated air conditioner hummed loudly in the background.

Her fingers clenched tightly onto the foreign sheets, fear gripping her heart as she struggled to make sense of where she was and why.

Questions and fears raced through her mind. Why was she here? Who had brought her here? As her heart pounded in her chest, Sage couldn't help but imagine the worst possibilities. Kidnapping, rape, human trafficking.

Sage's heart raced as she scanned the room for an easy escape route.

A door opened and Sage caught a glimpse of black leather sweeping into the room. She whimpered, more from fear than from the excruciating pain still pulsating in her head.

"You're awake. Good." Grey chuckled as he dropped onto a creaking and threadbare chair by the window. "You get one freebie."

"What the hell does that mean?"

Seeing Grey was marginally better than Zack, but just as confusing. How had she ended up with him? Were he and Zack working together?

"That vampire back there was about two seconds away from turning you into a darkling," Grey tossed out with all the concern of discussing the weather. He was still wearing the leather coat and dark clothing from the previous night. He had the whole daywalker vibe working for him, all except for that stupid fedora. The hat ruined whatever effect he was trying to go for. "You're welcome."

"I hear words coming out of your mouth, but can't understand any of them." She winced, reaching for the back of her head to find the source of her pain. Thinking only made her headache worse. "Why the hell am I here? And who the hell are you, really?

"I told you before. We're special, you and I." Grey stretched out casually, his boots thudding onto a tiny wooden coffee table. "But you have to be willing to learn the truth."

"We're back to this again, are we?" Sage groaned. "Last time you threw your story at me, you left in a huff when I asked for proof." The idea of a practical joke had long since passed, but given the circumstances, she'd much rather that was the case. "Now what? You'll lock me in until I agree to go with you?"

"If I had my way, I'd have let the vampire take you," he replied sharply. "But my bosses say I'm to bring you in… willingly."

"Not sure how they do things where you're from, but kidnapping isn't the way to get people to go anywhere with you… willingly." She threw the stupid jerk's words back in his face, hoping they would land as hard as the smack she'd love to give him. Moving amplified the headache, and she was doing her best to remain as still as possible. The pain eased when she closed her eyes, but—now that they were open and she was on dangerous ground—that wasn't a luxury she could afford.

"I saved you from the vampire who was luring you into the dark." Grey might not be openly hostile, but he wasn't exactly friendly. That fact was obvious in his aggressive tone. "Usually when someone rescues you, the appropriate response is thank you."

"There's that word again. Vampire." Talking hurt nearly as much as thinking. The last time they'd spoken, it was all fantasy turned reality mumbo-jumbo. Gods and magic.

"You've grown up in the human world with a human mentality. But you're not human, Sage."

Hearing her name spoken like that transported her back to her childhood, being yelled at by her mother. It wasn't the anger she responded to. Beyond the harshness, there was an undertone of care. Fear and frustration that—if the importance of the message wasn't heeded—something worse would happen. Despite the fact it wasn't her mother speaking, the tone still held sway, and Sage resigned herself to listen.

"Fine. Tell me about this other world." She stood up slowly, taking time to balance and put one foot in front of the other, as she wobbled toward the ensuite bathroom to grab a towel.

"That's not really my place." Gray's nonchalance ruined the previous effect his words had had on her.

"And yet you expect me to take you at face value and follow you, when clearly I already made that poor choice with the guy back there." Moving only made her pain worse. Ice would help. Sage shuffled around the room with all the speed of a grandma after hip surgery to gather supplies. She grabbed the ice bucket from the dresser and stuffed a handful of ice into a small towel. "What did you call that guy back there? Vampire?"

"You couldn't tell?"

More condescension. That was what she needed from him.

"How was I supposed to tell he was a creature that isn't supposed to exist?" Makeshift icepack in hand, she used her hair tie to close it, and set it on her aching head.

Grey snickered, but she wasn't about to take grief over her first aid skills. She pointed to her head. "Life hacks."

"Where were your life-hacking skills back there?" Grey doubled over with laughter. "You completely missed the fangs and how cold and pale he was."

So much for showing off. He had her there.

She had recognized something *other* about Zack at the bar. But beyond drooling over a cute guy giving her attention, she'd ignored the clues. He did have unusually sharp teeth. His eyes were unnaturally blue. She should have paid better attention to the inner alarms screaming at her. So much for that win she'd wanted. "We met in a bar at night."

That wiped the smile from his face. "Famous last words."

"Yeah. I get it. Game over." Ice worked to cool the angry throbbing of her head, but embarrassment turned up the temperature in her cheeks. "I'm paying attention now, and if you think I'm just going to gallivant off with some jerk who lurks in the shadows and is trying as hard as he can to get me to follow him into the unknown, then you have another thing coming, mister."

"Oh, tough girl," he taunted. "Did I hit a nerve?"

She scowled. "Does it make you feel like a big man or something, taking pot shots at me?" "Feel free to take a shot of your own, if you can."

Tempting as it was, she wasn't in fighting form. "Maybe when I've recovered."

Grey let his feet drop to the ground and opened his arms wide. "Anytime."

He might have saved her, but his bedside manner made Sage wish the vampire had just taken her out. There was no escape at this point, though despite his attitude, he'd piqued her curiosity enough to wonder how much truth he had to tell. "Give me some reason to trust what you say."

"I saved you from him, didn't I?"

"That remains to be seen. What exactly was he going to do to me? Drink my blood?" Sage cringed.

"For starters, yes." His reply came without any sense of irony.

"So he was going to kill me?"

"Worse."

Extracting information from him was only making her head hurt worse. She was sure she'd get more information talking to a brick wall. "Explain."

"You're not human." He whipped a finger at her like an accusation. "You wouldn't just die. Vampires, as a species, are an abomination. Stolen magic. Once human, they are made immortal through removing that which makes them mortal and replacing it with the essence of magic. But what they gain comes at a price. They're cursed creatures. And because of that, their kind can do significant damage to our people."

Every answer she got created more questions, and sent her further down the rabbit hole. "But aren't we already immortal?"

"Yes, we are. And should they remove from us what makes us special and replace it with their curse…" He let the words trail off as if expecting her to understand.

She didn't. Sage shrugged and shook her head, utterly confused. He might as well have been speaking a different language.

That earned her a disappointed groan. "He would have drained your body of blood, extinguishing your inner light. Taking away your magical essence. In other words, you would die!"

"But you said—"

He growled with frustration. "Between the final moments of life and death, he would share his blood with you. And as that happened, all sense of self and consciousness would be erased from your body. All that would remain would be your strength. You'd become a mindless slave, with him as your master."

She wished he would crack a smile or give any indication of joking, but his deadpan delivery rang with more truth than she was prepared to handle.

"Why?" The words escaped her mouth in a whispered breath before she could stop herself.

"We're considered neutral on the supernatural spectrum. Good and evil are always battling for the upper hand."

"How is that an advantage?"

"They gain a very strong and sun-resistant slave." Grey shrugged.

"And what of the other side?"

"Other side of what?"

"Good and evil. If evil makes you a lifeless zombie, what do the good… creatures… do?"

"Good by nature does not do evil," he replied snarkily.

"Okay, so I stay away from vampires and my life is perfect. Thanks for the tip. I need to go home now and eat a bottle of pain killers." Sage stood to leave, feeling woozy from the rush of sudden movement.

"We're neither good nor evil. We balance both sides. Is that what you're passive-aggressively trying to ask me?"

"You know, if you'd just be a little more helpful with info, this would go so much easier. Just lay it out there for me." Sage clutched at her forehead as if she might grasp the pain and pull it out. The ice from her makeshift pack had melted enough to saturate her hair, and cold water began to stream down her face like tears. She'd have allowed herself to cry if she were alone. Between pain and confusion, Sage felt near the point of cracking up.

"We are the agents of order among the warring supernatural factions. There are three base classes of magic." He counted off on his fingers. "Elementals can control and manipulate the elements. So like earth, air, fire, water, metal, and so on. They can remake what's already there. Ethereals can create something from nothing. Shades work within the realm of the unseen. They're the most unknown element of magic. They're the ones that can creep into your mind. They can hear thoughts. Manipulate desires. Probably the most powerful of all."

Grey closed up his hand and turned his wrist over, revealing his mark. "Just like the tree of life is our symbol, it's a roadmap of how the branches of magic have evolved. From the roots all the way to the crown, you have a base that branches out hundreds of different directions." He ran his finger along the pattern, following it outward to the circle of leaves surrounding it. "From those base classes come all the other levels of magical creatures."

Spoken like a well-rehearsed speech. Grey might as well have handed her a pamphlet.

Her thoughts suddenly shifted to Matt. He was as normal as they came. Human, like she thought she was. "And where do humans fit into this equation?"

"Humans are the most deadly of all. They can never know of our existence. That, all sides agree on."

"Why fear them? That makes no sense."

Grey all but rolled his eyes, scoffing at her comment as if she had just told him the sky was green and the grass blue. "Humans outnumber us on every front and are prone to extreme acts of violence when provoked by fear. They'll eradicate their own in order to destroy a threat."

"So we're the balance, you say? Like a supernatural police force? While keeping the humans from knowing about us?"

"If you must dumb it down to that level, sure." Grey pressed his palm to his head with a groan. "First thing you have to understand is that no race is good or evil. It's the individual that chooses how to use their gifts. Those whom you might perceive as angelic might be as slippery as that guy you met in the alley tonight. And those whom you consider demonic can be as sweet as candy. It is not for us to decide who is what. We're the ones who bring back order when rules are broken, or the balance has been shifted."

His words were beginning to make sense, a reality scarier than any nightmare she'd ever had. But the way he was handling her during this terrifying revelation only made things worse.

Sage gave herself a moment to calm her nerves and slow her heart before responding. Beyond all the scary stuff, it did seem as if he or the ominous bosses he claimed to work for had things relatively under control. That meant there was order and protection, and maybe even people who could teach her with patience and understanding. "Why us?"

"Because our people can't be affected by the things most supernatural creatures can do. The vampire, for instance, couldn't compel you."

"No. He just sweet-talked me into a dark alley. Then knocked me out." Sage bitterly rubbed her sore head.

"He was smart. They're all getting smarter, unfortunately. But the bottom line is, so long as our inner light burns bright, no magic affects us. We're not only neutral in the fight between good and evil, we're naturally and completely, magically neutral. No spells, no enchantments, no hypnosis, nothing otherworldly will have an effect on you. For that reason, you're well suited to this job."

"And I have to take it?"

"No. You can die. Or be turned into a darkling. You've used up your one freebie with me."

Whoever his boss was, Sage couldn't wait to meet them. If for nothing else, she could complain about the horrible way he'd mocked and ridiculed her with every breath. "This is what my mother did." The memories came trickling back. Her mom had always been sent away on business trips. Sometimes she came back battered and bruised. An agent at ASSET.

"That's how I knew to look for you. The Phoenix office called in your location and description when Miranda was reported dead."

Mark had often tried to get her to come to work for him. If he were in on the secret too, she knew she'd be okay. He was the closest thing she had to family. "ASSET," she whispered to herself.

"That's a shell company. Anonymous Supernatural Security and Elimination Taskforce."

"Supernatural? I thought the first S stood for Strategic?"

"You really think we'd put the word supernatural right out there for all the humans to see?"

He had a point there.

"ASSET has offices in every major city in the world."

As fantastical as it all seemed, the pieces fit. Mark had protected her as the next in line every time her mother had been sent out, knowing that if the worst happened, she'd be awoken. "Why didn't my mom tell me?"

"Look, I don't do the emotional breakdown thing, so don't start crying." Grey held up his hands to silence her. "My job is to bring you in. Once you get there, you can do the whole, why me thing with senior staff."

Between a rock and a hard place, she had no choice. The truth was staring her in the face, no matter how much she wanted to ignore it. And at this point, talking to anyone other than Grey would be better. "Fine. Whatever. Take me to ASSET."

THIRTEEN

Sage clung to Grey as they roared through the streets of Las Vegas on his roaring motorcycle.

Wind whipped her hair into a frenzy, lashing her chin like a cat-o'-nine-tails. Exposed to the elements, she could feel the dirt clinging to her skin. A thin film of grime coated her arms as her sweat dried in the air. She'd never ridden on a motorcycle before. Who would want to? Death traps. Grey had better be right about the whole immortality thing. Nothing separated her from a major case of road rash—or worse—if his insane weaving through traffic led them to an accident.

She squeezed her eyes shut, and mumbled, "Magical immunity" as a mantra as Grey brought them speeding down a thin line between cars stopped at an intersection. Sage reminded herself that her mom had worked for ASSET. She was heading toward knowledge and understanding. Answers to all the insanity. If they made it alive.

"Tell me when we get there." She cringed and buried her face, closing her eyes as they narrowly missed the side mirrors jutting out from cars.

"You sure you're really the daughter of Miranda Cynwrig?" His mocking laughter and condescending tone deserved a slap upside the head. Maybe after they'd parked, and he took the helmet off.

Sage smiled at the idea as they traveled toward the center of downtown Vegas, squeezing into an even tighter web of densely packed one-way streets. Before she could get her bearings, Grey turned into a parking garage and drove down into a basement-level space.

He pulled off his helmet and flashed a strange, knowing grin. "Know where we are?"

"Not really." Rule number one when living in Las Vegas. Avoid Downtown and The Strip at all costs. "Short of a few parking fines and jury duty, I stay far from the old casinos and official city buildings."

"Something else you'll have to get used to, then." He laughed, as if causing her any inconvenience improved his day. "Welcome to your new home."

Who referred to work as *home*? She might have to agree to work downtown, but home was her comfortable apartment with Matt and eventually his boyfriend Josh. Because there was no way Sage was ever letting the best roommate in the world go.

She stopped short and reached into her pockets, fishing for her phone. In all the commotion, she hadn't let Matt know what was going on. He'd be worried when he noticed she hadn't come home.

But these weren't her normal jeans. Still in the leather ensemble from the previous night, Sage couldn't remember the last time she'd held her phone or her wallet. They could be anywhere. The bar. That hotel room. Or Zack might have taken them off her during the hours of blackout that left a hole in her memory.

Shit!

"You coming?" Grey stopped short in front of a bank of elevators.

Reality trumped the fantasyland Sage was about to enter. Credit cards would have to be canceled. She'd just been laid off. How was she going to find money for a new phone? Stress riveted her in place. She'd have to get a new ID card, too. How exactly was she supposed to make time for all of that?

"What's wrong now?" Grey groaned.

"My purse. My phone. My life?" Panic sharpened her tone. "Pick one."

"Check the saddle bag." He pointed toward the motorcycle. "Hurry."

A small win—her purse and wallet were there, as was her phone, although it was dead. Trivial things, but in her current state, they meant the world. She could breathe again and focus.

Back in Phoenix, ASSET had a gorgeous white high-rise, flooded with light from every angle. The kind of place that felt welcoming and inviting, giving the illusion of transparency and truth. Little had she known what lay hidden in plain sight.

"This is ASSET, right?" The building gave no sign it belonged to a company at all. No signs. No placards. Even the parking lot was bare of names for its employees.

"Welcome to the Vegas branch, yes." Grey led her into the elevator and they rode it all the way to the top floor, exiting into a vast and open space with offices and conference rooms on either side. A large reception desk stood sentry at the center of the lobby. Behind it, there were hallways leading to more of the building. Back home, they had a lovely large cafeteria for the employees and training rooms where she'd watched her mother practice with the latest equipment. She'd loved seeing the dance of daggers and had even been offered chances to try her skill at knife throwing. For a kid, it was like a playground. Knowing better now, if this place housed the same space, it would be for serious work.

A tiny girl with silvery-blue hair sat at the large receptionist's desk, answering phones, and jotting down notes. She smiled at Sage and Grey as they passed. People scurried like little ants, paying no attention to Sage or Grey, as they traveled from one office to the next.

"This way." He guided her toward one of the glass-enclosed offices that sat just beyond the reception desk.

Inside, a fierce woman sat slaying the keys on her laptop, her turquoise eyes glued to the screen as if it held the secrets of life itself. Behind her, an impressive assortment of medieval-style weapons were mounted on the walls. Swords of folded steel were the first thing that caught her eye. Inlaid with patterns and magical symbols, they seemed to shimmer as they caught the light from the window. One had a cross guard ornately decorated with gems. It couldn't possibly be used for fighting. Just the kind of weapon her character would use on game night. If her phone hadn't died, she'd have taken a picture to show her RPG group. Magic users loved their pretty, shiny weapons, but used them more for decoration. It was her spells that did the damage in dungeon raids.

Sage's eyes darted all over the room, marveling at the vast array of pointy, shiny things. A large war hammer, probably too heavy to mount, sat propped against the back corner of the office. All of it amounted to an impressive collection Sage desperately wanted to reach out and touch. But first impressions and all, Sage didn't dare reach a hand out. By the looks of the office, the lady busy at her computer was a grand high muckety muck of some kind. With any luck, good behavior might earn Sage a chance to play later.

"That was faster than we expected," the woman said, and pointed over her computer screen to the seats opposite her desk. Her fingertips looked as if they had been covered in lace. The pattern reached to her forearms, surrounding the tree-shaped marking that designated her as a Terra. The tattooed gloved might have been henna or some form of tribal ink. Grey had said they were immortal. Maybe this woman was *that* old. Her tree looked darker, but with all the changes happening, Sage wondered if her mark would darken, too. Before Sage could take a good look at the patterns surrounding the special mark at her wrist, the woman barked, "Sit. Wait. I'll be finished in a moment."

Not exactly the warm and fuzzy welcome Sage had been hoping for. Mark had always been the most gregarious of guys, even as the director of operations. The grandest of the poohbahs at ASSET Phoenix, Mark was cheerful and welcoming to anyone who crossed his path. Maybe Sage should have taken him up on the offer to work there. The vibe she was getting at the moment was neither happy nor welcoming. Still, this was all new, and she'd made it this far, so it was time to see if she could get the answers promised.

"We had some trouble with a vampire that helped sway the decision to come in," Grey responded, and took his seat. "They're still pretty riled up. Might want to send some peace keepers."

Sage followed his lead and took the remaining chair, wondering what trouble Grey was referring to. She'd only met one vampire, but his words implied more.

"Understatement of the century, Maddox," the woman replied with annoyance. "They're out for vengeance. I've got reports of vampires and Shades openly attacking patrols. Together. Thanks to last week's little kerfuffle, we've got the beginnings of a line being drawn in the sand." Her fingers nimbly clacked away at the keyboard while she spoke. The words might have been chosen to make it sound less threatening, but the meaning came through loud and clear. Sides being picked for a battle. Vampires and Shades.

Sage had yet to learn which side was which at that point. She turned to Grey, wanting to ask what was going on, but held her tongue. Getting answers out of him had already proven to be as hard as pulling vampire teeth.

"Word on the streets is they're looking for something," he said casually.

"Do we know what that something is, Mr. Maddox?" The woman's response came as sharp as the blades hanging on the wall behind her.

Grey's eyes said yes, but when he spoke, his casual tone didn't betray the lie. "If I knew, I wouldn't have called it *something*."

"I have the ethereal factions breathing down my neck, new recruits to locate and retrieve, and let's not forget the budget and maintenance of this building. Don't bother me with *somethings*. It is your job to know. Do your damn job!" Even as she reprimanded him, the woman kept her eyes locked on the computer screen.

Grey didn't seem to be bothered by it. Not surprising. Given the abrasive attitude he'd displayed with Sage, she expected he was used to getting it back in spades from upper management. He sat casually in the chair, his fingers toying with the grip of a blade sheathed in his belt. A sword, based on the length of its handle, but short enough to prevent her from noticing it, hiding under his leather coat. *Dagger perhaps, or maybe a machete.*

The longer she sat, the more regretted coming. She'd expected some kind of welcome, or at the very least, acknowledge her being in the room. But for all the attention she'd gotten, Sage might as well have been one of the ornamental weapons hanging on the wall.

She let out a sigh loud enough to remind them of her presence.

"Do you have any training?" the woman finally asked.

Sage stood and looked down over the top of the computer screen to meet the face of her would-be new boss. "Hi. I'm Sage."

Those turquoise eyes glared up at her. "I know who you are. I'm looking at your file. What training do you have? Weapons? Martial arts?"

Everyone in the Las Vegas office had the same brick wall mentality when it came to conversation, it seemed. Sage took a breath and plastered a sweet smile across her face as she replied, "I'm sorry, what is your name?"

Scowling in response, the woman tapped the end of her pen on a nameplate at the edge of the desk. Director Ava Masters. "Training?"

"I take mixed martial arts twice a week," Sage responded in her best saccharine tone. "And my mother taught me how to use a knife."

"No training." Ava all but rolled her eyes as she shoved the pencil she was holding into a knotted bun at the top of her head for safekeeping.

"I just said—"

"You take classes, honey. And you've played with knives. That's not training," Ava replied. "Another newbie to be coddled. Just what I needed on my plate."

"Sorry to disappoint you." Sage threw the same snarky tone back at Ava.

"Training wheels, dear." Ava stood, and a smile replaced her scowl. "You're grounded to the premises until we get you adequately brought up to speed."

"Wait. I have a life. My apartment—"

"Had," Ava cut her off. "We will assist in closing your affairs."

"You can't do that. That's kidnapping."

Ava pressed a button on her phone. "Rina. I need you to process Sage Cynwrig's paperwork." A moment of silence held the room in thrall before a tiny voice over the speaker replied, "Yes, Ms. Masters." And just as quickly, Ava returned her commanding glare to Sage, waggling a finger of disappointment as she continued her lecture. "You're far from a child. And I'm sure Grey's already warned you what is out there. With the Vampire and Shade factions threatening war, I have Terras with nearly a century of experience being taken out… daily. I can't afford to watch out for one little girl who misses her boyfriend."

"That's not fair. My mother had a life and home."

"And your mother, ancient as she was, lost her light to exactly the same type of creature you ran into. She's a darkling now. You want to join her?"

Ava's words hit her like a slap to the face. Mark had told her mother was dead, that her plane had gone down in the Atlantic. No one had said anything about *darklings*. Sage opened her mouth to speak, but words failed to come. Tears, however, screamed with anguish as they leaked unchecked from the corners of her eyes.

"I'm sorry to be so blunt, but that is the fact. You are important, untrained as you are, and I'm not risking the safety of anyone under my command. You'll have to put aside your old life for the time being and learn your job. Understood?"

Ava didn't wait for her to answer. Not that Sage could have summoned her voice if she'd wanted to. Miranda might still be out there? As a darkling, whatever the hell that was. Why wouldn't Mark tell her the truth? And to hear it from such a cold and unfeeling woman—it was like hearing she'd died all over again, with all the pain that accompanied it.

A few more keystrokes and the printer came to life. Ava whipped out the document and handed it to Grey. "Take her to quarters and then see she's introduced to the trainer."

FOURTEEN

Sage stood, a slip of paper clutched in her hand—bunk number four. The door to the dorm loomed before her, indifferent to her unceremonious induction into a magical police force without so much as a signing bonus. Come to think of it, she hadn't signed anything at all.

A brick-like weight sunk in her pocket—the dead phone within offered as much solace as the empty corridors around her. She couldn't even call a friend or reach out to Mark as a lifeline. This wasn't her home. She felt neither welcome nor a sense of belonging here. Aside from a stupid mark on her wrist, she had nothing in common with any of the people she'd met. And that Ava woman had a serious stick up her ass. She didn't need kid gloves, but a little compassion given the circumstances might have helped smooth this transition along.

Sage reached to the necklace from her mother. Her fingers found solace in the cold silver, tracing the delicate branches of the tree pendant. She was a Cynwrig. What would her mother have told her?

You are not ready for the darkness in this world, but you must find strength in the days to come… Find the light within yourself and allow it to illuminate your future.

Remember that true strength comes from determination… Defeat is not an option.

The phantom echo of her mother's words wrapped around her like a shawl. Though it was far from ideal, Sage had to give this new reality a try. If for nothing else, to honor the memory of her mother. She'd worked for ASSET, so there had to be some good here.

Sage crossed the threshold into living space, divided by necessity rather than design. Two bunk beds were pressed up against the wall with a tall chest of drawers separating them. Each drawer bore a number matching the associated bed. She'd been assigned number four—lower bunk and bottom drawer. At least she wouldn't have to climb over anyone when it came time to sleep.

Despite being on the top floor of the building, the room had no window, and the only light came from a fluorescent lamp above. Its harsh, unforgiving glow set the feel for how her life would be in this facility. So much for the fantasy. But maybe that was the point. Admittedly, she wasn't ready to face the truth of all magic could be. Cold, drab, and ordinary might actually be a relief at the end of the day.

"You ready yet?" Grey knocked on the door but kept his distance. "We're due in the training hall."

She hadn't realized how long she'd been standing there in the room. He'd told her to drop her things and be ready. That must have been a while ago. "I've got nothing to train in, remember?"

"Newbies." Grey pointed to the drawer. "Suit up." She didn't see him retreat, but heard his footsteps as he wandered down the hallway.

Drab gray shorts and a matching t-shirt. If only she had been allowed to pack a bag before they left. As much time as she spent in the gym, half her closet and dresser at home were active wear. The other option in the drawer looked like some kind of space age jumpsuit. She'd save that for later.

When Grey returned, he crooked a finger and started walking away.

She followed silently in his wake as he gave her the dime tour of the facility. The entire upper floor was the agent-level. Training halls, sleeping quarters, cafeteria, laundry, infirmary, and computer stations. There were other levels to the building, but when she asked, Grey evaded as usual, saying that was *need to know info*, and of course, she didn't need to know just yet. She remembered prisoners being brought into the ASSET building back in Phoenix and suspected they had a space dedicated to prisoners as well. Not a place she wanted to see, anyway.

Grey led her down one hallway and through another until they came into a large space with padded floors that reeked of sweat and faint traces of blood. Punching bags had been hung from the ceiling in the back corners of the room. One wall was dedicated to mirrors, and along another wall was a line of benches next to cubbies filled with various sparring equipment.

"Welcome to the non-lethal training room." Grey's smile was almost mocking. "Try not to die in here."

"Your confidence is so endearing," Sage shot back, hoping to knock that stupid hat off his head before the day was over. "Careful now. Someone might think you actually cared about me."

"She's all yours, Dev," Grey shouted to the empty room.

"Miss Sage, we meet again." Devon appeared as if blinking into existence, startling her with his sudden proximity.

"Where did you—" she started to ask, but realized she didn't need an answer. Her kind were the ones with negligent powers. Materializing out of thin air was more than she could ever do. Which of course meant that Devon was some kind of *other*.

"Told you I knew you were special. I don't let just anyone into my gym." Devon gave her a hug, throwing his massive arms around her so tightly she thought she might pop.

Finally a familiar face, though he was undoubtedly going to kick her ass during their sessions together. Tough as nails, Devon held nothing back. Brutal honesty was his manner, and that instilled a sense of trust that Sage knew she could count on.

Smiling for the first time since she'd arrived, Sage pulled back to meet her trainer's eyes. "So you're a…" His were not the turquoise she'd become accustomed to, understanding that was a trait of her people. Nor were his the icy blue of the vampire she'd had a run-in with. Devon's were a silver-gray. "Not a Terra." She didn't know what to call him. Words had been thrown around her since she arrived, with none really making sense. Shade and Ethereal sounded magical, but she had no idea what they signified.

"I'm no Terra." Devon snickered, as if privy to an inside joke. "I'm not… *special*… like you. But I'm on your side."

"But also not human, either?" she asked.

Devon gave a sideways glance to Grey. "She hasn't been briefed?"

Gray shook his head.

"They skipped orientation." Sarcasm slipped out before Sage could bite it back.

Devon rose to his full height, cracking his knuckles and flexing his muscles as he towered over Sage. "I'm what you might think of as an ogre."

He hadn't used magic. Not that it should have any effect on Sage, being a Terra, but with just those subtle movements, she could have sworn Devon had doubled in size. Short as she was, looking up gave her a neck ache. She stepped back a pace to get a good look at him. Ogres were supposed to be big, ugly things. At least, that was what she'd come to expect from all the RPGs. They were meat shields because of their size, but that was all just gamer stuff. He'd said it with no sense of humor, almost as if proud to use the term.

"But you don't look—"

"What? Ugly?" Devon's voice was sharp as a blade.

"I didn't say that. You did!"

"You didn't have to. I could see it in your eyes."

"I guess I just thought… you know… movies, games, there is a sort of character type."

"Propaganda!" Devon scoffed. "My people are cunning fighters. We're the masters of warfare." His chest swelled with pride as he thumped it with a fist.

It was all she could do to keep a straight face. Some stereotypes fit.

"This whole supernatural *other lives* thing is all a bit crazy town. You don't look like…"

"Did you expect to see some burly green monster?" The corners of Devon's mouth lifted in amusement.

"Yeah. I guess." Sage shrugged. "I mean, where's the magic? The otherness?"

That earned a genuine smile from Devon. "You're not ready for the scary shit yet."

"Might make this whole thing more believable." *Rip the bandage off, as Matt would say.* Sage sighed, but it failed to release her tension. "I mean, how am I supposed to just know someone is special, when everyone I've met, apart from my troll of a boss, has looked like an everyday Joe?"

"It gets better." Devon's eyes flicked to Grey, then back, sharing an unspoken thought. "But you really need to prepare yourself or you might just go mad the first time you meet an Ethereal."

"I need to get going." Grey stepped toward the door. "You got her?"

"She's in expert hands," Devon replied.

Once Grey vanished through the doorway, the air in the room lightened perceptibly around Sage. Turning toward her mentor, she peered into his assessing gaze. "So how do I tell who is what? Everyone looks so normal."

That seemed to amuse him. "Enjoy the normalcy. It's the ones you meet out there that will surprise you."

Maybe she was just so used to seeing the unusual that she'd never recognize the differences. More questions with no answers. Par for the course. "Did you know? When you met me?"

"I saw your mark." Devon pointed to her arm. "Dead giveaway." Sage moved her right hand instinctively to cover her wrist. "That's why I agreed to train you. Some of us have glamours. Keeps humans from seeing our true selves. You Terras with your birthmarks are like walking billboards."

"Wait, so is that why I was seeing my boss turn into a troll? Glamour?"

Devon snorted. "Bet that was a shock, eh?"

"I might have screamed like a little girl."

"You are a little girl. We need to work on that." He pointed to the mat. "Which is why you train with me. No mercy. We need to get you into fighting form before you're sent out to battle."

"Wait? Battle?" Her pulse quickened as she absorbed his words. "Are we at war?"

"Figure of speech. Your people are, for lack of a better word, the enforcers of law. Which, at times, requires a bit of force to be applied."

"So you're going to teach me how to kick magical butt. I'm cool with that." Sage sank into a ready position.

"How about we learn how not to get our non-magical butts kicked first?" He assumed a defensive position. "You'll be up against people accustomed to using their magic. Since it has no effect on you, that levels the playing field some, but doesn't stop them from being able to drop your scrawny butt."

Brutal honesty. But at least she knew it came from a place of good. Devon inspired trust, where Grey had just been an asshole picking on her ignorance.

"So, do all creatures have special powers?" Sage kept her hips loose, ready to move in either direction, expecting one of Devon's meaty fists to slam into her at any moment.

"Creatures?" His chuckle preceded a teasing jab. "What are we? Pets or something?"

She deflected his fist across her body. "I don't know the proper word, okay? Cut me some slack."

His next strike came low. "Be respectful when you speak. There are many races within our realm."

"So each one has unique"—avoiding his foot, sweeping her legs, she hopped back—"abilities and gifts?"

"Better!" Devon smiled.

Compliments from him were few, and distracted by his quick approval, she dropped her guard long enough to allow him to get in a nasty blow.

The wind escaped her lungs as she collided with the padded ground. But knowing he'd be on her in a second, Sage blindly rolled to her left as she fought to regain her breath.

"Some of our kind have active powers and some, passive. You, for instance." He didn't pursue as she retreated from his last attack. "Completely passive. Which is why you need to be able to fight."

"I'm magic neutral." She panted as she backed toward the far wall. "Not passive."

"Could have fooled me." Devon stood in the center of the room, arms crossed, unimpressed by her retreat. "You're not able to absorb or use magic, which means you can't be fooled by it. But what you lack in active magic, you can make up for in skills, if you ever gain any."

She finally gained control of her breath. "And your power?"

"The patience of a god." He tapped a foot.

Her ribs ached as she stood. The fall had bruised more than her ego, but he'd warned her. *No mercy.* "You can be affected by magic, right?"

"Correct. Not that it will help you in this fight, Miss Neutral."

He wasn't offering his secrets, which meant he had some she'd eventually have to discover, but now was not the time. "Trolls?"

"Not the prettiest among us, but they have glamour for that." His stony expression faltered for a fraction of a second. "Keen mind for numbers, though. Just don't piss them off. Terrible tempers."

"What else?" Sage came forward again and reset into fighting position, watching Devon's hands, looking for a sign of his next move.

Devon smiled and relaxed, letting his arms unfold as he walked, creating a perimeter around her. "You have your standard shifters."

Light feet, loose hips, ears like a radar listening for direction and proximity. Sage paid attention, determined to stand her ground this time.

He circled around her twice. "Shape-changers can morph into anything living and copy the physical identity of other people. Hybrids, like the werewolf, can change only into the animal form of the thing that cursed them. They're a kind of stolen magic. Same with vampires. They're humans infused with dark magic that alters them irreparably. They may have immortality, but it comes at a steep price."

A hand landed lightly on her shoulder.

"Silver bullets and sunshine?" She twisted to the side and took hold of his wrist, bringing it around with her.

"Yep." Devon replied, breaking her flimsy hold. With practiced skill, he turned her momentum into his advantage and before she knew it, he had her by the arm. Tweaking it with just the right amount of pressure, he crippled her. One wrong move and her wrist would snap in half. She screeched as she worked to maneuver into a spot where she could gain any kind of leverage. "No mercy, Sage. Life or death. How do you get out?"

Every move she made, he countered, keeping in control while she remained in eye-watering pain. The more she struggled, the harder he pressed on her pressure points, so she stopped struggling. She allowed herself to relax and submitted to his control.

The moment she did, Devon's grip loosened. "This is how you fight back? Giving up?"

She gauged the proximity of his body as she stood in place. *No pain, no gain,* she told herself, as she threw her head back, hitting Devon in the jaw. The sharp sting shot through her skull, but his grip relaxed enough for her to pull away.

Sage ran to the other side of the room, and as soon as she reached the wall, she turned and set herself for his attack.

"You can't always run from your problems," he taunted, rubbing the spot on his jaw where she'd struck him.

"Live to fight another day?"

"That's a victim's mentality. You'll never be an agent at this rate."

"No one asked if I wanted to be an agent."

"More victim's mentality. Quit that shit right now. You're part of a world very few are privy to. Be proud. Your people are regarded with the highest of reverence, next to the damn gods."

"But…" *There's always a but!*

"But I want to cry like a little baby because life is hard." Devon mocked her with words she'd expect to hear from Grey.

He was right. She got dealt a hand she'd never expected, but rather than see the silver lining, she'd been focused on all the negatives. Sage crossed back toward him. "You're right. I'm a god-damned superhero."

Devon snorted with laughter. "I'll make you a deal. You shape up. I'll make you a cape."

"Purple," Sage demanded.

"What?"

"My favorite color." She took the moment of confusion and came at him, fists flying for his jaw. "Oh, and how about crushed velvet?"

He deflected, countering low to throw her off balance. "You're going to be the Plush Wonder?"

Her ankle sagged as she twisted awkwardly and tumbled to the mats.

"More like roadkill." Devon's foot was already in motion when she looked up and narrowly missed his heel drilling down toward her stomach.

She made it to her feet as fast as she could, but Devon was almost on top of her. With his hulking form towering over her, she knew she had to topple the beast if she hoped to gain the upper hand. "Captain Trainwreck at your service." She threw the full weight of her body into his abdomen, the edge of her shoulder hitting the target of his belly button.

He didn't go down, but she knocked him off balance enough to get in a single punch as he fought to stay standing.

"Enough for now." Devon held his hands up. "You're definitely a train wreck, but I like that you're attempting to think on your feet. Knowing an opponent's center of balance will increase your chances of using leverage against them."

"Was that an actual compliment?" Sage clutched her chest with an exaggerated gasp of shock.

"You haven't earned a gold star yet, but you have promise." He smiled. "Thinking on your feet will be key for you. Not every encounter will be a physical one, but when backs are to the wall and you're up against someone who's used to using magic to do their battles, they will come at you hard and fast... physically."

"Don't we get weapons?" Sage had pulled an impressive assortment from the boxes that belonged to her mother. Throwing daggers and knives of all sorts. She could do some damage if given a bit of refresher with those. And that thought excited her more than it probably should have.

"If you know how to use what you have right here"—he grabbed hold of her hands and shook them for effect—"then you don't need to worry about other weapons."

"I'd still feel safer with something sharp and pointy." She pulled away.

Devon narrowed his eyes, sizing her up. "A sharp mind trumps a pointy object any day. When you come up against the Elementals, that's the only weapon that will work."

"Ele-what-now?" More words she had yet to learn the meaning of. People around this place seemed to enjoy throwing around terms that sounded ominously broad.

"Special people whose magic works on physical objects. The general classification is Elemental."

"But you said magic doesn't work on me."

"You may not be hurt by magic, but that neutrality doesn't always extend to the items you hold." Devon nodded toward some benches. "Take a seat. I'm going to get you some reading material."

"We have study guides?" Sage snickered as she started walking.

"Yeah, we do. Pretty smart, huh?"

"Maybe open with that next time," she suggested, with as much snark as she could muster. "Wait. So does that mean there will be a test?"

Devon disappeared through a doorway that she'd have never known was there if she hadn't seen him open it, which made her wonder what other secret passages might be right in front of her nose. And if there were secret passages, it would stand to reason that there were hidden rooms and cameras. She could be being watched at that very moment. Sage turned around, taking stock of the room with new wonder. Her eyes landed on the mirrors. Typical of most gyms, but this wasn't a typical gym. Instinct said was being watched. And probably graded. Her stomach churned with anxiety.

Devon returned with spiral-bound books in hand. "First thing you have to remember about magical *others* is we are neither good nor evil. We're individuals." He handed over the small stack of three books. "These will give you some basics on the most common of our kind you might run into and how they're classed."

"And what am I supposed to do when I run into them?" She still wasn't sure of exactly what her role would be.

"That will be based on individual assignments when you're ready." Devon looked down his nose at her. "And based on today's performance, you've got ways to go. So let's not worry about that now." He must have sensed her low mood, because his tone softened as he put a hand on her shoulder. "We all have to start somewhere. You just got dropped into a world you didn't know existed. I'm kind of surprised you're acting as cool about it as you are."

"You'd be the first. Everyone else I talk to expects me to just roll with the punches."

"Of course they do. Keeps you from being allowed to feel the sheer size of things. Management needs good little soldiers, not people who are freaking out and causing a scene."

"You don't care?"

"I'm not management. Just the hired help." Devon winked.

"So you don't live here?"

"You've seen my gym. I have my own business. I help here as a favor to the organization."

"Why?"

"Because I believe they do good for this world."

"I thought you said it's about balance, not good or evil?"

"Balance is good for everyone. Too much evil leads to death and corruption in all aspects of life."

"And too much good?"

"Makes people complacent and easy to manipulate."

"I'm the one feeling manipulated here." Sage suspected Grey or maybe Ava were behind the mirrors, secretly grading her.

"You are. For the moment," Devon replied, with his usual blunt honesty. "But once you're more familiar with things, it will make sense. Trust me."

Sage hugged the new books close to her chest as she stood to leave.

"Study up and get some sleep. You and me, first thing in the morning. You want that superhero cape? You better be ready to bring it."

FIFTEEN

Books were good for one thing. Information. Answers without having to ask the right questions. Devon had given her a wealth of material to study. Most read like character guides for the games she played, but one in particular was filled with intriguing mythologies.

Sage traced charts of various pantheons of the gods, seeing familiar names from her childhood history lessons. Every culture in the world had their own take on the beginning of time and who ruled the heavens. While this book provided no confirmation of one god over another, it tied together links and similarities within the various mythologies.

And before them, came a small group of beings that appeared to predate human mythology.

The great gods before the dawn of man each blessed the Earth with their creations.

Ethereals connected to the heavens and knowledge.

Elementals connected to the physical realm.

Shades connected to the world unseen.

Blessed with unique abilities from the deities that sired them, each claimed supremacy, believing it their destiny to rule over all who dwelled within their realm. The earliest of the demigods were violent warmongers who quickly learned they could absorb and manipulate magic from those they destroyed in battle. An ever-growing lust for power saw entire races of demigods wiped from history as the war for supremacy raged for centuries.

The original gods who left their creations to cause chaos had long since lost interest in the world, leaving only Mother Earth to provide a solution and ensure the survival of the other creatures inhabiting the world. From the blood-soaked battleground, a magnificent tree sprouted, reaching high into the heavens. Its roots tapped into the very core of the earth. A great tree of life.

It bore the fruit of a new race of beings. Terras. Rooted in the heart of the earth and connected to the life force of each race that had come before them, they were bred to counter the problems of the other three. Terras were light to the Shades, physical form that Elementals could not manipulate, and like a sponge, they could absorb the magic of the Ethereals without taking any of the effects. Mother Earth's most perfect creation, Terras were the counterbalance of all that had come before them. Through their efforts, peace and order were established among the races, allowing the world and all of the lesser creatures inhabiting it a chance to flourish.

The way her people were described in the books infused Sage with a sense of pride she didn't feel worthy of. The Terra race seemed superior and noble. Gods with a little *g* in the grand scheme of things, but outside the pages, Sage was no god. How could she count herself among such special creations? Her mother, on the other hand, had been truly special. Miranda had undoubtedly been a Terra, fighting the good fight to keep safe all the people of the earth.

Her mother's words echoed in her mind. *Know that I have never once left you vulnerable, and even in my absence, I have thought of your protection.*

She grasped the tree-shaped charm dangling around her neck. Her mother had always been a protector, even when she left Sage behind as she went off on assignments around the globe. Now Sage knew it was all in the name of keeping the world, and by extension Sage herself, safe from harm. Miranda Cynwrig proudly continued the legacy of the Terra race until her light had been extinguished. And now that same duty fell on Sage's shoulders. The weight of that mantle threatened to crush her. She wasn't ready. Her mother had known it.

You are not ready for the darkness in this world, but you must find strength in the days to come. Our family is special. We all share an inner light that is passed down from generation to generation. Find the light within yourself and allow it to illuminate your future.

Remember that true strength comes from determination. Like your birthmark, you must find new avenues when one becomes blocked. There is always another way. Defeat is not an option.

Admiring the silver tree pendant, she turned it over in her hand, comparing it to the markings on her wrist. The tree of life. More than just the mangled veins below her skin, it was a branding of her gods, a reminder of her connection to the world, rooted in the blood of the earth and linked to all who shared that blood.

Her mother's final wish had been for her to keep the pendant close to her heart, so she would remember the light they all shared. Even before she'd found the pendant or read the letter, her mother's light had found her. Disguised in a dream, Miranda had already visited to say her goodbye and awaken that light within Sage.

She traced the pattern of branches with the tip of her finger, following each one as it twisted and twined with other branches down to the trunk of the tree. Set within that trunk was an infinity symbol that reminded her of the connection they shared. She pressed on it, clicking it like a button, and opened a hidden chamber in the back. *More secrets.* A tiny maroon-colored pebble tumbled into Sage's hand. Insignificant as it looked, in her hand, it felt heavy as a stone. She picked it up, wondering what secrets it held. Precious gems had special cuts to make them twinkle. This chunk of rock had none of that luster. As plain as it appeared, Sage sensed it was important all the same. Something to bring up the next time she spoke to Mark.

Her phone sat charging on the edge of the bed. She'd picked it up numerous times and laid it back down just as quickly. For all the explanation Mark might be able to provide to her, she hadn't yet come to terms with the feelings of betrayal, knowing he'd kept this all a secret from her. He'd always been like a father. He'd protected her and kept her safe, and because of that, she'd trusted him. Yet even after she had come down to retrieve her mother's things, he'd stayed silent about all of this magical destiny crap. Had he told her the truth, then and there, she might have stayed. But he'd remained quiet. He'd let her leave, thinking Miranda's plane had gone down in the ocean. Why lie? Why let her learn the cold, hard truth from someone just as icy?

As much as she wanted to confide in Mark, her emotions ran too raw. Time would soothe them, and then she would confront him about hiding the truth.

She stared down at the tiny rock again, wondering what secrets it held. Nothing was as it seemed. That was the only certainty.

Alarm bells sounded. A red light flashed above her. Sage's first thought was that this was some kind of training exercise to test her reaction, but in the hallway, sounds of frantic footsteps said otherwise.

Sage quickly secured the stone in its hidden setting and rushed out to see what was going on.

More lights in the hallway flashed red. The alarm continued to blare. A fire, perhaps? She followed the direction others were running and headed toward the main lobby.

A fight had broken out. Agents against agents, or so it seemed. Sage had no way to distinguish each person from the others. Though some of the fighters looked as if they had seen better days. A woman whose eyes sagged with deep purple bruises fought with a fierceness that belied her frail appearance. Like a corpse reanimated, all the color had faded from her skin, but she moved just as quickly as any of the others. Sage watched from the sidelines as a blade sliced open the woman's pale skin, sending a splatter of black blood to the ground.

What was the word Grey had thrown around? Darkling? Were these the beasts he had warned her she might become, if not for their care and safekeeping within the walls of ASSET?

Weapons whizzed through the air, and painful shrieks preceded the thudding of bodies hitting the floor. Still, above all the sensory overload, alarms screamed their staccato warning.

Trapped, weaponless and uncertain what to do, Sage clung to the sidelines, hoping against hope that she wouldn't be spotted. With any luck, the battle would end before the fighting found its way further into the building.

"You should be in your room." Grey startled her, coming up from behind. Holding a machete in one hand and a large dagger in the other, he looked as if he'd already seen action. Both weapons carried the stain of blood.

"What's happening?" she squeaked, fear gripping her throat so tightly she could barely speak.

His face was speckled with the same thick black blood, but he still managed to keep that stupid fedora on his head. "Remember what I said about darklings?"

Sage nodded, wishing she had not already guessed the truth. "Yeah."

"Now you know why they're so dangerous. Go back to your room and lock the door," Grey ordered, as he returned to the fight.

No way in hell was she locking herself into a room with no exit. She'd seen plenty of horror movies end badly for people who made stupid mistakes. But staying in the thick of it all was just as bad. The elevator was out of the question, but there had to be stairs somewhere. Sage crept around the edges of the battle, hoping if she followed the hallways to the other end, she might find another way out. She kept watch on the fight in front of her, slowly backing away from the fray, until she butted up against something that was not a wall.

"Sorry—" Her voice faltered as she turned to see what she'd run into.

Eyes that had once been turquoise stared down at Sage. Black as night and circled with blood. They held a deathly gaze that betrayed no recognition, though they clearly had a target.

"This can't be possible." Sage's heart thundered as if it were trying to punch a hole through her chest. It was the nightmare all over again, only this time she was wide awake. Sage pinched herself just to be sure, but the pain only sharpened her voice as she called out, "Mom?"

SIXTEEN

Miranda Cynwrig loomed before Sage, a shadow of her former self. Sallow skin hung loosely from her bones. Her once beautiful turquoise eyes had gone dark and seemed to drain the warmth from the room.

Sage's heart raced. Panic clawed at the edges of her resolve. Instinct urged her to flee, to escape the nightmare, but she remained anchored to the spot. The woman, the creature, darkling… No matter what had happened to her, this was Miranda Cynwrig. Her mother. The one person in this world Sage had been desperate to see.

The silence stretched as Miranda's scrutiny traveled from Sage's eyes to the delicate skin of her neck. Outside, chaos reigned among those transformed, yet Miranda stood still — an anomaly that ignited a flicker of hope within Sage. Perhaps not all was lost.

She'd prayed to any gods that would listen to return her mother, and here she was, her own personal superhero. If anyone had the strength to overcome dangerous magic, it was Miranda. She had to be strong enough.

The alternative was unthinkable.

Slowly those black eyes returned to Sage's face, but the recognition she'd hoped to see wasn't there.

"Can you hear me, Mom?" Sage reached out a shaking hand.

With viper-like speed, Miranda took hold of Sage and twisted, wrenching her arm up behind her back.

Sage threw her head back with a cry of pain and heard the muted crunch of bone as she connected with Miranda's face.

The moment her arm was released, Sage spun back around to face her mother. "I don't know if you're still in there, but please stop this."

Black blood poured out of her mother's nose, but she showed no sign of discomfort. The scrutiny in her eyes remained.

"Mom. You can fight this. Listen to—"

Before she could finish her sentence, Miranda lunged forward, her hands clasping around Sage's neck. Panic surged through Sage's veins as Miranda squeezed her windpipe with an iron grip, cutting off her ability to breathe. Still, Sage choked out the word, "Please."

Her vision faded, darkening at the edges. Every gasp for air felt like shards of glass scraping against her throat. Her arms fell slack against her body as the lack of oxygen drained her strength. Seconds without air felt like an eternity, and Sage's eyes began to roll backward.

All the fight left her body. Sage's knees gave way as unconsciousness called her home. She felt herself slipping away, hanging limply in her mother's grip, dangling between life and death.

And then, the pressure released.

Gasping for breath, Sage crashed to the ground, desperately sucking in air as if it were a lifeline. She blinked away the stars in her vision as the fog in her head cleared.

Where her mom had been standing, crushing her windpipe, she found Grey, weapons dripping with fresh blood.

"Don't look," he warned.

Never one to listen, she had to see for herself, and instantly regretted the decision as her eyes fell on the decapitated corpse of her mother.

"What the fuck!" The scream rose in Sage's throat as she recoiled in horror, crashing into a nearby wall. She couldn't believe what she was seeing. "Why did you do that?"

"Would you rather she killed you?" Grey's voice was cold and emotionless. Blood, thick and black as tar, dripped from his sword, joining the growing pool forming beneath him on the floor.

"Mom." Sage reached a trembling hand toward her mother, but stopped short, letting it hover over the body.

"That thing was not your mother, Sage." Grey's tone struck her like a slap to the face. "She might have looked like it, but your mother died a long time ago. This was merely a shell."

She refused to believe his words. Shell or not, her mother had been there, standing before Sage with a glimmer of recognition. She'd seen it. The hesitation. It might have been buried deep down, but there had been some small flicker of Miranda Cynwrig. Grey could have stopped her. He could have restrained her. Locked her away until they could bring her back. But instead… She gasped for air as if still choking, her lungs refusing to take in a deep enough breath to satisfy her speeding heart. He killed her. Blood pooled around her mother's body, and try as she might, Sage couldn't tear her eyes away from the sickening sight.

"You're lucky she didn't kill you," Grey offered, more gently than he'd previously spoken to her. As if that was some kind of consolation prize. Luck had nothing to do with this.

Whatever had been done to her mother was not lucky, nor was Sage having to bear witness to her death. And knowing who this woman was to Sage, Grey couldn't even bring himself to sound remorseful for ending her existence in the most final way possible.

"She… I…" Struggling to breathe, Sage couldn't get the words to make a connection from her mind to her lips. Lies. Everything had been lies. Her mother's death. The dangers of being out in the open. The safety behind ASSET's walls. None of it had been true. She'd let herself be manipulated by stories and lies. Crying solved nothing, but the dam of her emotions had broken. Tears flooded her vision, blurring the image of her mother along with the man who'd dealt the deadly blow.

"I… can't… be… here." Sage sobbed as she tried desperately to stand. The weight of her grief bore down on her shoulders, threatening to crush her.

"I've got you." Grey lifted her into his arms and carried her away from the sounds of fighting still echoing from the main lobby. "You can lob death threats at me when you catch your breath."

SEVENTEEN

"I've got a hot mess for you, Rina," Grey called out, as he set Sage down on a bench in the cafeteria.

A tiny voice responded, sounding distant but still able to be heard. Sage hadn't met Rina before, though she'd heard the name back in Ava's office. Another lackey of the agency.

"You got this?" Grey walked away, leaving his words hanging in the air unanswered.

Sage's eyes were swollen with tears as her face contorted in a twisted mask of despair.

Her world had shattered, leaving her lost and broken. Every gaze in the room bore down on her as her mind replayed the final moments of her mother's death. The urge to flee was overwhelming, but her legs remained rooted in place, betraying her and leaving her paralyzed in agony.

"Nice to meet you, Sage." Rina's voice broke through Sage's tempest of thoughts. "Kind of a shitty way to make a first impression, but maybe coffee will help."

Rina approached with a steaming cup of coffee in hand. A slender figure with shimmering silver-blue, shoulder-length hair, she was an enigma wrapped in ink and defiance—the tattoos decorating her right arm in intricate patterns contrasting with the image she envisioned of Ava's prim assistant. A tiny diamond glinted from the stud on her nose as she settled next to Sage, placing the aromatic brew tantalizingly within reach.

"I mean, I wish I had met you earlier, when Grey brought you in, but you caught me between assignments. Ava keeps me busy." Rina offered a friendly smile as her attempts to start up a conversation turned awkward. "I met her once—your mother." She spoke more reverently than Grey had, but that did nothing to soothe the raw pain.

Sage pressed her lips together as she turned away, knowing that if she opened her mouth, nothing good would escape.

"For what it's worth, I'm so sorry. Those bastards deserve to be put down for what they've done to our people." Rina's statement was laced with a bitter resentment that mirrored Sage's feelings. "They killed my father, too. A while ago," she added quietly. "But that's how it goes. The death of a parent conscripts us into a war we'd never known nor wanted to be part of. A never-ending war."

Rina wasn't any different from Sage. They shared the same pain. The void left by a loved one was not one easily filled. And that brought a new painful realization. Someday, the cycle would repeat should Sage ever have a child. As long as the cycle endured, this agony would be passed on to the next generation and the next until the end of time. No. The cycle would not continue with her. She wouldn't have children.

"I'm sorry you lost your father," Sage offered gently.

"I still miss him. But at least I can carry on his work." Rina smiled weakly.

"You're an agent?" Sage hadn't meant it to sound so rude, but she'd only been introduced as Ava's assistant.

"We're all agents first. I'm not very good in a fist fight, but I slay in the board room." Rina giggled at her joke.

In her current state, Sage was humorless, but out of courtesy, she attempted a chuckle when she caught the falter of Rina's friendly smile.

"I can serve ASSET better behind the desk than I can out in the field." Rina's tone darkened. "The undying paper pusher."

"We all have our strengths," Sage replied mechanically, still trying to gain control over her emotions. Rina hadn't been the one to put her in this position. She hadn't decapitated her mother. She hadn't lied or manipulated Sage and didn't deserve to be on the receiving end of her animosity. "I'm sorry I'm bad company. You don't have to babysit me. I'm sure there are others in more need of your care."

"Don't apologize." Rina reached out and took hold of Sage's hand. "You got a raw deal. When things calm down, I have a bottle of wine we can share."

"Much good it would do. Ever since Mom died, I've found I can't even get good and drunk to numb the pain."

Confusion flashed across Rina's face for a split second before she reined in her expression. "That sucks. The awakening affects some people differently, I guess. We'll come up with some way for you to work through the pain."

Sage dropped her gaze to Rina's hand, still clasped tightly around her own. On her left wrist, she wore a leather cuff much like the one she'd seen Mark wearing. The leather was dyed blue, but it still bore the symbol of the tree of life on it like a branding. That was the kind of thing she would prefer to wear to cover her deformity. "Where do I get one of those?" Sage hadn't meant to ask out loud, but the words left before she could stop them.

"It was a gift from my dad." Rina showed off all angles of the cuff for Sage to admire. A fat strap of suede leather, stitched with white thread, closed around her wrist with a two-pronged belt buckle. It was perfect, and wide enough to cover her birthmark completely.

Sage pulled the necklace from under her shirt. "My mom gave me this."

"At least we have something to remember them by." Rina's eyes lit with excitement, and she reached a hand out toward the necklace, her fingers dangling in the air just shy of the pendant. "It's beautiful." She let her hand hover for a moment, as if hesitant to touch it, and then turned toward the door. People were coming in. "Duty calls. Keep that safe."

Rina fell right into place, attending to the wounded being brought in.

Sage tucked her necklace back under her shirt. Her coffee had long since cooled, sitting untouched on the table next to her, but she gulped it down all the same, needing the boost of caffeine.

No one seemed to notice Sage as they passed her. She picked up on conversations in snippets, overhearing details of death counts and the occasional mention of the word, *darkling,* but no one seemed to know why they had been attacked.

She'd seen so much in the last few days. Her whole world had come unglued. Fantasy and reality blended into a nightmare she couldn't wake from. And at the top of it all was her mother. Darkling, or whatever they called her, Miranda had been there, standing in front of her. Maybe she'd been drugged. Maybe she'd been brainwashed. Those sounded so much more plausible than the explanation ASSET had offered.

Either way, her mother was gone.

And just as Rina had said, 'the death of a parent had conscripted her into a war she'd never known about nor wanted to be part of.' Everything she'd been forced to endure was because of that stupid mark on her arm.

Devon had accused her of being passive, of having a victim's mentality. He warned her to be strong and fight. And letting herself be told where she was supposed to be and what she was supposed to do was about as passive as it got.

This place felt neither safe nor where she belonged. And rather than accept what everyone else wanted from her, it was time she dictated her own destiny.

Rina met her gaze from across the room with a friendly smile. Sage returned it with determination.

Sage gathered her things and changing into her own clothes before heading back out to the main lobby elevator.

"Where are you going?" Ava barked at her just as she'd pressed the button to call the elevator up.

Sage's heart jumped. She clenched her fists to steady her nerves and stared straight at the elevator doors, praying they would open.

"I expected better of Miranda's daughter." Ava sounded as if she was getting closer, but no clip-clop of footsteps confirmed it.

"Then you shouldn't have killed her." Sage ground her teeth to hold herself together. She kept her eyes straight ahead, knowing if she turned around, Ava might crack her resolve.

"Haven't been paying much attention, then, have you?"

Pain sharpened Sage's tone. "I watched her die!" If she were truly immortal, she'd have to live with the image of her dead mother for an eternity.

"You watched a creature wearing your mother's skin." Ava's cruel tone cut like a knife. "And yes, *it* was executed." She drove the pain deeper with each word. "Before it killed you, I might add. You should thank Mr. Maddox for saving you."

If she never saw Grey again, it would be too soon. How did you face the man who decapitated your mother? No. She wouldn't thank him. She'd punch him in his stupid face. "You all have these stories and fantasies. Slap a funny name on it and expect people to buy into the mystique. I have my eyes, and I know what I saw."

"Eyes can be deceived. But I'm not here to tell you what you should believe. You've seen for yourself what fantasies are out there. Fancy names or not, you know the truth."

Sage pinched her eyes shut against the burn of tears that should have come, but she'd already spent them earlier. "I don't know what truth is anymore."

"Well, here's a truth for you." Ava cut her off sharply. "Out those doors, you are on your own. No one here will risk themselves to keep you alive. And you can bet your fate will run the same direction as your dearly departed mother."

The elevator doors opened.

Sage stared into the welcoming space, willing herself to take a step. *One foot in front of the other. Leave now before you're dragged back down the rabbit hole.*

"You may have that mark. But it does not make you one of us," Ava added. "That choice must be yours."

Part of her wanted to understand. She had seen more in the last few days than she'd ever imagined. Things that blockbuster sci-fi movies were made of. But beyond the special effects, Sage felt in her gut that she was in the wrong place.

She walked into the elevator, pressed the button for the basement level, and finally allowed herself to look Ava in the eyes.

She expected anger or maybe even hatred, but though Ava's sharp tone cut her deeply, all she saw in the director's eyes was disappointment.

"I'm sorry." Sage let the doors close.

EIGHTEEN

Determination carried her all the way home, but the moment she set eyes on her front door, Sage hesitated. She'd thought of nothing but the journey, saving no consideration for the destination, or what kind of shitstorm she'd walk into. There were bound to be questions, and she didn't have satisfactory answers, even for herself.

Matt opened the door before Sage could get the key into the lock. The hard look on his face confirmed that he'd been waiting, worried. "Where the hell have you been… dressed like that?"

"You wouldn't believe me if I told you." Sage feigned a meek smile.

"First, we're going to discuss your wardrobe." Matt pulled her into a bear hug, squeezing her so tight she felt as if she might pop. When he let go, she caught the worry and strain behind his eyes. "Then you're going to explain why on earth you left me hanging on game night."

"Dammit!" *Of all the nights to be trapped in fantasyland.*

"Hard to raid the dragon's keep without your entire team." He taunted her with a mixed glare of teasing and anger. "Where the hell was my healer?"

"I'd have much rather been here, trust me," Sage's voice trembled as she spoke. Thankfully, she'd made it out alive. Magic or no, resurrection wasn't a thing that happened in the real world. At least, she hoped not. She couldn't erase the memory of her mother's twisted face, corrupted by dark magic, before her life was violently taken. The image of the bloody pool at her feet, with her mother's severed head lying just out of reach, flashed in her mind once again, causing her to shiver uncontrollably.

Matt's expression turned from curious to worried as he saw the fear and pain etched on Sage's face. "Beer?" he asked, already on his way to the fridge. It was code for, *Sit down, we need to talk.* As an unwritten law between them, delivering bad news always had to come with a drink of some kind. Though lately she'd lost the benefit of alcohol's numbing magic.

"Was the gang mad I couldn't make it?" Sage took her seat at the table.

"Worried. With good reason." Matt set two amber bottles down and popped the cap off each. "I know you're going through a lot. I won't downplay it."

"I'm sor—"

"Let me finish," he cut her off. "I'm here for you. No matter what, okay? A shoulder to cry on, confidant, and your unlicensed therapist… you know I have access to the good meds." He winked in that adorable way that never failed to bring a smile to her face.

"If only you took my insurance." She snickered.

Although he should have laughed too, Matt's smile faltered and his expression turned serious. "Speaking of that… I opened your mail while you were gone." He slid one of the beer bottles in front of her slowly. "Honey, why didn't you tell me you lost your job?"

"I…" She'd forgotten about that. So many other things had stolen her focus over the last few days that being laid off by her troll of a boss had been the least of her worries. "It was so sudden… Marcy…" Should she mention the shape-shifting boss, and how she'd screamed like a girl? Or maybe how she'd been accosted by a vampire and swept off to the secret agency of magical assassins? She'd sound utterly crazy talking about crap like that, and Matt already thought she'd gone off the deep end. True or not, any explanation she could offer would only confirm her psychosis. Maybe someday she could show him what she'd learned. But even then, how was she supposed to do that? She was magically neutral, or so she'd been told. Couldn't use it. Could be affected by it. So what would she show him?

Matt stared at her as she fumbled for words, his jaw set tight, ready to lash out no matter what she said.

"Life just keeps taking one shit after another on me." Sage sighed, throwing up her hands in defeat. "I don't know what else to say."

"Sorry, for starters!" he roared at her. "I half expected to find you lying in a ditch. Don't you ever scare me like that again." Tears glistened at the edges of his eyes, but his voice was pure rage. "I don't care what's happening." He took a long swig of his beer. Sage recognized the maneuver, covering his face to hide the emotion and maintain the guise of manly aloofness. He'd chug the whole thing to give himself time to regain composure if that's what it took.

And she felt completely deserving of his rage. She hadn't meant to make him worry. She should have called or texted. Given him some reason for her absence. It tugged at her heart to see him fighting to look strong. He deserved more respect than she'd given him. "I'm so sorry!"

"Where did you go?" He wore the mask well enough, but behind those watery eyes, she saw cracks in his stony exterior.

"You wouldn't believe me if I told you." No truer words had been spoken, but she knew he'd demand a real answer, so before he could follow up, she added a few nuggets of vague truths. "I went for a walk. Stayed in a hotel. I was safe enough. I just needed to step outside of my life for a moment and see it from the outside, you know?"

"You could have called. You could have texted. I was worried sick, counting down the hours until I could file a missing person's report."

A dead phone was the lamest of all excuses, and Sage didn't dare to use it. Matt deserved better than that. Phones were everywhere. She could have found some way to get a message to him. She'd thought of it while at ASSET, but with all the crazy going on around her, she hadn't made the time to pick up the phone. His anger was more than justified. "You're right. No excuse. I was an ass. How do I make this up to you?"

"I'll think of something." He reached across the table and grabbed her untouched beer, claiming it as his own.

"I mean it. I'm sorry. I'm having a really hard time dealing with Mom's death. I didn't realize how much it would screw me up. I'm a total jerk."

"That I believe," he scoffed.

"You've always been a momma's boy." She hoped a little good-natured ribbing might lighten his mood.

Matt set his bottle down and burped loud enough for the neighbors to hear. "Proud of it, too."

Emotions bottled up like a knot in her throat. He didn't know how lucky he was to have his parents alive and well, living only a few short miles away.

"Maybe we should go crash Sunday night dinner?" he offered, as the silence between them grew stale.

Tempting, but Sage didn't think she could handle it. No matter how good a cook his mother was, it would only rub salt in the wounds. "I don't think I—"

"You said *anything*." He glared at her over the top of the beer bottle he was lifting to his lips.

"That's not fair!"

"Nor was letting me think you were lying dead in a ditch." He slammed the bottle down.

"You jumped to conclusions."

"You left me no reason not to. You're not yourself. You're freaking out over every little thing. You're hiding things from me. We used to talk about everything. I get that losing your mom is hard. But there's something else going on with you, Sage, and for whatever reason, you don't want to tell me."

"I need help. You're right. I'm screwed in the head. And when I figure out which way is up, you'll be the first to know. Okay?"

He rolled his eyes. "Sure, Sage."

"And if it means that much..." She let out a deep sigh, knowing she'd regret it. "I'll go to dinner at your parents' house."

"I'll call them and let them know to expect us this weekend." Matt's smile looked forced. He stood and cleared away both beer bottles, tossing them in the recycling bin as he headed toward his room.

"Where are you going?" He'd gotten what he wanted. Why storm off in a tizzy?

"It's my turn to leave you hanging." Matt's voice echoed slightly, as if reverberating off of the walls. "But don't worry. I won't stray far." A moment later, she heard the shower.

Matt, being mad at her, ranked up there with the other tragedies that had happened this week. Telling him about her little revelation would be the right thing to do for their friendship. But short of any tangible proof, what could she say? She needed answers from someone she could trust.

Sage headed into her bedroom, locked the door, and turned on the television for background noise. Not sure of how the conversation would go, she didn't need Matt overhearing anything and getting the wrong idea. He was already mad enough as it was.

With a reluctant sigh, she picked up her phone and called Mark Sorenson.

NINETEEN

The phone had barely rung before Mark answered. "I was hoping I'd hear from you."

Sage collapsed on her bed, staring at the ceiling, not sure how to begin. Anger was at war with sadness. He was her last true link to the past. To home. Mark might not have lied outright, but omission was just as bad as a lie, and he had failed to tell her what was happening. He might have saved her from a lot of trouble if he'd convinced her to stay. Anger won the battle, sharpening her voice. "Why didn't you tell me when I was there in Phoenix?"

"It's quite normal to be skeptical during such a new transition period," Mark replied flatly. His usually friendly voice betrayed no emotion. "A breaking-in period is often necessary. If you recall, I extended multiple offers of employment."

That was a lie. He'd asked her once. He offered her a place to work, as he always had. But that was hardly more than small talk. Had he really wanted her to stay, he could have given her a reason. And as she'd found out, in the worst possible of ways, there were plenty of reasons. Yet he'd remained mute. He was being strangely distant. Even the tone of his voice was off. Lacking personality, he spoke to her as if she were a client.

Maybe calling was a bad idea, but she needed answers. Truth. Understanding of what was real and how she fit into it all. "What am I supposed to do?" Sage huffed.

"You've been contacted by the Las Vegas office, correct?" he asked, though he had to have already known the answer. Grey had told her earlier that he'd been given her file by the Phoenix office in order to locate her.

"Oh, they rolled out the welcome wagon for me." Sage countered his neutral tone with snark.

"Miss Cynwrig!" Mark said her name with impatient annoyance. That tone was familiar. Mark had pulled rank on her many times during her youth.

"Yes?" She threw the word back at him. She was not his daughter. Nor would she allow him to talk down to her. He'd relinquished that right—as far as she was concerned—when he'd failed to reveal the truth to her in person.

"I'm sorry," he whispered. The sudden shift in his tone made her wonder what was going on at his end of the conversation. "You're right to be angry at me. I should have sat you down and told you, but…"

Sage held her breath in anticipation, but Mark left the words hanging in the air.

"But that's… in the past now." He sounded like a man itching to say something while at the same time struggling to bite his tongue. "Ava's got an excellent team in the Las Vegas office. You'll be well prepared for duties in due course."

The cryptic shift in conversation only added to her confusion. "What happened to coming to work with you?" He'd asked her every chance he could to come work for him, even before she'd gone off to college. It had always been the family business.

"Unfortunately, Miss Cynwrig, you're out of my jurisdiction." His answer came swiftly, and as cold as any she'd received from Ava back at ASSET.

That wasn't like Mark. "What are you not telling me?" she demanded.

"I assure you, they're a topnotch agency with an excellent record. You'll be well protected there."

He had to be speaking in some kind of code. She believed he was concerned for her safety, but there was a lie in his delivery. What was he not saying? "And I wouldn't be safe with you?"

"As I've already said, you're out of my jurisdiction. Your concerns have been noted, but at this time, you will have to report to Ava Masters, the director of the Las Vegas office."

"Vegas or bust, eh?" she asked, trying to decipher his message, searching for the clues in his ambiguous answers. It went against everything she'd ever known of Mark to push her away, when he'd kept her safe all her life. If he thought she was better off where she was, then there had to be some reason for it.

"Educating yourself is a very good place to start. Perhaps you should take some time to research Terras and the beginnings of ASSET," he suggested. "It might lessen the concerns you're having during this transition phase."

"Aren't you Terra as well?"

"Of course." His business-like tone faltered for a moment. "And the library within the ASSET facility is an excellent resource—"

"Has something happened there? What are you protecting me from? I need the truth, Mark. I need real answers. From someone I can trust." She couldn't hide the desperation in her voice. In the long pause that followed her outburst, she heard her roommate fumbling around the hallway. She'd have to choose her words carefully too from this point on.

"I heard that the ASSET facility in Vegas was hit." Mark dropped his voice to barely a whisper, as if he too was trying to ensure his words were not overheard. "I'm more relieved than you can know to hear you're safe. Our facility did not fare as well. Do not come back here."

"Then nowhere is safe." Sage remembered the sirens and the dark things pouring in from the elevator. She'd never felt so scared in her life.

"There is no better place for you right now than within their protection." Mark loudly touted ASSET's security. "Ava's office is known for having skilled agents capable of handling any situation."

"Is this normal? Being attacked at the office? I don't remember Mom ever—"

"No," Mark cut her off with another whisper. "We're in the midst of a war with the magical factions the likes of which have not been seen since the dawn of time."

"Bad time to be awakened," she replied.

"It's *why* you were awakened! These skirmishes are only the start of the devastation that could spread across the globe. Their attacks are targeting the best of our agents." His voice remained low, but she caught the desperation in his tone. "Agents with centuries of experience have been mowed down in the field, turned dark, and sent right back after their own people. And when one Terra dies, the next in their line awakens. As you were. Leaving us with nothing but trainees to protect the world from the battles to come. If this continues, it will cripple us. You aren't ready—"

"Because no one trained me," she snapped back at him. "If I had been told what my destiny would be, I might have been prepared to fight." Secrecy was screwing the agents of

ASSET, not newbie Terras being awoken. If they had any sense, they would at the very least train their children, so if they were awoken, there wouldn't be this *transition period*, as Mark had called it.

"The Las Vegas office library has copies of our training manuals for you to peruse." Back to business again. "You could benefit from reading *The Great Tree, The War of the First Race,* and *The Mother's Cure.*"

"Reading. Got it," Sage grumbled, still gaining two more questions for every answer she got. At least he'd given her some place to start with research. Reading she could do. And Devon had already given her some books to start with.

"Open your eyes as well as your mind," Mark insisted. "You see the truth in front of you. Now you must take your place within the organization."

"But what do I do about my life here? My friends?"

"Protection is the duty of all our agents at ASSET."

"How am I supposed to do that?"

"By returning to ASSET and completing your training!"

"That's not fair! I have a life."

"You have a duty that goes beyond what you've already experienced."

His cryptic answers were really beginning to grate on her nerves. "You know that's not fair. Seeing Mom. And then watching her die."

"I heard about that." He sighed loudly into the phone.

"You didn't even bother to tell me the truth about her."

"I hadn't been given complete intelligence on that agent's whereabouts. She failed to check in after an assignment. Her last contact reported her missing. We assumed the worst and followed protocol." He lowered his voice again, whispering so quietly she almost couldn't hear. "You wouldn't have been awakened if your mother's light still burned within her. The fact you were experiencing the changes and starting to see the real world around you was proof of that."

"So when I came down there, you didn't know for sure?"

"I had it on good authority when I called you, and seeing your mark begin to change proved it."

"And you still couldn't tell me the truth when I was right there? Face to face."

"I truly didn't want to believe it myself. For that, I'm sorry. You deserved to hear it from a trusted friend."

"Instead, I was lied to, and manipulated by the person I needed most."

"You're right to be angry at me. And I hope in time I can earn back the trust I've lost. You're like a daughter to me, Sage. I never meant for this to happen to you. Miranda was the kind of warrior who should have fought for centuries. You should have enjoyed a normal life, married someone nice, and started your own family. That was what we wanted for you. Not this. We never wanted to involve you in this world's troubles. But now that you've been awakened, you must understand what you are." His sudden shift back to being the company man nearly gave her whiplash. But she understood the need to sound like business as usual if there were potentially untrustworthy ears nearby. "There are dangerous elements out there, Miss Cynwrig. All Terras must band together now to protect each other and fight for the greater good."

"Who's good?" Sage huffed.

"Peace. No good comes from war. Our people are the bringers of peace. You'll learn that as you read the *Mother's Cure*."

"And yet we're warriors?" Sage clarified.

"Peace rarely comes without some struggle, which is why our people need to be well trained."

"Has there ever truly been peace?" she asked.

"Yes," he replied, a little too swiftly to be believed.

"What happened to change that?" She hoped that if she kept prying, she'd finally get to the bottom of it.

"I wish I knew," Mark whispered more urgently this time. "Darkling armies are a significant concern at the moment. Especially since they used them to gain access to the facility."

"And you still think I'm safer there?" If what he said was true, then the answer would have to be no. If Darklings could make it into ASSET facilities, then she was no safer with them than on the street.

"ASSET has the resources to protect its people and the magical archives held within," he proudly boasted, and the sudden shift in volume made her pull the phone away from her ear.

She was ready with a snarky retort to what seemed was another one of his vague replies, but she caught the fact he had volunteered the words, *magical archive*, and held her tongue.

Mark paused long enough to justify his next statement as a reply to her unasked question. "Things that might be dangerous for other magical creatures to use have always been held safe in the hands of our people."

"Because we are the peacekeepers?" she asked.

"Who better to store and protect the most sensitive of magical artifacts than those who are immune to magic?"

She lost the train of thought, realizing he was pointing her to an answer, but she wasn't sure of the right question to ask to make his direction clear.

"*The Great Tree* is an excellent read if you're looking for a basis in our history. The *Mother's Cure* as well. Those two books will help to clarify your place at ASSET."

"Okay, then." She'd asked for truth, and what she'd gotten was homework. Though vague, he had given her a few important clues on what to research, maybe even the answer to what was in the magical archives that would be worth sending in an army of Darklings to retrieve.

"Shall I alert Ava of your return, then?" He sounded hopeful.

"Don't worry about me, Mark. I'll be safe." She ended the call and reached for the books Devon had given her.

The Mother's Cure.

Blood joins all creations, great and small. The forgotten gods, whose names cannot be uttered by human tongues, were known as the mother and father. They splashed their blood upon the earth, and life sprang forth. The air, the land, and the places the sun had not yet found defined the form each creation took.

The dawn of magic shaped the earth for all the creatures that followed. The forgotten gods smiled upon their children, giving them dominion. The father turned his eye toward the great beyond, but the mother kept a distant watch over her children.

Through their magic, the first lords of the earth shaped the world. Fertile lands, crystal clear waters, shimmering rainbows that danced between clouds. Beauty was the gift of those of the Ethereal magic. All that they laid eyes on was to be made glorious to look upon. Not to be outshone by the creations of their brothers, Elemental magic shaped the land, raising mountains of fire and ice and infusing the ground with minerals that hardened into stones of beautiful color. Magic of the Shades turned the earth so that where there was light, darkness could exist, and revealed the twinkling starlit sky as the sun gave way to the moon.

A Weapon of Magical Destruction

Magic and blood created life, and so too did the first lords of the earth. Like the mother and father before, they shared that blood, passing down gifts to the next generation.

They filled the newly created lands, each claiming their right to dominion. Wars soon stretched across the earth. Waters that once ran clear turned murky and undrinkable, polluted by the dead. Magic shattered the land as battles raged on, with no end in sight. All the beauty of creation turned to ruin. Blood and magic destroyed life just as easily as it had once created it.

The great mother could not stand idly by and allow her children's squabbling to ruin the world she had given them. From each branch of magic, she made a sacrifice, binding their blood to a lone fruit tree growing among the ruins of a recent battleground.

With her careful tending, the tree grew strong and tall. Drinking in the blood-drenched soil, its bark hardened to a deep crimson. Its deep green leaves turned brown, but fortified by the mother's care, the tree bore fruit the likes of which had never been seen. Sweet nectar, clear as pure running water, plumped the pulpy fruit. Skin so pale yellow it almost looked translucent, allowed a glimpse at the nourishment just below its tender flesh. The fruit tempted any who happened across the great tree.

Water washes the blood clean, and so too did a bite of the fruit.

Rendering powerless those who had eaten it, each hungry warrior was marked by the tree so the mother could see who had been changed.

Only once did the tree bear fruit, but from that single harvest, thousands of enemies were neutralized.

The mother plucked the last of the fruit from her great tree, saving it should she need its magic again. The tree withered and returned to the ground, and the mother gathered her newly changed, fashioning them into her own army to fight the destructive forces of magic.

Sage yawned and set the book aside, wondering how much of what she'd read was the imagination of whoever had written the story. Mythology and fantasy often ran in similar veins. She half-expected to see mention of a dragon fighting in the magical wars.

Powerful magic creatures ending the wars instead of fruit. Though she couldn't ignore the parallels to modern religious mythology either. Special fruit. Was that the thing they were looking for? Was that what was hidden in the archives? Magical fruit? Doubtful, unless it was petrified.

Her stomach growled. It had been hours since her last meal, and if she waited much longer, she'd soon look like a withered old piece of fruit herself if she didn't get something to eat.

Sage was two steps from the front door when Matt called out, "Where do you think you're going?"

She'd excuse his tone this time. He had a right to be annoyed with her. And what better way to make amends than with a night out? "Want to join me for a greasy burger down at the pub?"

"Not really." He waved her off, returning his attention to the TV. "I deal with enough barflies at work."

What Sage wanted most was to be around someone she trusted, but she wouldn't push Matt. She'd find other ways to get back into his good graces. At least at the bar, she could be around people and not feel so alone. Julie always looked out for her, and no doubt, her favorite server would be interested to hear about how her night out with Zack had gone.

"When will you be back?" Matt didn't make eye contact. He was playing with her. Pretending not to care, but she knew him better than that. He wouldn't have asked unless he was desperate to make sure she would return.

"I'm not going to leave you hanging like that again. If I decide to run off into the sunset, I'll at least leave you a Dear John letter."

"Don't even joke like that." His voice soured.

"It's just a burger and maybe a beer... or two." Sage shouldered her purse and opened the door.

"Hey." Matt called her back. When she turned, he was standing, holding his hand out. "It's dangerous to go out alone. Take this."

Always looking out for her. She smiled and accepted the pepper spray. "I'll be back... soon."

"You'd better."

"Allons-y!" She winked and made her retreat.

The night felt a little less friendly as she stepped outside the confines of her home. After the things she'd learned, about the world hidden within the one she thought was real, Sage was practically jumping at every shadow. A sense of unease quickened her steps as she took the short path to the outer gate of her apartment complex.

She'd always known there were bad people lurking in the shadows, but now the shadows themselves could be evil. The persistent nag of hunger drove her forward. The pub was no more than a five-minute walk. Two, if she ran.

Setting her pace with the promise of a hot meal, she reached into her purse and gripped the small bottle of pepper spray. She'd rather it be one of her mother's daggers, but short of a proper weapon, this would do. If nothing else, she'd make anyone who dared come at her scream in pain.

Flickering streetlights, the sound of car doors slamming in the distance.... everything that she'd ignored in the past was making her anxiety shoot through the roof.

"You'd think by now you'd have learned not to walk alone at night" A voice called out from behind, causing Sage's heart to jump into her throat.

She turned to find Zack, his face twisted with a predatory hunger. Every instinct in her body screamed for her to run, but fear paralyzed her limbs.

TWENTY

Sage stood rooted in place, her breath held hostage by the shock coursing through her veins as she tried to summon the will to run or attack.

"Have my hypnotic eyes silenced you?" Zack cast her a smug grin, revealing a set of teeth Sage was all too aware were as lethal as they were porcelain perfect. "Don't beat yourself up about it. I've yet to encounter a woman who can withstand my... allure."

Smooth as ever. His silver-tongued charm had lured her in the last time, but she wouldn't fall for that again.

"You're wondering whether I'm going to hurt you." His expression darkened. The glint in his eye sharpened with all the intensity of a viper, ready to strike. "Good. That means you know exactly what a vampire can do. Especially to a Terra like yourself."

Sage sucked in a sharp breath. Her blood turned to ice in her veins.

Zack took a long sniff of the air. "Do you smell that? Fear. Such an intoxicating aroma.

"You want to come at me? Fine. Bring it." Sage gripped her keyring with the bottle of pepper spray her roommate had given her. It wouldn't kill a vampire, but it was all she had to work with. "After the week I've had, I've got nothing to lose. But I promise I'll make sure you regret messing with me."

Zack stood still, his eyes fixed on Sage as if considering his options.

In the silence that stretched out between them the frantic thumping of Sage's heart anxious heart betrayed how close she was to letting her fear take over. If Zack moved, she had to be ready to fight.

Sage clenched her fist and brought the pepper spray up to eye level.

Amusement replaced the hungry expression on Zack's face. "You seem like a decent person. I'd hate to kill you." He delivered the line with a disarming wink.

Dread evaporated the moment she recognized the words and where they came from. "You seem *less* like a decent person." She breathed a sigh and lowered her hand. "And I'd hate to die."

"You were warned, I'm sure, to stay away from vampires."

Despite his attempt to quell her nerves with nerdy catchphrases, Sage couldn't fully let her guard down.

"Aren't you supposed to be dead?" Her memory was still a bit fuzzy on the details of what had happened the last time they'd met. As badass as Grey pretended to be, he should have killed Zack. Why leave a vampire like him alive?

"I am. In a way." Zack turned his head to reveal scars on his neck. "But don't worry. All the equipment is still in working order. I could give you a demonstration, if you like."

A shudder threatened to reveal her disgust, but she held herself still. He might just as easily take it as fear. She couldn't show that, no matter how much her heart was racing, given that she was within striking distance. "Why didn't Grey didn't kill you?"

"Kill me?" Zack clucked his tongue. "That's no way to treat a compatriot. As if he could." He puffed his chest with pride as he closed the gap between them in a blur of movement. "Your pal Grey asked me to scare you. He needed you to see reason, which you still clearly have not. Should I try harder this time?"

"That bastard!" Sage growled. Anger overtaking her fear, she shoved Zack away. "He played me just like you did."

"We all must bend to the whims of you Terras, eventually." Zack bowed low in a mocking gesture. "From time to time, when it's worth my efforts, yes, I willingly aid the cause."

"You say it like it's a bad thing." Sage threw the words back at him, but she felt their meaning all too well.

"Circle of life." He waved a dismissive hand. "But my involvement ended when they brought you in."

She wasn't buying that. He wouldn't be lurking in the shadows near her home if that were the truth. Grey's little spy. At least Grey was smart enough not to come himself. He was the last person she wanted to see. "So why are you slumming around here still?"

"It is dinner time." Hunger returned to his eyes. "But don't worry, little one… You're not on the menu. Terra is an acquired taste."

Zack gave her the creeps. "If you dislike my kind so much, why are you working for them?"

"Oh, our kind. Does that mean you've joined the rank and file?" His taunt made her pause to look at her wrist. He continued before she could open her mouth to speak. "Having that mark means you're special, but are you truly ready to say you're one of them?"

She'd been led to believe that it was her life's mission. Bearing the mark meant it was her duty to join the ranks of

ASSET. But could she actually say she was one of them? Especially after the way she'd left?

"Your kind people the world, you know?" Zack said before she could come up with a worthy retort. "But not all of them operate behind the shield of ASSET."

He was being awfully cryptic. "And you're telling me this...why?"

"Because when I first met you, I was serious about guiding you to a place where you could find out more about your special markings."

"Because you were being compensated by Grey, right?" She all but rolled her eyes, expecting him to give her the company line. If he couldn't scare her, he could always try the righteous route. Make her see the greater good and all that bullshit. More manipulation.

"He's not the only one I know who can help you."

She snatched at the opportunity to reply before he could go on. "No, he was just the first to pay up, right?"

Zack smiled, putting all his sharp teeth on display. "Everyone has a price."

"Guess that makes you a double-dipper, then?"

"Consider it being entrepreneurial for a good cause. You don't understand who or what you are, and I happen to know people who can educate you. Everybody wins."

"Except me. All these people who claim to know are just going to use me for their own ends."

"You can only be used if you allow yourself to be. Knowledge is power."

He had a point there. She was walking blindly through a world she didn't understand. Other than the books she'd taken with her, there was little else to teach her the way of things. "True enough. And you've already outed yourself as a player for both sides. So I know you're full of shit."

"Good and evil aren't sides to be played. Thinking that is your first mistake." He tapped her on the head lightly with his index finger. "No one wakes up in the morning eager to check off their evil to-do list, though plenty of righteous people will never let you forget their victories. All people are self-serving. Good and evil are just labels."

"Well, I have no money to pay for your service. So… Thanks, but no. I'll figure it out on my own." Sage stepped back to put a few feet between her and the vampire.

"Suit yourself. But allow me to give you a word of caution before you go. Your people's strength relies on teamwork. Alone, you're nothing but tasty prey for those with a… discerning palate."

She fought to hold off the shiver working its way up her spine. "I should be glad you're no connoisseur, then?"

"If I were, you'd already be in my thrall."

Fear was the greatest enemy of all, and despite the brave face she tried to show Zack, when she opened her mouth to throw an insult back at him, all that escaped was a squeak as she remembered the creature her mother had been turned into.

Zack's brows pulled together as he closed his eyes. A moment of silence passed, only breaking with the sound of his frustrated sigh.

"I've been in your place." Zack surprised her with sudden gentleness in his tone. "New to a life I couldn't possibly understand. Uncertain of what lay ahead of me."

"You stole your immortality." She threw the words at him, unable to control the tremble in her voice. She balled her fists in anger, part of her wanting to take a swing at the asshole for threatening her, the other part realizing just how much she should fear him for what he could do *to her*. Thankfully, he hadn't, but how much of that was because he'd been paid not to?

"I stole nothing." Annoyance flashed across his face, but to his credit, Zack held to his softer tone. "I was gifted it… by my lady love."

"The same *lady love* I saw you dismissing the other night?"

"No. Dead more than fifty years, but I can still remember her sweet smile." Zack gripped his chest, wincing as if the memory caused him pain. "Ours was a love that spanned more than a generation before she was taken from me."

Anger and distrust morphed awkwardly into a sad sympathy, but Sage held firm where she stood. "I'm sorry."

"I was the poor farm boy to her Buttercup." He paused, allowing Sage to make the connection. The last time they'd met, she'd had a laugh baiting him with fantasy references. Now it was his turn, and the effect disarmed her better than anything else he had said. "When she was turned and taken from me, I searched night and day to find her. She was my true love." He took a breath and let go of his chest. "When I finally found her, she'd been changed, but I loved her no less. I had promised my heart to her, and she accepted it. In return, she gave me the gift of immortality. We shared our hearts in the truest of senses. So don't speak to me as if I'm some thief in the night, stealing magic I don't own."

Embarrassment replaced the haughty sense of importance she'd thrown at him moments before. She'd been a Terra for only a few days, but had already developed prejudices from her ignorance.

"I wasn't always a vampire," Zack reminded her sternly. "The learning curve was steep when I was turned. I can appreciate where you're at now, being unaware for so long of what destiny had in store for you. Mock me if you want, but no matter what I gain from helping you, ultimately it is you who will benefit most."

"How did your lady love die?"

"She developed a discerning palate." He smirked. Just the reminder Sage needed to keep her guard up. "Will you come now and let me lead you toward a new mentor?"

"I'm sure you can understand if I don't trust you to be my guide."

"Trust the streetlight above us. Or the people walking along the roads with us. I'm not leading you into the dark. Where we are going, you'll find more light than even I can stand to be around." Zack waved a hand for her to follow.

Ten minutes later, they arrived at the Bulwark gym. Devon's place. "Here? This is my trainer's place."

"You trust him, then?" Zack asked, as if he already knew her answer.

Of all the people she'd met, Devon had been the most open with her, but being connected with Zack didn't sit well with her. "I guess."

"If you can trust him, then you can trust I'm not leading you into another trap."

"That remains to be seen." Who else was in on this double-dealing business? Grey, Zack, and now Devon. Of the three, Devon was the least likely to blow smoke up her ass. And he'd already given her more information than the others. She supposed he was the lesser of three evils.

The doors were closed, but the inner lights were still on.

"Have fun storming the castle." Zack attempted to bow out before Sage knocked, but as her hand touched the glass, Devon appeared, as if blinking into existence.

Looking both shocked and relieved, he pulled them both inside his gym. "I thought the worst when Grey said you'd disappeared."

He had to mention that bastard!

"I didn't feel safe there."

"ASSET us the safest place for you to be right now," Devon said.

"Don't you work for ASSET?" Sage threw her words like an accusation. "How can you say that after what happened?"

"I work with them, not *for* them," Devon replied.

"Because you believe what they do is good, right?" She repeated the same words he'd said to her earlier, hoping the meaning might elicit some real truth this time.

"Generally, yes." A look of unease spread across Devon's face.

Zack scoffed. "ASSET is responsible for the recent attacks on my clans."

"ASSET only goes after problems," Devon said defensively.

"Depends on your definition of a problem." Zack all but rolled his eyes.

"Clearly, not everyone holds your same view of ASSET as the good guys."

Devon eyed Zack for a moment as if having a silent conversation. "Yesterday's attack was unprecedented, I'll give you that."

None of it made sense. But the way they talked further solidified her position. Leaving ASSET had been the right choice. Whatever was going on, she was not safe there. But was she safe anywhere?

"Not from where I'm standing. ASSET is far from being the good guys." Zack's tone dripped with disdain.

"Enlighten us then." Devon speared Zack with a look that chilled Sage's blood. As predatory as the vampire was, she'd put her money on the ogre to come out on top if they came to blows.

"There are whispers among my kind." Zack took a step backward, edging toward the door. "The word on the streets is, agents have been clearing house without provocation. They have a new kind of weapon. A week or so ago, an entire coven were reduced to dust."

"I've heard of no such thing," Devon retorted.

"Why would you? You're not an agent. You're just the hired help." Zack slowly backed toward the exit. "Go ask your pretty boy, Grey. Bet he knows."

If she didn't know better, Sage might have thought the vampire was scared, but after learning of his entrepreneurial aspirations, she guessed he wasn't being paid to divulge the juicy details. Sage moved to block the vampire's exit. "What kind of weapon could do that?"

Zack shrugged as both she and Devon glared at him, waiting for answers. "I'm not sure, but if the rumors are true, ASSET is overstepping their mandate. Good reason for the *plebs* to fight back."

"By turning agents into mindless meat shields?" The memory of her mother resurfaced. "My mom was in that group sent to attack us."

"I had no part in what happened there." Zack held his hands in surrender, looking as frightened as Sage felt. "I want that made very clear."

"Above your pay grade?" She threw the words at him, finding strength in her anger.

Even at her full height, she was still a head shorter than Zack, but he cowered all the same at her aggressive stance. "I may not be in love with ASSET, but I'm not stupid enough to be party to an attack on them, either. I did what I came here to do. I delivered you to someone who can help you. Consider it a freebie. I did my good deed, and now I'm leaving."

"I think you have more to tell us." Devon moved with impossible speed, as if blinking in and out of form, appearing at the doorway and completely blocking Zack's retreat. "If what you say is true, and ASSET has a destructive weapon, wouldn't it be prudent of you to make sure you're seen as being on their side?"

"You might as well let him go." Sage glared at the sleazy vampire. "Informants are only interested in how much profit they can make by playing sides. I bet he doesn't even have any information to sell."

Devon locked eyes with Zack. "There is always a reckoning. Remember that."

Zack scooted through the door without another word.

"I'm surprised you let him go." Sage laughed as she saw the vampire disappear into the night. *Run, you bastard.*

"He'll be back. Spineless as that one is, he knows how to ally himself with the winning side before the axe falls." Devon turned to face Sage. Exhaustion hung like heavy luggage under his eyes. He heaved a sigh and joined her, taking a seat on the benches along the wall. "If what he said is true, I'm not sure which side is which."

"Truth time. What exactly is your role in all of this?"

"I'm a combat-readiness trainer."

After all that, he dared to give her such a vague answer. "Okay then. I'll be on my way."

"Where are you going to go, Sage?"

"I don't know. Somewhere where people are honest and tell me what the hell is going on."

"ASSET is not an evil agency. It is, however, a very large organization, and because of that, is sometimes subject to the whims of the higher echelons of power. Is that what you wanted to hear?"

"Better than what I have been hearing." She hadn't meant to sound so mean, but frustrated as she was, her ability to sugarcoat her thoughts had all but vanished. "I read that book you gave me. My… people"—she struggled to say the word—"were created to solve problems."

"You read mythology. The problem with that is it can't be proven. It's a story, although a good one that probably gave you all kinds of warm fuzzies about being Terra." He nudged her with his elbow.

Sage appreciated the gesture. He was at least trying to be on the level with her. Brutal honesty was his motto. She'd take that over the alternative. "So I shouldn't be proud of what my people have done?"

"That's not what I'm saying. Don't take everything as gospel truth. No one, not a single creature walking this earth, is good or evil because of what race they are. People choose to do good or evil." Devon stressed the point. "Even the Terras."

As many times as Sage had heard that phrase, it might as well be on a t-shirt. "So, what if people inside ASSET are doing evil?"

"That's what has me worried." To his credit, Devon had not bothered to downplay that thought. "If that's true, then we could be on the brink of another magical war. You read the history."

"Mythology?" she corrected.

"Both have nuggets of truth. Magic has the potential to destroy more than just lives. War could tear apart the very fabric of our society. Best we figure out what is going on. Until then, maybe you shouldn't go back to ASSET."

Her jaw dropped. She'd expected him to tow the company line and drag her kicking and screaming back to the barracks.

"I'm not saying it's safe for you out here, and I can't guarantee your protection. But if your gut told you to walk away, you'd better listen. Your gut is a much better voice of reason than you think."

"They killed my mom." Sage shed a tear. "That's why I left."

"Was she..."

He didn't need to finish that sentence. Sage nodded and wiped away her tears before he could get to the final word.

"It makes sense now. The wounds are fresh. It's hard enough having an awakening at your age, but to see the reason why is more than anyone should have to bear." Devon pulled her into a bear hug, and she buried her face in his hard chest.

"We're going to figure this out. And you'll see. Your people serve a noble purpose. You should be proud of what you are. Now go home and get some sleep. I'll let you know the moment I find anything out."

"And what do I do in the meantime?"

"Keep reading. Learn all you can. Who knows? Maybe there's something in those books about a weapon to destroy magic."

"Isn't that what we were created to be?"

"You're magic neutral," Devon said reverently. "What Zack described is annihilation."

TWENTY-ONE

"Honey, I'm home." Sage trudged through the front door, exhausted, reeking of alcohol, and stone cold sober. Devon had fed her, and after she'd revealed her newfound resistance to alcohol, he tested her shot-for-shot. "See, I told you I'd be back."

"I had my doubts." Matt sat staring at the television, clenching the remote in his hand as if ready to crush it. "You've been acting strange, and that's saying something."

"If I didn't know better, I'd say you were trying to insult me." Sage marched to the fridge and grabbed two beers. "But I'm glad you're mad at me. Shows how much you care." She came around, placing herself in line with the TV, and held a bottle out to him. "Peace offering?"

He couldn't resist. Even though he looked ready to strike, when he faced her, the anger melted away. "You're like a sister to me. I don't want to see anything bad happen to you." Matt snatched the beer and made space for her on the couch.

She settled down next to him and snuggled close. This was home. This was where she felt safe and loved. Where no one was trying to manipulate her. But it was also a place where she had to keep a dangerous secret. Normally, she could unload all her troubles and trust that Matt would help her work through them. Smart, sensitive, and at least toward her, non-judgmental. But this was the first time she couldn't just let it all out and feel better. There was no explaining this without proof. Even the most open-mined person needed to see the magic to believe it. She'd only sound like a raving lunatic if she unloaded all she'd learned to Matt, especially now that there was some kind of weapon killing supernatural things and starting wars. Her problems had increased tenfold thanks to what she'd learned from Zack, and not even a tray full of tequila worked to deaden her nerves. She'd grabbed the beer out of habit when what she really needed was a gallon of water.

"Where's my easy button?"

"If only." Matt chuckled. "And don't even think you're getting control of the remote tonight."

"I wasn't even going to try." Being there next to Matt was soothing, and she didn't want to get up, even if her throat burned for water. He flipped through channels, looking for something to watch. Hundreds of channels and nothing seemed interesting, but Matt continued to press the remote as if the next channel might be a winner.

Sleep must have claimed them, though Sage barely remembered closing her eyes. But when a knock woke her, the sun was sending down piercing shafts of light through the window blinds.

"Not it!" Sage might not have felt the alcohol the night before, but that did not spare her the headache to end all headaches.

Matt pushed her off of him and tossed the TV remote in her lap. "If it's a damn clipboard, I'll beat them with it." He lumbered to the door and checked the peephole.

"They can shove whatever they're selling straight up their—" Sage's stomach lurched as she tried to stand. She ran to the bathroom before the regrets of the previous night came back to haunt her.

"It's for you." Matt's voice echoed all the way into the bathroom.

"I'm not home." She rushed to brush her teeth to rid herself of the lingering dragon's breath.

Grey's voice stole her attention. "Sage, we need to talk."

"Of course he'd have to show up." She threw the toothbrush at the sink.

"You okay?" Matt appeared at the bathroom door. "Want me to get rid of him?"

Their eyes met through the reflection of the mirror. Sage wanted nothing more than to be rid of that asshole. But everywhere she went, there he was in some fashion or another, cold and unfeeling, with a smirk she'd be happy to smack clean off his face. But telling Matt to send him away wouldn't work. He'd just find more nefarious ways to get Sage's attention. And the last thing she needed was another vampire showing up on her doorstep. "No. I'm fine."

"Which one is it?" Matt looked confused. "Should I tell him to go?"

The headache wasn't helping either. Not fair. She shouldn't have a hangover if she hadn't at least gotten to enjoy the alcohol that caused it. "Let him in," Sage groaned. She'd be damned if he thought she was going back to ASSET, though. If nothing else, she'd make that perfectly clear. Grey could go stick his machete where the sun didn't shine, if that was his motive.

Splashing water on her face and making quick work of taming her hair, Sage managed to look human by the time she made it back to the living room.

Grey was standing in the kitchen like a soldier at attention. In the light of day, his fedora and leather duster combo failed to resonate the badass vibe he was going for.

Matt took his place next to Sage like her personal bodyguard. "New boyfriend?"

"Boyfriend?" she snorted, completely ruining her mad-dog stare. "Hell, no!" She'd rather punch him in his stupid face than kiss it. How could Matt even think… She took a breath to stop her laughter and tried to reclaim the angry glare she'd hoped would solidify her position of defense with Grey.

"That's a relief." Matt elbowed Sage in the arm. "We were going to have to have a serious talk if you were." "You two are hilarious." Grey locked his eyes on Sage, as if Matt weren't there. "I came to make sure you were okay after what happened."

Liar. He already knew she was fine. His little vampire lackey had reported her whereabouts. But she couldn't call him out on that with Matt standing there.

Matt turned his scrutinizing gaze at Sage, all humor fading to concern. "Something you forgot to tell me?"

Sage crossed her arms and stared back at Grey, willing him to feel her contempt. How dare he come here and stir up trouble, especially when he knew she had a roommate? A human roommate, at that. "If your intent was to start drama, leave now!"

Matt cleared his throat to get Sage's attention.

"I'm fine. We're fine." She struggled for the right words. "He's just an antagonistic prick, here to make my life hell."

"Can we have some privacy?" Grey acknowledged Matt with a sidelong glance.

"You've got some balls, don't you?" Matt scoffed. "She doesn't seem to like you very much."

"Yours are bigger," Sage nodded to her roommate, feeling the sudden surge in testosterone threatening to suffocate her. "Let's go for a walk, Grey."

"You know how I feel about that. We can talk here, if your bodyguard gives us some breathing room." He jerked his head toward Matt. "Don't worry. I'm not going to hurt her."

"Do you have to work at being an asshole, or are you just naturally good at it?" She regretted telling Matt to let Grey in. That man was more drama than her aching head could deal with.

"Not a boyfriend. Not a friend I've ever met. Why is it we're letting him in our house, rude as he is?" Matt glared at Grey, as if sizing him up.

"Friend of the family, unfortunately." She forced her tone to remain civil. "Here to make sure I'm not losing it after Mom died." She didn't let on that Grey had been the one to strike the final blow, but the restrained anger in her voice was enough to set Matt off.

"She's cool. I'm taking care of her. Go tell Mark she's not going back to Phoenix." Matt took a step toward Grey.

"She can speak for herself, I think," Grey responded threateningly.

"Its fine, Matt." She threw her hands into the air. "Just give me a few minutes, please. I'll hear whatever Grey needs to say and send him on his way."

"I'll be in my room if you need me." With a huff, Matt turned and headed toward the hall.

She'd pay for his restraint later. One problem at a time.

"You have five minutes." She glared at to Grey. "Why are you following me?"

"You know why."

"I used up my freebie, remember?" She threw his words back at him.

"After what happened, you're not safe. And our numbers are dwindling as it is." Grey's tone softened, but the look in his eyes remained sharp. Ever the company man, through and through. If he'd had half a brain, he'd have told her the same thing Devon had. His agenda had nothing to do with her safety.

"You people have been nothing but rude and manipulative to me. Why the hell would I go back there?"

"Because you belong." Grey held up his wrist so she could see his mark.

"Says the guy who used a vampire to trick me," she replied bitterly. "Screw this damn mark! It's ugly. Just like that prison of an agency you keep trying to incarcerate me in."

"Zack served a purpose, providing a safe way for you to see what you will be up against next time you run into someone more dangerous."

She nearly slapped him. Asshole was too good a name for him. "Don't give me that, *teaching me a lesson,* crap. It was manipulation, plain and simple."

"What do you want? An apology?"

"No."

"Good. Because you're not going to get one. I'm trying to help you. What happened to your mom can and will happen to you out here in the open." His voice was strained, as if desperate to control his volume.

"I might have believed you if you'd been honest with me from the start. But you're no better than the other scumbags out there. I'm done being a pawn in your little game. If all you came here to do was drag me back into that place and lock me away, you can go to hell."

"I tried. Remember that." Grey turned and stormed out of the apartment.

Sage growled as she slammed the door behind him. When she turned around, Matt was standing there looking like a deer caught in the headlights. "See? They don't give up. And I will not go back and work for the people who killed my mother." She shouted loud enough for Grey to hear, although he had already left the apartment.

Matt opened his mouth, but no words escaped.

"Momma was a badass, but I'm not her."

"Could have fooled me, honey." Matt retreated to the couch. "Too bad. He could have been cute if he lost the ridiculous hat. Made him look like such a tool."

"You can have him." She threw herself onto the couch next to Matt. "The nerve of him coming here."

"Something you want to talk about? What did he do?"

She caught the innuendo and answered quickly to stop him from rushing out the door to defend her honor. She shivered at the thought of being close to that jerk. She'd sleep with the vampire before considering a scumbag like Grey.

"It's okay. We all have regrets. As long as he didn't force himself on you."

"You and I both know I'd have ripped his nuts off if he tried."

Matt choked on laughter. "And you say you're not a badass."

"I talk a good game."

"You know you can confide in me. No matter what. I know you didn't just go stay at a hotel when you were gone."

"I can't—"

"But," Matt cut her off. "I also know about secrets. You've got one, and there's probably a good reason you haven't told me. So, out of respect for our longstanding friendship, I won't dig deeper. Just please know I'm your non-judgmental confessional when you need it."

"Bless me, Father, for I have sinned," Sage snickered.

"That will be five Hail Marys and you're buying breakfast." Matt elbowed her in the ribs.

"You are one of the few people in the world I can trust. And it's because of that I have to keep you in the dark. Mom was into some crazy stuff at work, and I'm unfortunately having to clean up a few messes she left behind."

Matt nodded. "Tell me when you're ready. Until then, I propose we hit the DVD collection, since there's nothing worth watching on TV this early in the morning."

"No magic. I've had enough of that crap to last a lifetime." She could avoid it for now, but no matter how done she was with ASSET or supernatural bullshit, she'd have to deal with the fallout of sending Grey away sooner or later.

TWENTY-TWO

After twenty-four peaceful hours of normalcy, Sage almost felt like her old self. And then Devon called her to come down to his gym.

Daylight somehow felt safe, though deep down Sage knew it wasn't true. Creatures of magic existed in all shapes and sizes, but only vampires had issues with the light. Still, she welcomed the fresh air and sunlight as she strolled toward Devon's gym.

A sign on the door read, Closed, but she peered inside, spotting faces she'd never seen before.

Sage knocked and waited for him to appear, as he'd done so many times before.

He opened the door, his face tightening as his eyes met hers through the plate glass. "Before I let you inside, I need your word that you'll listen and do as I ask."

"Something up?" He'd called her down. Why the sudden subterfuge?

Devon stepped aside and let her in. "I've called some of my personal friends. They're good people, but the presence of a Terra might make them nervous."

"I'm not one of them," Sage said arrogantly. The people of the Vegas ASSET group had already shown their true colors. No way in hell was she claiming to be party to their nonsense.

"Your word, please." Devon took hold of her arm before she could pass completely through the doorway.

"Yes, okay. I'll be good." The moment she crossed the threshold, Sage was on display. The assembled group regarded her curiously, but rather than look her in the face, they looked at her arm. To her birthmark. Would there ever be a day when it wasn't the first thing people saw?

"Terras are the peacekeepers." Devon lowered his voice. "So in a way, you're…"

"A party crasher?" She finished his sentence, understanding his implication. No one invites the cop to a party when they know something illegal might go down.

"To put it mildly." A lopsided grin cracked Devon's stony expression.

"I'm here to learn," she said, loud enough for others to take note. "Not to condemn people I know nothing about."

"Outing yourself as a newbie might not be smart either." Devon's hand found its way to her back. "This is Sage. She's my charge for the moment. Her mother's light was extinguished recently, and she's a refugee from the recent attack on ASSET."

The room resembled an AA meeting from the doorway. Chairs were arranged in a circle and people were settling in with coffees in hand. Two women and a man so far, but more chairs sat empty. One for Sage, one for Devon, and at least one more.

With his hand pressing gently on her back, he guided her toward the group. At first glance, they looked as bland as any people she'd have passed on the street, but the closer she came to them, Sage realized they weren't people at all. Not in the normal definition, at least. None had moved or made any visible attempts to alter their appearance. But in the blink of an eye, their appearance shifted, leaving something completely different sitting in their place. Every one of them changed. By the time she made it to an empty seat, the group had transformed into creatures she hadn't learned the names of. They were, however, beings of active and powerful magic if they were using a glamour. Finally, she might see for herself what all the fuss was about.

One woman, who at first glance looked like a librarian, with a messy bun of dark brown hair and vintage-looking horn-rimmed glasses, had shrunk down so much she hardly stood taller than her mug of coffee. "You're new then." The petite lady sprouted wings and flew up eye-level with Sage. Her skin gave off a luminescent, rosy glow, but her eyes were pure amethyst. "I'm sure we're all a sight to you, aren't we?"

"You're absolutely gorgeous." Sage admired the way the woman's delicate wings fluttered with the speed of a hummingbird at her back.

"Thank you." The winged creature smiled and bowed. "Call me Nyx."

Devon leaned into her ear and whispered, "She's an Ethereal. You might know her kind as a pixie or a sprite. They can manifest things with magic."

Try as she might, there was no way to hide her excitement at being in the presence of real magic. It added a much-needed perspective to all that had happened over the last few days. She turned to her left, where a man with green-gray skin sat. He had an ageless quality to him that made it hard for her to guess how long he'd been around. Slits flapped at his neck as though he was in water, and his chest rose and fell with each breath.

She held out her hand. "I'm Sage. Nice to meet you."

He shook it with a curt nod. "Quarn."

Sage leaned over to Devon. "Aqua man?"

Quarn responded. "If that makes it easier for you to understand, yes."

Another woman—much taller than the pixie—with hair and skin that blended into the shadows floated rather than stood in front of her. The whites of her eyes contrasted so sharply, they demanded to be looked at. But as Sage tried to look at her, she flickered in and out of focus as if she were a hologram having bad reception.

"Sylvia," the woman introduced herself and shifted form, becoming a person-sized black cloud. "Shadow runner."

"Nyx," Devon interrupted the introductions. "Can you set up a perimeter? I'd like to be alerted if anyone tries to magic their way into this meeting."

The pixie flittered around the room. At each corner, she threw out a handful of shimmering specks that glittered in a rainbow of colors as they joined to form a magical barrier encasing them in a bubble.

Sage's mouth hung open as she admired Nyx's handiwork.

"You can see it all, can't you?" Devon looked around, but his expression didn't hold the same level of wonder.

"Can't you? It's gorgeous." She held her hand out and skimmed the edge of the magical barrier with her fingertips. Smooth to the touch, like glassy water on a calm lake, but when she penetrated it, Sage found only air on the other side. She shoved her hand through and back again without popping the bubble encasing them, or causing so much as a ripple on the surface.

"You're magic neutral, remember?" Devon came up and put his hand out, but where she could puncture the bubble, his hand stopped short, finding the barrier impenetrable. "You can see the magic as it is used, but none of it affects you."

She nodded, still testing the edges of the barrier.

Nyx fluttered by, giggling, and tossed a shower of glittering magic around her. "Have you never truly seen magic used?"

Sage twirled as shimmers danced around her. "What is this?"

"A parlor trick for you." Her tone sharpened. "But if I threw so much as a single speck at Devon, he'd be on his knees, begging me to end his suffering."

Sage looked at her trainer.

"Pretty things are often the most deadly." Devon answered.

She read the message loud and clear. Reining in her amusement, Sage set her jaw and claimed one of the unused seats.

"Are we ready to talk now?" Sylvia's form solidified for a moment as she spoke, looking every bit a woman ready to hit the runway in a flowing gown of ebony gauze. But when her words trailed off into silence, her body evaporated into the black cloud floating a few inches above the ground.

"Yes." Devon claimed his seat. "Whether they have affected you or your clans or not, I'm sure you've all heard the rumors floating around about ASSET."

"Not rumors." Sylvia snapped into focus. "I knew members of the vampire coven that was attacked."

Quarn leaned back in his chair. "Too bad we don't have one of their representatives here to respond to that. Perhaps you should have called this meeting in the evening."

"We don't need them." Sylvia hovered around the group, circling slowly.

Sage noted the unease that passed around in her wake. She remembered the dream and the floating shadows that killed by passing through their enemy. Sage held her breath and prayed her innate neutrality would protect her.

"I'm close with the vampire covens in North Town. They're all but decimated." Sylvia floated toward Sage. "And those who have come forward say it was the ones bearing the mark who attacked them."

Devon shook his head. He put a finger to his lips, but rather than shushing Sylvia, it seemed as if he were stopping himself from saying something.

"To be clear," Nyx asked, "the mark of a Terra? The tree of life?"

Sylvia rounded on the pixie and they met each other at eye-level. "Is there any other race that bears a special mark?"

"Do you know what happened during the attack?" Devon blurted his question. "What weapons were used? Silver? Stakes?"

"Stakes?" Nyx scoffed, fluttering lower to hover at Devon's level.

"I'm trying to gather information," Devon replied. "If the Terras were responsible, there would have to be a weapon."

"Their magic was taken. And... they all died a final death," Silva responded.

"Death is not the end. Nor is it final, even for the leeches who steal their magic. The Mother and Father bound us in their blood, and when spilled, it returns to the earth where it first granted life." Quarn spoke as reverently as a priest giving a sermon.

"Spare us your fervor for the Mother and Father." Nyx flitted around above everyone's heads. Soft snickering sounds made it seem as if she was laughing, but no one responded angrily to her. "They turned their back on us ages ago, leaving the precious Terras our keepers."

Sage held her tongue. Responding to that bait wouldn't help her make friends.

"Parents teach their young by allowing them mistakes and seeing if they learn. Never have they wavered in their care of us." Quarn spoke his words, looking directly at Sage, though they were clearly meant for Nyx. "The Terras were but another lesson. Have we learned? Perhaps not."

"What exactly is this weapon rumored to be?" Devon asked.

"That we don't know," Sylvia replied. "Those who were there died."

"And who is said to have used this weapon?" Devon continued his line of questioning.

"The Terras, of course." Sylvia threw the accusation like a dagger in Sage's direction.

"Terras only act in response to crimes," Creases formed across Devon's brow.

"No crimes have been committed." Sylvia turned her deadly gaze to him. "Our city has been at peace."

"Terras don't need reasons to show off their muscle." Nyx giggled, but the sound carried a sinister edge. Unnerving the way she sounded so sweet, yet at the same time Sage understood the pixie was as deadly as the Shadow looming at her back. "They only need targets."

"You guys don't like them very much, do you?" Sage asked.

"We don't like others interfering in our affairs." Nyx's voice turned cold.

"Terras are the lesson from our great Mother. The folly of our ego. And a warning that should be heeded, lest we summon the gods back and invite their wrath." Quarn was the only calm voice in the room.

His words resonated with a strength that surpassed anything the angry ladies had spoken. "ASSET, on the other hand, flexes their muscle with as much ego as our people. They must learn the lesson as well. The folly in their ego could someday to bring about the wrath of our great Mother."

Sage tried to recall the passage she'd read in Devon's books. The Mother was supposed to have saved the last fruit from the tree of life.

But before she could open her mouth to say as much, Sylvia jumped in. "Terras ensure we are all aware of their power. Leaving them out of things can be seen as a crime."

"Not true." Grey's voice startled the assembled group.

Nyx changed form, her pink tone burning brighter into a deep crimson as she grew twice her size. She held her hands out, and two glowing spheres of light formed at her palms.

"Peace." Grey held his hands up. "I come in peace." He walked into the gym as if he owned the place, passing through the barrier Nyx created as if it were nothing but air. "ASSET holds the fragile peace in our community together."

"Who invited him?" Sylvia shrieked. "This is a trap!"

Devon jumped to take position between himself and Sylvia. "No trap. Grey, what are you doing here?"

"I came to talk to you about Sage, but I see you've already taken her underwing." Grey kept his hands up, standing his ground. "I'm not here to start trouble. I'm trying to do as you are and find out what caused the attack on ASSET."

Devon and Sage exchanged glances. She'd already told him off once for being a liar and using dirty methods to get his way. But as she opened her mouth, Devon interrupted her.

"Let him talk. Grey might have information useful to us. We should hear from the Terras if they're being accused."

"You can't trust him." Sage protested. "He used a vampire to trick me."

"It was Zack." Grey offered in defense. "We all know how harmless he is."

Devon chuckled. "True."

Grey strolled up beside Sage. "I'm not apologizing for anything I've done. I had my reasons, so hate me all you want."

Sage's lip curled as she balled a fist ready to strike.

"As to the rest of you," Gray addressed the room. "I want to know what is causing this uprising, because it puts all our people at risk."

How dare he pretend to be so noble to the others while showing her nothing but disrespect? Her knuckles went white with the strain of holding her hand clenched, but she couldn't throw the punch, no matter how much she wanted to. It would only make her look bad. She'd give him what he was owed soon enough.

Sylvia floated toward Grey. "Your people have pushed too far this time."

"What have we done?" he asked.

"You have a secret weapon and laid waste to an entire coven," Sylvia replied with spite.

"How?" Grey asked calmly, meeting her eyes. "Where are the bodies? Where are the spent ammunition shells? Where were the signs of a fight? You say my people did it. What proof do you bring?"

"They were turned to ash," Sylvia replied.

"Fire, then?" Grey confirmed. "Why have I heard no reports of arson on the news?"

"Not fire—their light was extinguished. Their magic taken back, leaving them dust in the wind." Sylvia's words brought the room to an uneasy silence.

All eyes were on Grey, waiting for him to answer the accusation.

"What you claim is a weapon of magical origin," Gray spoke slowly. "Think about it. If the weapon was of magical origin, my people couldn't use it." He held up his arm to show his mark. "If it were anything else, there would be evidence."

Nyx fluttered around, shifting between colors as she circled the group.

Sylvia hovered, as if contemplating what she'd just learned.

"The boy speaks the truth," Quarn broke the silence. "When the gods created our people, we were all blessed with magic. But the Mother denied her children the Terras. They were created to oppose magic."

"Then we have to ask ourselves two questions." Devon collapsed back into his chair. "What is this weapon supposed to be? And more importantly, who is using it?"

"Three," Sage added, drawing attention from everyone in the room. "Why are the Terras being blamed for it?"

TWENTY-THREE

"Terras are the great weapon," Quarn offered, pulling out a book from a satchel under his chair. He opened it and searched for something. "From the great tree, the Mother brought forth fruit that held within it the power to neutralize the magic-fueled war threatening to destroy the world she and the Father had created."

"Neutralize, but not annihilate," Grey countered.

"Balance. Yes," Quarn responded mechanically, as he continued to page through his book.

"ASSET is not about balance. It is control and manipulation." Nyx landed on her chair in a huff. "Who's to say they haven't employed others to do their dirty work?"

"ASSET does have many magical employees." Sylvia planted a hand on her hip and glared at Devon. "Lackeys who do their bidding willingly."

Sage hadn't considered that. Terras might not have been able to use magic, but if they employed people like her trainer, who was to say they didn't have other magical creatures in tactical positions?

"We don't have lackeys. We work with the magical community. We're peacekeepers." Grey tensed. Twitchy muscles flexed as he brought his hand up to his coat as if preparing for a fight. Sage knew he used machete-length blades. And he hadn't bothered to sit down since arriving. Chances were he had them under that stupid leather duster, along with who knew what else. Blades were the weapon of choice for the Terras, and Grey had certainly shown his proficiency with them when beheading her mother. How quickly could he unsheathe them if things went sour? She'd seen enough blood to last a lifetime and prayed to whatever gods might be listening that this meeting wouldn't end with more deaths.

"Peacekeepers," Nyx scoffed. Her open hostility toward Grey spoke volumes about the interaction she'd had with the Terras, or perhaps just with ASSET. "The man reaching for a weapon wants me to believe he is no threat." She fluttered up, eye level with Grey, and her skin shifted color again, glowing a vibrant blue. "Violence at the core of your being."

To his credit, Grey remained still, and kept his blades sheathed, even as the blue pixie creature hovered close enough to strike him. "Terras are no better than any of us," Nyx sneered. "And yet somehow they gained dominion."

"Balance." Quarn shocked everyone with the sudden volume of his reply. "Not dominion. They have iron and steel where we have magic." His voice held power, like a wizened wizard, speaking truth to the masses.

Nyx's side remained quite clear in her haughty retort. "Too bad we can't hurt them."

"Punch him," Devon replied. "He'll feel the blow." Devon moved to Grey's side, as if he wished to act as a spotter. Sage didn't like the direction things were taking—openly inviting violence. Devon, however, remained calm. "Cut him. He'll bleed. A great deal more than you, I'd wager."

Sylvia floated up alongside Grey, too. Two on two, each within striking distance, it if they were chess pieces moving in for a checkmate. Sage held her breath as Sylvia's body turned to vapor. She sent her wispy smoke-like form through Grey's chest.

Grey sucked in a breath, as if expecting pain, and squeezed his eyes shut. Sylvia passed through him as his breath released, and her body again took its human shape. Grey remained standing, his breathing a little quicker, but no worse for wear.

Sage waited in stunned silence, knowing how deadly and quick Grey could be. Sylvia had stepped over the line with her demonstration. He would be well within rights to react, yet to his credit, he didn't. With tension mounting, how much more would he allow before retaliating?

"He's immune to my natural abilities." Sylvia turned her anger back to Devon. "Therefore not equal. There's no balance."

"You can steal someone's life with a touch, and you want to argue that someone being immune is not balanced?" Devon asked. "I'm not immune. I could easily be bent to your will by the mere threat of your power, as many were in the dawn of time. Powerful magic required a powerful solution." He jabbed a finger at Grey. "And all his people got was immunity."

Sylvia evaporated and for a moment Sage thought she had left the conversation, but a moment later, she reappeared across the room, floating in a circular pattern as if pacing.

Nyx still hovered close enough to pose a threat, but her skin had cooled, turning a light shade of lavender. It was probably best to keep her on the lighter side of the spectrum. Sage and Grey might be immune to magic's touch, but they were the only two.

"As for what people work with ASSET, yes," Devon said. "I work to help train their agents, but I'm not privy to anything outside of my gym."

"All magical personnel are limited. Only Terras are assigned to fieldwork." Grey lowered his hand back down to his side. "And we agents of ASSET swear an oath to fight for peace. We use force only when necessary."

"As did the first Terras." Quarn pointed a finger at the book he'd been looking through.

I am rooted in the earth that bore me. Blood of the ancient magic runs through my veins. The Mother's light has blessed me, and I am ready to take my place in the great cycle.

As the Mother has shared her light, I will share it and spread her glow around the earth.

As the Mother has given her blood, I will protect that blood from being spilled.

As the Mother has shown patience, I will not be quick to judge.

As the Mother has punished her children, I will punish those who break her laws.

As the Mother has forgiven, I shall remember temperance and mercy when punishing others.

As the Mother has buried her children, I shall remember the great cycle of life ends.

As the Mother has made me her soldier, I, and those who follow in my bloodline, shall follow her orders, from now until the end of time.

"Not exactly the oath we say today, but it sounds about right," Grey agreed.

"Terras are so noble," Sylvia scoffed.

Quarn stood and held his book to read. "The Mother offered the fruit of her great tree in peace to those who would have it. Once tasted, their lust for war was quenched by the sweet juices. They ate the fruit whole, leaving not one seed to fall back to the earth. After consuming the fruit, those who had once been at war found they'd lost the magic that had fueled their desires for power and superiority."

"The fruit that took away their magic," Sage said, remembering the passage she had read in Devon's book.

Quarn cleared his throat, silencing the room before continuing. "Fearing they would be vulnerable to their brother's power, one by one they fell to their knees, begging for the Mother to restore them. She made them each swear this oath. They, and their children, and their children's children, in perpetuity, would all be bound to the Mother until the end of time. As a symbol of their agreement, each was branded with the image of the tree, a reminder of the oath they swore, and a way for the Mother to know her people. So long as the oath was honored, they wouldn't need to fear their brothers."

"And we don't," Grey said casually. "We still honor the oath we swore as peacekeepers."

Sage snorted. "You've got a funny way of honoring things." She'd meant to say it under her breath. But he'd heard her.

"You still blame me for your mother?" Gray turned on her. "She was dark. Her light had been extinguished. I didn't kill her. I saved you from that fate."

"And using a vampire to bait me into joining you?" she threw at him. "Was that saving me, too?"

"Would you rather I had kidnapped you? Forced your compliance? Or was showing you what threats might be out there really that underhanded?" he replied just as quickly.

She had no defense. His methods left a lot to be desired, but even she had to admit he'd done them with good intentions. She'd still punch him in his stupid face before long, though. "Whatever. You're a boy scout. We should all learn from your example."

"What we should do is stop squabbling amongst our-selves." Devon cleared the air with his booming voice. "Quarn has pointed out that perhaps there's a link between the fruit from the tree of life and whatever this weapon may be."

"Fruit would rot." Quarn closed the book. "But the seeds within… those could have been preserved."

"The book you gave me said something about the Mother saving some of her fruit, in case she needed their power again," Sage offered.

Grey held up a finger. She could see the wheels turning behind his expression as if he knew something, but wasn't sure what to say.

"The book speaks to the juice of the fruit quenching the lust for war. It could stand to reason that the seeds actually took away the power." Quarn nodded thoughtfully.

"Like a sponge," Grey finally said, his eyes growing wide with newfound realization, though his words were oddly chosen. "Not long ago…" He winced as if struggling for words. Sage could almost see the smoke rising as he gathered the power to run his Neanderthal brain. "I remember… a code word. *Sponge*. It had to do with an artifact bound for the Eu-ropean archives. A week or so ago, it came through our office with a special team."

"So you admit to using it?" Sylvia hissed at him from across the room.

"Are you listening? We can't use it!" Grey roared back at her. "I never saw it, though I do remember heightened secu-rity as it was scheduled to pass through our office." He turned to Sage. "Your mother was on the team taking it to Europe."

Sage's heart lurched. He'd been one of the last few to see her alive. "Did you know what it was she was carrying?"

"I knew it was special, that's about all." His revelation, for all the potential it had, only gave them more questions. Grey appeared to be struggling for something more he could offer. "I was nosy. I asked one too many questions, tried to chat up the people who were transporting it, and got assigned newbie training as a result."

If nothing else, his new information gave the group something more to do than squabble. For a few moments, silence fell over the room. Sage should have been thinking about the weapon, but all she could see was her mother's face. How dark it had been. Miranda was the best. Why would anyone have turned her? She couldn't have been party to any of the deaths. Terras were not able to use magic. Had she been aware of what was going on, or was the weapon stolen from under her nose? Questions she might never get the answer to.

"When it passed through the Las Vegas office, were there any disputes?" Devon asked.

"Like I said, I don't know. We had it here for about a week. There were lots of closed-door meetings. But when I got nosy, they reassigned me to all the shit details that kept me away from the office," Grey replied.

"Well, clearly it was used during that time," Sylvia reminded the group. "A bunch of vampires were destroyed."

"But not by ASSET," Grey pointed out. "Terras can't use it if it is magic."

"No one said anything about Terras," Sylvia snarled back at him. She had a point. But it still didn't seem feasible to have someone from another branch of magic handling it.

"But if someone else tried to use it," Sage mumbled, thinking out loud. "They'd just as easily be drained of their powers."

"Don't make assumptions about things you don't understand." Sylvia had a response for everything that made her or Grey look bad.

Sage bit back her angry reply, choosing to let others with more knowledge take the heat.

"Do we know for certain that the weapon made it to the archives in Europe?" Nyx asked.

"If she went, she never returned alive," Sage said in a reverent whisper. Her hand instinctively reached for the necklace her mom had given her. She clutched it tightly, hoping to feel some part of her mother still with her. "But I would guess, based on what happened next, that her team never made it off the ground."

"Her mother was made a darkling," Devon translated. "Sage has had a rude awakening."

Nyx fluttered close to Sage's head. "I'm sorry, dear."

"Not as much as I am. That's how I got mixed up in all this." Sage sucked in a deep breath to get a hold of her emotions, fumbling idly with the pendant, letting her fingers trace the tree's design.

"So we must work under the assumption that the weapon is a seed. And its last known place of record is here, in our city. But we still don't know how it was used or by whom." Quarn brought everyone back on point.

"We need details about what happened to the seed while it was here. Where did it go? Who was guarding it?" Devon listed the questions on his fingers. "That's in-house stuff for you Terras to figure out."

Grey nodded.

"We also need to know more about this seed. Are there any records of them being used in the past? What are their properties? How is their magic activated?" Devon pointed to

Quarn. "Do you have any other books pertaining to the old myths?"

"You're welcome to join me for a look through my library." Quarn bowed his head.

"And what am I supposed to do?" Sylvia asked.

"We need information—or better yet, witnesses," Devon replied.

"I'm to be a spy, then?" She huffed, but didn't reject the idea outright.

"Sylvia, you hold a unique position at the Sortilege agency. With as many of the classes as you interact with, there is no one better suited to locate witnesses." Devon spoke with unquestioning authority. "And Nyx, your contacts on the Strip will help us keep a finger on the pulse of traffic in and out of the city. If anyone can find a witness, I'll bet it's one of you two." Devon challenged Nyx and Sylvia each with a nod, as if inspiring each of them to be the first to find the answers.

"We must find out what happened to this weapon," Quarn added. "Because if it is still out there, it is our people at risk. More attacks will happen. The Great War could return. With four combatants this time. What would the Mother resort to then?"

"Phoenix reported an attack not too long ago," Sage offered as a new piece of information, though she wasn't sure how it fit into the puzzle.

"Sounds like someone is following a trail," Nyx added. "I wonder if the European archive has been attacked, too."

"I can try to look into that too," Grey replied.

"How did you know about Phoenix?" Devon asked.

For the first time, it seemed Sage knew something other people didn't. "Mark was like a second father to me." She shrugged, downplaying the connection she had to him.

"Sorenson?" Grey asked. "He's got very high-level access. Might be useful to contact him."

"If you can trust him." Sylvia snorted. "He is a Terra, after all."

"He's good people," Sage said. "I've known him my whole life."

"But did you know what he was?" Sylvia threw her doubt slyly, as if trying to plant seeds of her own to create more animosity.

"No. But he was the one to care for me when my mom was out on missions." Sage wasn't stupid enough to fall for her weak attempt.

"Protecting the next generation is the duty of Terras," she scoffed. "You were just another mission. A job that needed doing."

No wonder the shades got a bad name. Sylvia grated on her nerves almost as badly as Grey. But knowing this, she held her tongue. The Terra's oath replayed in her mind. *Temperance and mercy. Patience...* She couldn't afford to let Sylvia get under her skin, especially if they needed her to scour the dark places to bring back useful information.

Duty or not, Mark loved her like a father. Even when she had acted horribly, he did his best to guide her with patience.

"We'll have to bring you back in under the guise of changing your mind," Grey said, as more of an order than an offer of how to get Sage back inside of ASSET. "Time to go kiss Ava's royal ass. And when you return, you will follow my lead."

One way or another, Sage knew she'd end up back in that place. But did it have to be with Grey as her partner?

TWENTY-FOUR

After another harrowing ride through the city on the back of Grey's bike, Sage hopped off in the ASSET parking garage, crossed her arms, and stared him down through the visor of her helmet. "If I have to be stuck with you, let's get one thing straight."

"And that is?" Grey pulled off his helmet.

"You treat me with respect. No more lies. No more games."

"I thought you liked games. At least that's what it said in your file." He swapped the helmet for his fedora.

"I mean it. You be straight with me. We're supposed to be a team here. If I can't trust you—"

"Okay. Fine. No games." He cut her off before she could fully lay into him. "And what happens after you learn all the truths? Will you run and hide? Because our world can be a scary place."

"I'm not a coward." Sage grumbled. "But I need a reason behind my actions. Motivation based on facts, not lies and manipulation."

"Look. For what it's worth, I'm sorry." Grey sounded genuine, but the apology came too quickly to be genuine.

"Whatever." She swatted his words away like a fly. "Just don't screw me over when we get in there."

"I'm a boy scout, remember?" Grey patted the top of her helmet again.

That's what she was afraid of. He was talking a good game now about being a team player, but which team was he playing for? Sage still knew nothing about the world she was walking into and having to put blind faith into a partner who'd already screwed her over wasn't exactly comforting.

"You coming?" Grey nudged Sage with his elbow and headed for the elevator. "Our first order of business is to make you look like the prodigal daughter. Ava will want to talk to you about your return."

"I don't want to talk to her," Sage groaned.

"She runs this place. You have to follow protocol if you want to be taken back, even if it's under false pretenses."

Sage plastered a fake smile on her face and stepped into the elevator. At the top, the doors parted. She held her breath, expecting to smell the stench of death. The last time she'd been there, the carpet had run red with blood. But now, it showed no signs of the battle that had taken place. Everything had returned to business as usual. People milled around, walking between offices. Some were heading toward the back hallways.

Ava was walking out of her office as they headed toward the empty reception desk. She stopped dead and locked eyes with Sage. A satisfied grin ticked the corners of her lips. "You're wasting your time with this one, Mr. Maddox."

"I've convinced her how dangerous it is to be alone out there," Grey replied with a simpering *I'm a good boy* tone. He didn't seem like a kiss ass, and if this was his way of acting, Ava would surely see right through it.

"I don't need to deal with waffling newbies." Ava speared her with a look of dominance. "You hear me, Ms. Cynwrig?"

She'd offer to remove the stick up Ava's dark places, but doubted that would help their situation much. With all the self-restraint she could muster, Sage replied calmly, "You've given me no choice. Please understand what this has been like for me."

"Understand?" Ava shot back at her, slamming a fist on the desk. "I have no fewer than ten dead agents to deal with and locate their next of kin to bring in and train before they too are turned dark. A vampire uprising to quash. Repairs to our facility to arrange. And not to mention all the day-to-day complaints of my staff, who think I'm their personal den mother. Understanding is the last thing I have time to do. I need agents who can do their job, so shit like this does not happen again. I'll only ask you this one last time. Are you prepared to do your duty? Because if not, we'll locate your next of kin and make sure they are brought in after your death."

"Great talking to you, as always." Sage saluted and was about to turn on her heel when Grey snatched her by the arm.

"I'll take personal charge of her training. Assign her as my partner, and she can learn on the job."

"My two biggest troublemakers together." Ava laughed, but failed to convey amusement. "Oh, this should be fun." Her tone, married with that angry glare, was nothing short of menacing. "Fine. You're assigned to North Town tonight." Ava ripped a pencil from its perch at her ear and scrawled something down on a notepad. "I want you to see to the vampire covens personally. White flag and all, you let them know we are not assigning blame at this time. Truce. We were hit, same as them. Licking our wounds and counting the dead. Make sure they understand and try to get them to talk."

Grey's lip twitched. The look on his face was that of a man who wanted to protest but knew it wouldn't do much good. "You sure that's a good idea for a newbie?" He said the words casually, but there was definitely weight behind them.

"Did I stutter?" Ava barked, without so much as a second's pause to consider what he'd said. "White flag. Truce. This is an easy one for a seasoned agent like you. Get to it!"

They were being sent into a warzone. Grey didn't need to spell that fact out to her. Truce or not, anyone crossing enemy lines was at risk. And vampires? Weren't they the ones who could actually hurt the Terras? Was Ava trying to get them both killed, or was this meant as trial by fire?

"I'll have her suited up and ready to go out this evening," Grey replied, and loosened his grip on Sage's arm. He shook his head, a silent warning for her to not open her mouth and start an argument. She grudgingly agreed, biting her tongue.

"Ms. Cynwrig," Ava called out before they'd had a chance to escape.

Sage looked over her shoulder at the director.

"You made the right choice coming back. Once you lose the chip on your shoulder, you'll see."

Sage smirked and turned to walk away with Grey. "That went well."

"Better than expected." His tone didn't match the sentiment as he led her away from the main lobby.

"Is she always such a bitch?" Sage hadn't meant to say that out loud, but the thought escaped from her mouth too fast to stop it. She looked back to make sure no one had heard.

Grey had. "She has a reputation for not allowing anyone to get to close to her. You should see how many assistants she's burned through."

"Seriously?" Sage nearly choked on her breath.

"If she could use magic, maybe. Ava's a woman I wouldn't want to cross on a bad day. Thank the gods for making her a Terra." Grey chuckled.

"Were her assistants Terras? Or were they…" Sage wondered aloud.

"Ava's… no, Rina is Terra. Executive assistant positions are held by our kind, for obvious reasons. Usually those who are not field capable. We have to keep our secrets," he added, to make sure she understood. "Most of the un-agented positions are for specialists, like Devon, but some of the inactive magic races are clerical. Like the Trolls in our accounting department."

"So then what's our play? How do we figure out who could have had access to the," Sage lowered her voice, "seed?"

"Play it cool for now. We need to make sure everyone sees you here as someone meant to be here. We don't need someone raising an alarm if you're spotted somewhere you shouldn't be. We're going to go through the motions and swear you into the order."

That sounded suspiciously like a double-cross to Sage. She was supposed to appear to be an agent, not actually swear an oath. She opened her mouth to protest, but before the words made it out, Grey walked her into an office that looked more like a storage closet than an actual work place.

"Hey, Rina, I need to get this one in the system."

From behind a large pile of folders, Rina poked her head out. "Sage! I'm so glad you came back. I was worried something I'd said had set you off. You should have seen how mad Ava was." She rushed past the stacks and threw her arms around Sage. "But thank the Mother, right? I mean. You had to come back. You're Terra. How could you not?"

Way too friendly for Sage's liking, especially having only met this girl once before. They'd commiserated about lost parents over a cup of coffee, but did that really deserve this tight of a hug? Sage tried to pull away. After an awkward moment, Rina released her.

"Sorry. I'm a hugger. Especially when someone just saved my job." She chuckled nervously.

"Ava was really that mad?" Sage asked.

Rina looked around. "Do you see my new office? You tell me."

"Yay, we're all excited for this happy reunion. Can we get to work now? Some of us have a patrol tonight, and I can't wait around all day." Grey's interruption broke the awkwardness perfectly. Finally, a good use of his turgid personality.

"New recruit paperwork. I'm on it!" Rina turned to a towering stack of files. As she lifted her arm to pull the file, Sage noticed the bracelet Rina wore, which covered the markings on her wrist. When she had time, she was going to hunt down one of her own. That would be easier than explaining her marking all the damn time. Rina was covered in tattoos, and that camouflage probably ensured she never got a second look at her Terra brand. There was much nicer art on the other arm—a full sleeve with symbols of all manner of magic ran up from her wrist all the way to where the sleeve of her shirt fell.

Lost in thought, Sage failed to follow the conversation going on in front of her. And when silence accompanied two sets of curious eyes, she was left smiling stupidly, waiting for a verbal cue.

"We need a sample of your blood," Grey said with annoyance. "Follow Rina."

Sage did as she was told and walked through a doorway into a small infirmary.

Rina took a clipboard in hand and began rattling off questions about health and medicines, asking more personal questions than Sage cared to answer in the presence of a total stranger. Or Grey, for that matter.

She finished the questions and then held out a tablet for Sage. "Fingerprints. Follow the instructions and let me know when you're done." Rina turned away the moment Sage took the tablet and booted up a computer on the desk set along the wall.

"Seems like only yesterday I sat right there where you are," Rina talked as she tapped the keys. "My father used to tell me all kinds of bedtime stories about shadow creatures and great giants. Dragons, too. When I found out they weren't stories, I was beside myself."

Grey excused himself for a moment, promising to return before they were done.

Sage listened to Rina talk, mumbling, "Mmm-hmm," whenever a natural pause in her conversation needed it.

"Well, the dragons have yet to be proven. But I still hold out hope," Rina continued. "I love magic. It's proof that the world is better than we had ever dreamed."

Sage swiped each of her fingers multiple times on the tablet's sensor and waited as it recorded all ten of her fingers. "Hmm... Right. Done."

Rina turned and held her hand out to take back the tablet. "What sucks about it all is that despite the good being done to keep the peace, there are always those out there abusing magic."

"That's why we do what we do, right?" Sage asked.

"Unfortunately, yeah." A tear glistened in Rina's dusty blue eyes. "As much as I love magic, I would rather have my father around. In a perfect world, ASSET wouldn't be necessary."

"Nothing is perfect. But I guess that's the point really," Sage agreed. "But if we do our job, we can help make it a little better, right?"

"You sound like you've seen the light." Rina's smile brightened. "Glad to have you on the team."

"You printing her access card now?" Grey asked, surprising both girls with his sudden reappearance at the door.

Rina clacked away on the keyboard. "Just putting in the details. Let's get the blood now, and we can finish the medical stuff. Hang on for the nurse." She connected the tablet to the computer.

Grey smiled. "So you assign her rights to the building right here? Just a few clicks?" He leaned in close as if inspecting her handiwork. "We know who holds the true power here."

Rina blushed and gave him a coquettish shrug. "I wish. But I'm just the paper pusher. Not qualified to fight, or so they say."

"It's not all it's cracked up to be." Gray nudged her with his shoulder. Sage had never seen him acting so friendly. Was he flirting? Just the thought made her sick to her stomach. She was never more thankful for the distraction of the nurse coming in to do her medical workup.

Sage turned her attention to the large beast of a man who'd strode toward her with a tray of syringes in hand. For a big guy, he had a surprisingly light touch. He didn't say much, save for a few words about soreness, and to let her know she might feel a bit groggy after the shots. He drew blood and then injected her with a concoction of who knows what.

The nurse came and vanished like a ghost, moving so quickly that when he left, she couldn't remember the look of him or what name he'd had written on his badge.

"All done," Rina said triumphantly, and handed her a keycard on a chain. "Just need to be sworn in with Ava and you're officially an agent, Sage Cyn…." She faltered with the last name.

"Thanks!" Sage took the badge and hung it from her neck.

"Off to wardrobe now." Grey shuffled her toward the exit. "Thanks, Rina. We'll tell Ava you took good care of us."

"Please. Anything to get off the naughty list." Rina waved them off.

"Do you know her well?" Sage asked when they got out of earshot.

"Nope."

"Then why were you so friendly? You're never that friendly with me."

"Jealous?" Grey waggled his eyebrows. "It pays to be nice to the right people."

"Just blind flirting then?" Sage scoffed. Men were such pigs.

"Whatever it takes to make sure she wasn't paying attention to the keys being clicked." He quickened his pace, forcing Sage into a jog to keep up.

"We're not heading to wardrobe, are we?"

TWENTY-FIVE

Sage had always been ushered straight from the parking garage to the top floor, skipping everything in between. She'd almost forgotten there were other levels to the building. But when Grey pressed a different button, it piqued her interest.

"Oooh, Floor seven. Housewares." Sage sniggered. "Ladies' lingerie."

He stared at her as if she'd just spoken a foreign language.

She shrugged off his unspoken annoyance. "Elevator humor."

"Wasn't very funny."

"Neither are you, most days," Sage sniped at him. "You know, back there with the whole flirting espionage thing, I thought you might be lightening up."

"You want funny or professional?"

He' said it with such a straight face, but she couldn't hold back the laughter at his statement. "You think you fit into either of those categories?"

"I do my job." Grey puffed up defensively.

"So professionally, you hired a vampire to trick me into taking a midnight stroll."

"And you fell for it," Grey replied. "Who should be ashamed here?"

Sage refused to acknowledge that comment. He was an asshole, no matter how he tried to play the situation. Fake apology or not, Grey would do it again, if given the chance. She had his number. Knowledge was power, and he'd given her enough education to make her wary of taking anyone at face value.

"Now, if you're done playing around, swipe your card." Grey pointed to the little blinking box next to the door.

Super special secret access to a place forbidden by most people—the excitement of a new adventure overtook her annoyance. She held her ID up to the scanner and swiped it. A green light flashed, and the elevator doors opened. Sage bristled with self-importance, beaming as she looked to her partner. Where she hoped to find him just as pleased, she found little more than mild interest in his expression. Suspicion replaced the momentary sense of accomplishment. He was playing her again. *Dammit!* "I thought you said all agents have access to the archives."

"I did. We do." Grey brushed past her through the gaping elevator doors. "But I still needed to see if your card worked."

Could he be any more annoying? It was as if his mission in life was to piss her off. "You did that on purpose, didn't you?"

"Made sure you had access to the building? Yes." Grey continued down the hallway without as much as a glance over his shoulder. "Keep walking."

The offices on the seventh floor were more like dungeons, filled with prisoners chained to their in-boxes. Grey led them down one hallway that branched off at a T and took the left path, though neither looked any different.

This part of the building had a very labyrinthine vibe working for it, and given the creatures she'd already run into, it wouldn't have surprised her to see a talking worm meant to lead her down the wrong path. "The goblin king will be in the castle beyond the city," she recited, more to amuse herself than to start up another conversation with Grey.

"And here's the Bog of Eternal Stench." Grey pointed to a bathroom door as they passed.

"I thought joking was unprofessional." She wanted to laugh but wouldn't give him that satisfaction.

He stopped short at a door with keycard entrance. "Care to do the honors?"

"By all means, don't let me have all the fun." Sage wasn't about to let him play her again.

"This time you will need to." Grey held his hand out.

Sage ran her new card through the scanner, and when the light turned green, she let out a nearly silent, "Yes!"

"Proud of yourself? Must be hard… sliding your card."

"Shut up." *Teamwork,* she reminded herself, taking her frustration out on the door, pushing harder than necessary to open it. *Punching him in his annoying face won't help our cause just yet. But when this is over…*

Vastly different from anywhere she'd been before, the room held racks of computer towers all linked by cables and wires. The air had changed as well, noticeably better smelling and cooler than in the hallway.

"Server room," Grey answered her unasked question. "The best way for us to log into the database without drawing too much attention."

"But won't we be seen on cameras?" Sage asked.

"I'm giving you a tour of the facility," he replied. "When trying to get away with something, it's always best to act like you're not doing anything wrong." Grey headed toward a single computer station at the end of one of the many spider-webbed rows of cables and computer equipment. Tapping a few keys, he brought the screen of an old CRT monitor to life and began moving through files faster than Sage could keep up. She wondered how often he'd done this in the past. Only a practiced hand would know with such precision where to click and what codes to enter. Had he feigned not knowing about the weapon? Or was this the reason he'd been assigned newbie duty? Being nosey. If that were the case, Ava would already be aware of his computer-hacking capabilities. Sage's nerves prickled with suspicion, and Grey had already given her reason not to trust him. But she trusted Devon and doubted he would send her on a mission alone with Grey if he suspected the arrogant agent of being corrupt.

Where was her damned easy button?

Who should she trust?

So many questions. And at the top of her wondering mind sat a desire to know what Grey would find as he searched through the files.

"We all log in our own journal entries on cases we work," Grey explained, as he continued to open up and read files before closing them just as quickly. "If anyone had the weapon, it should be noted somewhere. I'm searching for keywords and agents that are associated with them."

She looked around nervously, searching for a flicker of camera lights or movement in the shadows, afraid at any moment someone might see what they were up to. She'd not yet seen the prisons here, nor did she want to. Curiosity trumped fear, and learning about the weapon and its guards definitely tipped the scales. "Didn't my mom have it for a time? She was on the team sent to bring it back to headquarters," Sage offered. Her hand found its way to her heart, feeling the pendant just under her shirt.

"Last name?" Grey asked.

"Cynwrig."

He tapped the keys, but when her mother's name appeared on the screen, a passcode request popped up too. Grey entered in a few different codes, but each returned the same error, blocking them from access. He growled with frustration. He balled up his fists as if to pummel the computer into obedience. His arm trembled, but he did not strike. With a defeated sigh, he said, "No luck."

"Do we know anyone else who was on the team?" Sage asked.

Grey tried a few more names. She didn't recognize any of them. But each one he pulled up was locked in the same way as her mother's. "Without admin level access, we're not going to find much."

Certain that hidden cameras were watching her every move, her first instinct was to give up and get the hell out of there, but this was their best shot at answers. And she knew someone who might have the kind of access they needed. Sage pulled out her phone and said a silent prayer she wasn't making a horrible mistake.

"What are you doing?" Grey asked.

"Seeing if I can get us access." She dialed Mark's number and waited for the call to connect.

"Sage! It's good to hear from you—" Mark began to say.

"No questions asked, please. I'm calling in a favor." Sage hoped to convey with her tone the dire need she had for him to just comply. She had made similar requests, over the years, but they had been for trivial problems like needing a ride home after drinking too much at a party and avoiding the wrath of her mother. This request she knew would trump them all.

"Anything," Mark replied, with a casual tone honed from years of practice.

She took a deep breath, holding it in for a moment before releasing it with her request. "I need your admin password for ASSET."

"Nope." His answer came with no hesitation.

"Seriously. I can't tell you why," she urged with whispered tones. "You know me, Mark. I wouldn't ask if I weren't desperate."

"There are things you should not see. Even with what you know now," he answered.

"The time for keeping secrets is over. Your silence has placed me in the middle of danger. The wolves are closing in, and I need a bone to throw at them or I'll be their next victim. I'm asking as your… your… daughter."

"Honey, you are like my daughter in every way possible, but… I can't… I'm trying to protect you." He sounded as if he were sorry, at least, but it was still a denial.

"If only you knew how wrong you were," Sage sighed. "Good-bye then, Mark." She hung up the phone before he could throw out more false promises with no truth. How could his silence protect her? That's what had landed her in the middle of this mess in the first place. All he'd had to do was come clean when she was in Phoenix. He'd had so many opportunities, but let her walk away all the same.

"Why did you do that? You just put him on alert. They'll be looking for someone accessing records now," Grey all but yelled at her. He kept his voice low enough, but the accusation was still there.

"I thought…" Sage grumbled with disappointment, more at Mark than herself. It was a good plan. She had thought her connection to Mark was stronger than that. He'd always promised to come to her aid no matter what. More lies. It seemed all things associated with ASSET were lies. No wonder the whole of the magical population had a grudge. Mark was supposed to be better than the rest, but even he had proven false. "I'm not sorry," she glared back at Grey, daring him to talk crap. She'd taken a shot, and she'd failed. But at least she'd been willing to try. If he wanted to be snarky, she'd give it back in spades. "We'll just have to find another way to look at the records."

Grey gritted his teeth and turned his attention back to the screen to continue his search. "We could look at the dates the weapon was here and see if anything else strange was reported or logged in."

Sage watched over her shoulder as Grey moved through the files. Her phone buzzed in her hand, and when she looked down, she saw Mark calling her. No use in answering, though. He'd already said no. She rejected the call.

"I'm seeing something labeled Sponge," Grey said excitedly.

"Do you people always use idiotic code words?" Sage tapped her phone against her thigh. Anticipation making her antsy. It didn't matter what stupid name they called the weapon, as long as he was able to find out the information.

"Would you prefer it be called Weapon of Magical Destruction?" Grey retorted.

"I might. At least that sounds like something worth looking at."

"Point made. But we don't want it drawing that kind of attention, even among our own people. Ambiguity has its benefits."

"Whatever you say. Just find it."

"Every record with the label of *sponge* is locked." He growled even louder this time and slammed his fist on the keyboard tray. Rejected again.

Sage's phone buzzed for the second time, and she wondered how long it would be before Mark alerted Ava about their call.

"You going to get that?" Grey growled. "It's distracting."

She sighed and made to put the phone on silent, noticing a text from Mark. Where there should have been words was just a string of three letters and three numbers with an exclamation mark at the end. Her eyes lit up, recognizing it for what it was. "Password," she whispered, and held the phone up for Grey.

"Guess he would do anything for his daughter." Grey tapped in the password and opened the file labeled *Miranda Cynwrig*.

"You were right. She had it. And she says, in the hands of a Terra, it is little more than a teardrop in size, garnet-colored, and easily mistaken for a dirty old pebble. They let a dwarf by the name of Hukkel hold it."

Sage leaned over his shoulder to read the entry herself.

Reported to the Las Vegas office for testing and cataloging of the item marked as Sponge. Dwarven weapons master Hukkel inspected the rock, which was no larger than a pebble. In agent hands, it looked dirty and unimportant. However, once in the hands of the Dwarf, the stone glowed orange as if it burned with an inner fire. He logged it in for testing.

The record was date stamped and then followed by another entry.

Weapons master Hukkel has suddenly taken ill. His records have noted the stone absorbs magic from anything it touches without activation. It glows in the presence of magic, intensifying as the absorbed magic is pulled into the stone. Three days layover in Las

Vegas has been extended to a full week due to recommended further testing for usage and range. Testing is being carried out by in-house staff of the Las Vegas office. Records request have been forwarded from the Phoenix office where the Sponge was located. My team has been given leave to enjoy the city while we wait for further orders.

Each entry was shorter, and Sage recognized the frustration her mother must have felt.

Las Vegas has us held indefinitely on the basis of further testing. Weapons master Hukkel is now reported as removed from duty. I have requested to be assigned guard watch over the weapon and been denied. Complaints filed with superiors. I await new orders.

That was the last entry with her mother's name on it. Possibly her mother's last words. Miranda had never left Las Vegas. Her death was no doubt the fallout from this further testing. "She talked to Mark. Made complaints, or whatever she called it. He should have told me that." Sage was growing more and more annoyed with the confusion. For every answer, she ended up with another question.

"He did tell you. In a way." Grey gave her a side-eye glare. "That's all I have from her. She and her team were never received in Germany."

"Why has there not been an uproar over the seed being missing, then, if they never reached their destination? And what about Hukkel? What the hell does 'removed from duty' mean?"

"News to me. I was told he'd gone to Germany with the team." Grey looked just as annoyed as she. "He was a good man."

"But no one ever left, did they?" Sage didn't need the answer. It was obvious.

"That's my guess. The weapon is still here. Which is why there was a raid on our facility." Grey replied.

"Wouldn't the leaders of the other offices then be putting pressure on Ava?" Sage tried to work through the threads of truth weaving all around her. Loose strands still lay frayed. Misinformation, lies, stories that sound valid on the surface thinly covered the truth. But it didn't quite add up.

The expression on Grey's face matched her own. Probably coming to a similar conclusion, only slower. The wheels were turning in his Neanderthal brain. It looked painful... thinking. "Have you seen how stressed she is?"

"True." If that were the case, Sage felt sorry for being so snippy with the head of the Las Vegas office.

"She's not the type to go blabbing her deepest thoughts and fears to anyone," Grey continued. "If she's trying to sort through all the lies herself, with the big wigs breathing down her neck, it would certainly explain the vein threatening to pop in her forehead." He snorted.

Sage thought back to her previous phone conversation with Mark. He'd sounded so strange, speaking as if expecting someone to be listening in on the conversation. Talking in code. "Mark too has been unusually reserved."

"He gave you the password, didn't he? After he warned you there were things you might not want to see."

It all made sense. And she *had* seen more than she wanted. Knowing that the seed was dangerous in the wrong hands she prayed that the pebble hidden in the necklace around her neck was nothing more than it seemed. But desire did not create truth. Denial wouldn't make it any less real. Sage knew exactly what it was without needing further confirmation. If her mother had felt it was being mishandled, Miranda would have done anything she could to send it away to the safest place she could think of. She'd trusted Mark with her most precious possession. Sage. So, why wouldn't she have trusted him with the weapon? That was why his office was raided. And why Mark had not bothered to push Sage to stay and work for him, when he had always wanted her to remain close. The trail would end with Miranda's death. Even if someone followed her back to the Phoenix office, the weapon would not be there. He'd sent the weapon to Sage, right under everyone's nose, disguised as the knickknack of a former employee. She was the secret keeper now, and no one could learn the truth.

"So what now?" Sage asked nervously, her hand seeking the chain around her neck again, feeling its weight more now than before.

"There are other records pertaining to Sponge in here, but those appear to be locked by Ava herself. And I doubt she's in a sharing mood. We're just going to have to do as we were instructed and go talk to the vampires."

"Is that safe? We know they were attacked… and retaliated." Sage didn't want to say it out loud, but the word *trap* echoed loudly in her mind.

Grey shrugged. "We have to follow the leads if we want to find the truth."

TWENTY-SIX

Sage hardly had time to send off a text message to Mark to say thanks before they were back on Grey's bike heading to Devon. He'd reported that Quarn had provided him with some reading material that looked promising. Information was the key. On that, they had all agreed, but Sage couldn't reveal the information she had, especially not to the others like Sylvia and Nyx. They seemed just as likely to turn on her as help if they knew the truth of where this weapon was.

They found Devon sitting in his office, his nose buried in the books he'd borrowed, scanning each page quickly before moving on to the next.

"ASSET definitely had it," Grey said the moment they came through the door. "And Ava has sent us to treat with the vampires, which tells me she thinks they know more about what happened to it than we do."

"Sage can stay with me. We have lots of reading to do." Devon tilted his head toward the small stack on his desk.

"I'm going with Grey," Sage answered back proudly. "My first official assignment."

"You're not ready for this," Devon argued. "Ava should have known better than to send the both of you. What is she playing at?"

"She's either trying to get rid of her two biggest trouble-makers, or…" Grey let the words hang in the air for a moment as he watched Sage's eyes widen fearfully. "She knows the vampires are not stupid enough to attack us under a white flag."

Devon set his book aside and stood. With his jaw set tight, he had the look of a man who wanted to counsel them against going but knew it would do no good. "Ava isn't new to the game, I'll give you that. But recent events are unprecedented. A full-scale attack on an ASSET building. Darklings turned and sent inside to attack. Nothing went missing, did it?"

Grey shrugged. "I don't know. We just concentrated on the weapon and where it might have gone."

"Vampires are smarter than that. They had to know ASSET was more than capable of defending itself. What were they hoping to gain by attacking?"

"Information about our defenses?" Grey offered.

Sage knew they were looking for the weapon, but then she realized they had attacked the main floor, where the agents were, not where any of the archives might be. "Is there a link between the vampire who turns someone dark and the darkling?"

Both Devon and Grey stared dumbstruck at Sage.

"We believe so. Why?" Devon asked.

"Revenge?" She hadn't really pieced it together, but offered her thoughts just the same. "Maybe they know the identity of the person who used the stone on them, and sent their army in looking to kill that one person."

"Why attack Phoenix, then?" Devon scrutinized Sage's face as if trying to see through her defenses.

"Some of the agents who didn't make it back came from the Phoenix office too. It's a long shot, sure, but if they were out for simple revenge, they might look to attack where they think their enemy feels safest?"

"I'm not entirely convinced it would be that simple," Devon said, scratching the stubble at his chin thoughtfully. "But wars have been started because of lesser insults."

"If the clans think we have the stone still, and know how powerful it is, why risk riling us up?" Grey added, with his usual arrogance.

"Because if they've realized, as we have, that the stone cannot be used by a Terra, then it would have to be from someone tied to the organization. Someone who might hide under the safety net of being *in* the building," Sage continued, relaying the thoughts as they came to her.

"All the more reason we need to take this mission. Talk to the vampires who were hit and see if they might give us something to go on." Grey nodded toward the door.

Through the glass pane, the gorgeous crimson and ochre stripes of the sunset were fading into the dusky colors of twilight. Time for the vampires to come out of hiding.

"Yeah, and don't worry about me." Sage stood her ground, crossing her arms in front of her, making a good show of determination even though fear had begun to creep up her spine. No backing out. She'd never hear the end of it. "I'll be fine. I have Grey here as my meat shield!"

"Already picking out pet names. You two do make a cute couple!" Devon's face remained as flat as his tone, but his words were sharply chosen.

Grey laughed as if Devon had just told the funniest joke.

"If he's your meat shield, what does that make you?" Devon asked.

Sage opened her mouth to refute his insinuation, but embarrassment held her voice in check when she realized the joke was on her. All she could do was wait until they settled down. She chewed the inside of her cheek but kept her head high, hoping to appear above their childish remarks.

"She's a damn newbie. That's what she is," Grey replied, wiping away the tears of laughter.

Devon whipped a finger at him. "Well, then, you make sure you have her back, you hear me… Meat Shield?"

Grey smirked. "I know my job."

"We'll be fine." Sage gritted her teeth, trying hard not to appear bothered by their taunting. "I can take care of myself."

"Famous last words." Devon's expression darkened. She'd walked right into a trap. Damn her pride. He was her trainer. He knew exactly how capable, or not, she was of defending herself. "Have you ever been up against a vampire?"

"Zack didn't seem all that tough." She shrugged in the hopes of downplaying her initial mistake.

Grey continued to laugh. "Zack dropped her little ass on the ground with one blow to the head."

"You paid him to do that," Sage snarled. "I hope I can return the favor someday."

"Worth. Every. Penny." Grey winked.

If she could smack that damn smirk off his face, she would. He really deserved a dose of humility.

"You two need some alone time?" Devon stepped in between them. "Zack's a pretty boy who knows how to use his charm and good looks. He's a powder puff compared to the real blood suckers."

Sage backed away, stepping out of the office to be clear of the testosterone filling the small room. Devon had been preferable to Grey so far, but even he had begun to grate on her nerves. "Okay, so what do I need?" She looked around the walls, noting the weapons Devon had mounted above the mirrors. "Necklace of garlic? Holy water? Wooden stake?"

Devon disappeared behind her. She knew, without a word, that another painful lesson was about to begin, but before she could ready herself, Devon struck. He moved more quickly than she could have anticipated, sweeping her leg in a flash of motion. Knocked clean to the floor, she lost her breath for half a second.

"How are you going to stake me from down there?"

One day she would learn to keep her damn mouth shut. She'd invited this, all because of her pride. It had been days since the last time she'd kissed the mats and was enjoying not being made a mockery of in front of others. If only she had just kept her head down and mouth shut! But she'd invited this, another patented and painful Devon-style no-mercy lesson.

Grey stood on the sidelines snickering, but one look from Devon silenced him.

"All the weapons in the world won't help you if you're on your ass." Devon glared down at her.

"Sorry, master," Sage groaned. Her butt hurt more than her pride at the moment, but not by much.

"Being cute won't work either." He held a hand out to help her up.

She reached for it, but the moment she did, his other came down hard, sending his palm into her chest. Sage fell backward harder than before, all the air knocked from her chest. She was certain she'd bruised her tailbone this time as well.

"Never trust a vampire!" Devon called out.

She wanted to reply that he wasn't one, but as she struggled to suck in breath enough to fill her lungs, there was nothing left to speak with.

"You need to be aware of what is going on at all times," Devon said with a side-eye glance to Grey.

He wasn't inviting that jerk into this lesson, was he?

She scrambled to put her back to a wall and cut off an attack from behind. Devon circled around to the left, and Grey slowly moved to her right. With Devon, it paid to expect the unexpected, but Grey was the unknown. She watched him closely for signs of movement. Scooting up against the wall, she made it to her feet and set herself ready for an attack.

Devon came at her first, aiming low to knock her off balance. She pivoted away from his lunge and found Grey's fist heading for her stomach. Two against one was unfair. They both had her on size and strength, and it was all she could do to duck and dodge each time one or both of them tried to swing at her.

Maneuvering the best she could, Sage took a brutal punch to the gut and nearly lost her lunch. She doubled over in time to miss another meaty fist aimed at her head and somehow found the strength to throw all her weight into an elbow, taking Grey down to the mats as she connected with his groin.

Devon stopped his attack, chuckling at Grey, who lay groaning on the ground, cupping himself with his hands. "I'll give you this. Your size puts you at an advantage sometimes."

"Thanks. I'll remember that." Sage clutched at her aching stomach, hoping she didn't have a broken rib. Even if she did, it was worth it to watch Grey strain to hold back the tears in his eyes. He struggled to his feet, and she savored his every grunt of exertion. It was only a small taste of the karmic payback she owed him, but definitely a satisfactory start.

"You'll heal fast, but only if you come out alive," Devon said. "And I expect to see you back here after you've dealt with the vampires. You will report in to me. Understand?"

She nodded. "Are we expecting them to fight?"

"Given recent events, you're walking into the lion's den. Expect anything," he replied.

"So what about weapons? I mean, I know you say I have all I need here, but I'd feel a hell of a lot safer with a wooden stake or something." Sage's gaze flitted up to an impressive set of machetes on the wall.

Devon's jaw tightened again. He too looked to the wall, as if knowing exactly what weapons Sage had in mind. "Your best weapons are faith and courage."

Odd reply! What faith am I supposed to have? In the Mother? As far as she understood, the gods really didn't care much to interfere in the day to day of the world they'd created. But before she could open her mouth to ask for clarification, Devon took one of her hands and balled it into a fist.

"Faith." He held her fist up and then grabbed for her other hand. "And courage."

"Those are terrible fist names." Grey found his voice, and it was still steeped in arrogance.

Tempting as it was, Sage did not unleash faith or courage on him, though she might offer him a taste of justice before the night was over.

"Call them what you will, these right here are your best defense. Don't give an enemy something they can use against you." Devon let her hands drop. "But if you must, take something sharp and pointy."

Sage remembered the box of her mother's personal effects. Miranda had had all manner of sharp pointy things she could use to defend herself with. "I think I know just the thing. But we'll need to stop at my home first."

TWENTY-SEVEN

"So this new job of yours… does it have good medical?" Matt asked the moment Sage came through the door.

"Yeah." She rushed by and threw up a hand to cover the biggest of the bruises blooming on her arm. Sage knew she looked rough, but didn't want to let on. This was only supposed to be a pit stop. No time for lengthy explanations, even though she owed Matt one.

Voices in the hallway followed, carrying all the way into her room. "You see that girl there? She's my best friend." She didn't need to see Matt to know he'd be a stone wall, not allowing Grey to pass into the living room. As scary as Grey could be, Matt had the advantage of passion to back up his muscles. "If you hurt her, I'm coming after you."

Those words bolstered her spirit. She felt Matt's love as strong as the beating of her heart. No matter what anyone told her, she was a Terra or whatever, Sage was his best friend. And Matt was hers. That was a bond worth protecting.

She waited to hear if Grey would reply. Given that men had their need to always one-up the other, he'd probably say something insulting. Though the aim of his ire would land on her rather than the man threatening to protect her. Either way, it could cause a fight. She held her breath, ready to throw herself between two hulking men if need be, but she never heard a reply from Grey. Maybe he had some smarts after all.

Not willing to take any further chances, Sage dressed as quickly as she could, in dark pants and an equally dark shirt. She opted for combat boots instead of the belted leather heels Matt had originally suggested when they'd last played dress up. By themselves, they made a very gothic-looking uniform. Only when she threaded her legs through the thigh straps on the utility belt, clasped it at her waist, and donned her mother's leather jacket did she transform from angsty to killer.

The jacket, well worn and surprisingly easy to move in, warmed to her body, welcoming its new owner. She was totally badass, and for a moment, as she caught her reflection in the mirror, saw the shadow of her mother as if looking over her shoulder with approval.

By the time she made it back into the living room, it looked as if both men were about to come to blows.

Jaws dropped along with fists as she sauntered in, suited up and ready for action.

"Oh, damn," Matt fanned himself. "You're like the Tomb Raider reborn."

"She didn't wear that much leather." Sage smirked at his admiration. If Matt said she looked good, there was no denying it.

"Selene," Grey said, with an over the top eye roll.

"If only. That chick was badass with a capital B." Sage giggled awkwardly, wondering if he'd meant to compliment her or if Grey was just trying to correct Matt's description.

"Cosplay is cool and all." Matt's expression darkened, worry creating lines in his brow that aged him well past his years. "Please tell me you both are going to a convention this late at night?"

"It's only eight." Sage rushed to the junk drawer to grab an elastic for her hair. They were heading into a war zone, and she didn't want to worry about tangles or strands getting in her way. "The sun's barely gone down." She rolled her eyes, hoping to give off the casual impression that they were heading out for fun, not work, as she weaved her long hair into a braid that rested over her shoulder. "There. Now I'm totally working the tomb raider angle."

"Wrong. All wrong." Matt shook his head and held his hand out. She'd never been able to do her own hair. But Matt had practiced hands. He took the elastic from her and unwound her poor excuse for a braid. "You know what I mean. I worry. And I don't particularly trust the Daywalker over here." In seconds, he turned her mop into a warrior's braid that would rival the one Miranda used to sport.

"What would I do without you?" She kissed him on the cheek.

Grey stood by, grinding his teeth. He could be bothered all he wanted, for all Sage cared. He had been nothing but a jerk to her.

"Please be safe," Matt whispered.

"I'll be fine. He won't let anything happen to me." She met Grey's eyes, daring him to say something stupid. They might not like each other, but they were working as a team, and that had to count for something.

"And yet you walked in hiding bruises." Matt whipped a finger at her.

She'd almost forgotten that. Her stomach still hurt from the sparring session earlier. "Training session. You know I have self-defense twice a week."

"Well, I hope you got in a few good punches of your own, then." Mat didn't look convinced. He stood with his arms crossed like an unpassable mountain between the living room and the kitchen.

"Just ask him," Sage giggled. "Good old elbow to the nuts."

Matt hissed and sent his hands to cup his crotch protectively. "Works every time."

"You have to trust me. I'm safe enough. This is what I was born for. My mo—"

"Died working for those loonies," Matt cut her off.

"She did. And I'll never forget that. Which is why I have a meat shield over here to protect me." She tilted her head at Grey, who grunted in agreement. The look on his face sat somewhere between disgust and boredom. "I'll be safe. And tomorrow I'll buy the coffee, okay?"

"I'm not asking questions now, out of respect for our friendship, but you will have a lot of explaining to do when this is all over." Matt's nostrils flared with each breath, but after a few moments, let his arms fall to his side and retreated to his room, muttering, "Skinny caramel latte."

"That's an oxymoron, you know!" Sage scoffed as she headed toward the door. Who orders something non-fat and loaded with sugar? Nutrition 101. A fight they'd had many times over the course of their friendship.

"Then don't make it skinny." His door closed with a slam. Matt's patience was wearing thin. She'd have to explain everything to him soon. At least he hadn't pressed her to talk in front of Grey. If he had, she'd be forced to spill all the secrets. Then he'd be up all night worrying after her, and that solved nothing. She had a job to do. She had to learn what had happened to the vampire covens. And now that the sun was down, she had to move quickly.

Sage sighed and ushered Grey through the door ahead of her. "I'll be home soon. Love you!"

TWENTY-EIGHT

Night unfurled its dark cloak as Sage and Grey arrived at a North Town club, pulsating with thumping electronica beats. A line snaked near the entrance, a mix of scantily clad figures eagerly waiting to step inside. Predominantly female, Sage observed as they parked discreetly at the rear of the building. The half-occupied parking lot led to a secondary entrance, where a handful of individuals lingered.

"Vampires running a nightclub?" Sage's voice dripped with disdain at the worn-out trope.

"We all play our parts in this world," Grey replied in monotone. "Survival comes in many forms."

Sage's gaze flitted to the figures loitering by the back entrance. She silently assessed who might be human and who belonged to another realm. "But isn't this a bit too..."

"It is what it is." Grey shrugged. "We don't police people's daily lives. Remember that. Our job is to keep the magic in check. Be on your best behavior now. We're on their turf."

"Got it." She smirked. "I solemnly swear that—"

"I mean it, Sage. You're going to see them, warts and all. Keep your mouth shut. We're here for information only. I don't need to pick a fight over skewed morality."

The strain in his tone said more than his words. They were crossing into enemy territory. Much as she wanted to be cute and snarky with Grey, it was time to get her head in the game. Vampires were the ones who'd turned her mom dark. They were the reason she had been awakened.

Sage crossed herself and then held up a three-finger salute. "Scout's honor!"

"Damn newbie," Grey mumbled under his breath, shaking his head as he started toward the edge of the parking lot.

Not going through the back entrance, she noted. Sage tried to look casual while keeping her eyes sharp as she followed Grey. A couple were making out, pressing themselves against the body of an old pickup truck. Two girls who looked like they belonged in an 80s movie, with giant hair and eye-assaulting neon leggings, were having a smoke under a set of stairs that led up to a private entrance on the second floor. A group of guys were arguing a few cars over. Words like *territory* and *rules* stuck in her ears. She realized that most, if not all, of the people out in the back parking lot were vampires.

A cold dread settled over her. She sought out the mark on her wrist, fingers rubbing it like a worry stone. The moment she realized what she was doing, she noticed the girls at the back stairs were watching her.

They recognized her for what she was.

Grey rounded the corner and came to the front of the building. At least most people there were human. That thought comforted her until Grey walked up to a large bald man with muscles that had muscles of their own. The bouncer was definitely not human.

"I need to talk to the boss." Grey spoke with a confidence that made her wonder how well he knew the vampires. He'd had a connection with Zack. It would stand to reason that he might have a working relationship or more with other vampires too. Ava had singled him out for this mission.

When the bouncer did not immediately let them inside, Grey held up his wrist, showing his mark. Without prompting, Sage showed her wrist as well.

A low grumble rolled up the bouncer's chest, audible even over the thrum of music leaking from the doors. He reached for his walkie-talkie at his waist and called into the small radio. "Terras coming in. Two of them."

"Keep up the good work." Grey pushed past the behemoth, giving him a pat on the shoulder as he entered the club. Sage was his shadow, not wanting to be separated at all inside the lion's den. Instinct said *run,* but Grey continued on into the dark. The temperature dropped as they passed through a curtained doorway and stepped down onto the main floor. Lights and lasers assaulted her nearly as much as the volume of the music—distractions that would make it easy to be ambushed.

She'd been in clubs many times, and expected loud music, the overwhelming stench of cheap perfumes, and sweaty bodies rubbing up against each other. But seeing vampires feeding right out in the open was a sight she could have never prepared herself to witness. Sage wanted to say something, but Grey had already warned her.

Books and movies had romanticized the idea of being fed on by a vampire. They made it seem sexy and passionate. But as they waded through the throngs of people, Sage could see pained expressions on some of the victim's faces. Music overpowered most of the other noises, but she could almost feel their moans reaching out to her. And they were definitely not the pleasurable sort.

"They won't remember a thing." Grey leaned in and whispered in her ear.

"They'll live, right?" Sage hoped the answer was yes.

"Not our territory, not our issue. Unless someone screws up and makes it our issue." His reply came without a hint of emotion. "Now wipe the disgusted look off your face before we piss off our hosts."

Devon had been right—she wasn't ready for this. Sage gritted her teeth and set her jaw as she fought to control the disgust in her eyes. Taking deep breaths helped. Focusing on air in and air out occupied her mind as she continued to follow Grey. He snaked around the dance floor, past the center bar, and headed toward a roped off VIP section.

"You two finally found each other," a familiar voice called out from behind her. The last voice she wanted to hear. It sounded far from friendly, though he took great steps to appear so. Zack came into view. His lips stretched wide enough to make sure Sage saw his fangs.

Determined to ignore him, she continued to keep pace with Grey.

Zack was suddenly at her side. "Of all the places I'd expect to see you, this never made the list. Enjoying the show?"

She refused to acknowledge his obvious attempt to get under her skin.

"You won't find welcome here, if that's what you think," Zack said, a little too loudly.

Grey stopped so suddenly, Sage ran into him as he turned around to face the vampire. "We're under orders, welcome, or not. Either escort us upstairs or go find yourself something to snack on."

Zack made a show of wiping his mouth. "How quickly we turn on our friends. No respect. No thanks." He took the lead toward the velvet ropes.

Another bouncer was standing guard, less intimidating than the one outside, but only by a fraction. Zack mouthed the word *Terra.* The bouncer grimaced, but opened the velvet rope all the same, allowing Sage and Grey to pass.

Zack stayed behind. "Nice knowing you both."

"Ignore him," Grey said.

"Oh, was he talking?" Sage smirked.

Halfway up to the VIP section, a door opened up on the landing. Sage recognized the woman peeking her head out as one of the twisted sisters who'd been smoking out on the back door when they came through. She held the door open but didn't greet Sage with any warmth.

The office behind the door was large, with its own back door exit. Sage made a quick mental note of the windows and doors, as well as the vampires sitting around the cozy room, hoping to avoid a fight but still wanting an escape route all the same.

Grey paid particular interest to the two women who had taken places at a very official-looking desk. Blondie, with the eye-assaulting green leggings, had the chair. To her left, perched on the corner of the desk, sat an equally 80s-inspired lady. Her face was concealed by a black mourning cap with matching lace trim hanging over her eyes.

"Who's the new leadership here?" Grey opened the meeting by speaking to the two women, but nodded toward two more gentlemen standing like bodyguards near the back door.

"Why? You here to take us out as well?" Blondie with the neon green leggings spoke first.

Her partner scowled but said nothing.

"I'm here for fact-finding. A truce," Grey assured them.

Blondie at hissed the word *truce,* her glare darkening.

"We believe someone is playing both sides against the middle," Grey continued, despite the obvious aggression.

"Now, I don't know about you, but I hate games—and being played is only causing us both trouble."

Fangs on display, Blondie did not appear to be in the talking mood. "You're the one in trouble right now, Terra."

"Hey! We've both taken heavy losses. Do you really think threats are the right response here?" Grey was the worst choice for a diplomat. His words might be well-intentioned, but his natural arrogance gave them a haughty edge that Blondie clearly picked up on.

"You think we're just going to bow and scrape before you? When the Terras speak, all must listen. You talk of losses. You have no idea what true loss is."

Blondie's partner nodded emphatically. "Terras have lorded over us all for too long. Thinking you're better than us. At the end of the day, you all bleed just like anyone else. And look how you come crawling when someone dares to challenge you."

"Do you see me on my knees?" Grey shot back at them.

Sage choked on her breath. *Wrong choice of words. He's falling into their trap.*

"If I wanted you on your knees, you'd be there," Blondie cackled.

"And if ASSET wanted you dead, we'd have finished the job you claim we started." Grey stood strong, crossing his arms at his chest and locking eyes with Blondie, daring her to keep taunting.

The men standing guard at the door looked ready for a fight. Their muscles tensed, and they kept their eyes trained on Grey and Sage as if waiting for the word.

Death was coming. Sage could feel it in her bones. This meeting would not end in words. It would end with blood. Her heart kicked into overdrive as she realized the odds were stacked against them. She might hold her own against one, but there were three more to deal with. Grey acted like a badass, but how good was he? Could he take on three of them?

There had to be another way. Something to calm the aggression and get them to listen. But what? She knew nothing of these people or what they cared about. No. She knew exactly what they loved. Blood. Blondie eyed her with a hunger that screamed predator.

Silence passed as Sage's heart thundered louder. The vampires could surely hear it. They were probably counting the beats, just imagining the blood flowing through her veins. Zack had called her an acquired taste. More out of reflex than intention, she nudged Grey, hoping he would bow out gracefully before they became the main course of the evening.

Grey spoke again, this time taking a lighter approach. "I'm not here to exact any revenge or punishment on behalf of ASSET. We're here for peace. I might not know loss, but she does." He turned his gaze to Sage. "Her mother was one of the darklings sent in the attack. She's afraid and alone in this world and just wants to know how it all happened."

"Aww, poor little baby." Blondie wasn't buying his change of tactic. Too bad. It had been a far nicer approach than the steamrolling he'd opened with. "If momma hadn't been sticking her nose in places she didn't belong, then this little girl would never know her place in the world." Blondie's laugh echoed throughout the room, with all her compatriots joining in on the joke.

"So much for appealing to your good nature," Sage groaned. "You clearly have none."

"Baby can speak? Adorable." Blondie's mouth twisted into a lopsided grin.

"I'm going to venture a guess here. You're new to your position," Grey said, drawing attention back to him. "Word is the vampire covens had a major shake-up recently. Lost a lot of old blood."

Blondie's expression sharpened. "You Terras would know all about that, wouldn't you?"

"It's our job," Grey replied just as curtly.

"To wipe out entire covens in the blink of an eye? You call *us* killers. Have you looked in the mirror lately?" Blondie threw her words like daggers.

"How could we wipe out entire covens?" Grey parried her angry accusations with practiced efficiency. "By what means were your clan harmed?"

Blondie smirked. "Keep fishing, honey."

"I told you we were after information." Grey's nostrils flared. "Whoever it is causing the rift, they're not just going after your people."

"But my people are the ones paying the price," Blondie snapped at him.

"And until we can get to the bottom of things, this kind of crap will continue to happen," Grey responded with equal annoyance. "More vampires dead."

"Maybe. Or perhaps the reign of the Terras will come to an end. It is after all your race lording over all the others that started this fight in the first place. The gods' perfect creations, sent to bring order to the chaotic magic ruining precious mother earth." Her voice dripped with sarcasm.

"Funny to hear that come from someone who's stolen their magic." Grey threw a dirty look at the cocky vampire.

"At least I have some," Blondie retorted, without missing a beat. "Your people are the worst kind of immortals—useless and without magic. But you can bleed."

The men who'd been standing guard at the door looked at each other and then at Blondie. She nodded slightly, and they took that as their cue to move in.

Grey unsheathed a large blade from his waist and moved like lightning to block. He connected with one target, but the other man continued toward Sage.

Sage's hand trembled as she reached for a small blade hidden in her belt. Folding it back against her wrist, she steadied herself, ready to face whatever came her way.

The male vampire approached with a cocky stride, a twisted smirk on his face. His appearance was grotesque, more beast than man, with a single fang protruding from his mouth and an empty socket where another should have been.

The look he gave her nearly froze her in place. Snaggle-toothed he might be, but still predatory in every sense of the word.

As he barreled down on her, Devon's words rang in her ears. This wasn't training. It was time to fight for her life. She couldn't afford to be a victim.

As soon as he was in range, Sage's instincts kicked in. She whipped her arm around in a frantic swipe, the edge of her blade making contact with his shirt but failing to halt his momentum. Determined not to give up, she swiped again, but he effortlessly knocked the knife out of her grip with a backhand blow.

The knife flew into the air, the metal glinting briefly before clattering onto the ground. And just like that, Snaggle-tooth was on top of her. Panic rose in Sage's chest as she struggled against his iron grip. His frigid breath brushed against her neck, sending shivers down her spine.

In a last effort to free herself, she sent her knee shooting upwards towards his groin. He let out a pained hiss and retaliated by slamming his head into hers.

Pain exploded in Sage's skull, her ears ringing as if the world was splitting apart. She could feel herself on the verge of losing consciousness, but she refused to give in. She had to keep fighting, to keep struggling as long as there was breath in her lungs.

Snaggle-tooth's body felt like an immovable wall, his arms pinning hers to her side and holding her weight entirely under his control. Desperation coursed through her veins as she realized she had no moves left.

Devon's words whispered again in her mind. *Use what you have.*

She had nothing. No weapon. No fists.

Sage squirmed with her legs and tried again to find the sweet spot between his legs, but he'd guarded himself this time. If nothing else, her struggling amused him enough that he had not yet finished the job. What else could she do? Vibrations from his mocking laughter reverberated against her cheek, pressed against his chest. She turned her head and bit down into his pecs as hard as she could.

Snaggle-tooth yowled and punished her with another smash of his wrecking ball of a head into hers. Unconsciousness took her for a few precious moments.

When Sage came to, she felt a searing pain like hundreds of needles piercing her flesh. Disoriented, she vaguely registered the sensation of a mouth clamped onto her neck, sucking at her lifeblood.

She had lost.

And then suddenly, the weight above her went limp. She was still pinned to the ground, but the pressure of his mouth was gone. Sage tried to turn her head and see what was happening, but it was no use.

Screams erupted in the room and blood splattered across her face, but she couldn't see from where or who had caused it.

Sounds of a fight raging around her continued to echo. Fear gripped her as tightly as the man crushing her body into the floor. Her heart would have been racing, but weak as she was from loss of blood, it barely registered a beat. Then, as if he'd grown wings or suddenly been filled with gas, her attacker floated off her. She rolled away and pushed herself up to her knees.

"We need to get out of here. Now," Grey shouted. He was covered from head to toe in blood and bits of something she neither recognized nor wanted to. "Can you run?"

Sage tried to nod, but her heavy head swayed more than moved under her will. She opened her mouth, but no words came out. Only the knowledge of how dead she would be if she stayed gave her strength enough to put one foot in front of the other and stumble after Grey.

He bolted the door leading to the club and turned toward the back staircase door. Pulling her along, they made their way down the stairs and into the parking lot. Sage clung to Grey as if he could keep her from passing out again.

When they made it to his bike, they found Zack sitting on it.

"Nice ride." He always seemed to have that cocky smirk on his face. His eyes lit with something like excitement as he looked toward Sage. "Someone's been naughty."

"Off the bike," Grey warned.

Zack slowly rose to his feet. "Had you come to me asking nicely, I'd have given you all the information you needed."

"You could have offered information willingly, too," Grey replied.

Sage vaguely remembered Devon asking, or maybe ordering Zack to find information. And the bastard had run cowering from his gym. If she'd had the strength or control over her body, she might have brought that fact up. As it was, she was barely keeping herself upright. And if someone didn't give her a place to sit soon, she'd take her final rest right there on the asphalt.

"That's something your kind are terrible at... asking nicely," Zack teased. "Might do to remember that next time."

"Are we done with the life lesson?" Grey asked.

Sage was sure he was stalling for time, and the rest of the coven would come down on them at any second. She tugged at Grey's jacked urgently, and the strength it took nearly toppled her over.

Zack's eyes followed her frightened motions and then sank lower from her face to the open wound in her neck. "Yes. You'd better move quickly." He retreated from the bike and let Grey mount it.

Against her moaning protest, it was Zack who helped Sage climb on back and ordered, "Hold on tight. Don't let go. Don't pass out."

Sage nodded stupidly, already halfway between worlds, but clung to Grey's body as ordered.

Zack closed in once more as Grey brought the bike to life with a mighty roar of the engine. "I'll give you this one for free," he whispered in Sage's ear. "The one who attacked my people wore the mark of a Terra. But that was a false glamour, one made of ink and not magic." He ran a finger through the bloody wound at her neck and licked it clean, smiling as Grey tore off out of the parking lot.

TWENTY-NINE

Fading in and out of consciousness, Sage clung tightly to Grey as he sped through the streets. Minutes might as well have been hours. Time warped and twisted as much as the bike, weaving through the blur of neon and moonlight. Sage fought to keep her grip through the tempting call of sleep. She replayed the moment those snaggle-teeth had sunk into her neck. Like serrated daggers, they ripped her flesh open. She'd never forget that raw and angry pain as long as she lived—though that might not be much longer.

Streetlights turned fluorescent as stars transformed into ceiling tiles. She'd moved, but not of her own accord. Someone had pulled her away from the death grip she'd had on Grey. When and how were questions that needed to be answered, but Sage couldn't get her mouth to form or find breath to push the words past her lips. She understood one thing as weakness forced her to accept the warm strength cradling her. She was safe.

"I told you to protect her!" Devon shouted. His booming voice unmistakably angry, but not the kind of anger she was used to hearing from him. When he shouted at her, it was meant to motivate, to force her to get up and fight. His tone now struck hard, like a punch to the gut. True anger. Grey had to be his target, but he didn't deserve it. Asshole that he was, Grey was the reason she still was still living. Sage wanted to answer in his defense, but those words too refused to come out.

Her vision faded. Halos reached out from the lights above, blurring the rest of the world so that all she could see was the bright glow. What she really wanted, desperately, was to allow herself to fall into darkness. Sleep. Rest. Time to heal. That's all she needed. Just a little time in the darkness, and then she would return.

She made that promise as her eyes shut. Then pain, as raw and as sharp as the teeth that had shredded her skin, shocked them open again.

"Stay with us!" desperate voices shouted. Both Devon and Grey were pleading for her to wake. "No sleeping, okay? Stay here for me."

Hands grasped her and shook her. A smack landed across her face, sending fresh pain blooming through her cheek. Anger was all that kept Sage clinging to the light, furious at them for waking her. She needed to rest. How could she heal without rest?

"We need to get her patched up. And get me some liquid iron." Devon shouted orders like a general in the field. He packed her neck with something warm and wet. It tingled at first, and then the burning began, like liquid fire dripping into her already angry wounds.

She hissed, agony bringing her vision back into clarity as she came fully awake.

Fine lines etched deeply across Devon's brow. "Yeah, it's going to hurt." But his voice lacked sympathy to match his worried expression. He forced her mouth open, poured in a bitter draught, and commanded her to swallow.

If she'd had the strength, she'd have wretched from the taste, bitter and coppery like the essence of pennies.

"As soon as you can stand it, we'll give you something to wash it down." Devon attempted a smile, but it didn't look convincing. She had to look pretty bad, maybe even worse than she felt.

"She's a tough one." Grey's voice came from outside her field of vision. "Newbie here tried to fend him off. You gotta watch those knees of hers," he chuckled. "And she's a biter, too. You'd be proud."

She had to look pretty bad if Grey was trying his hardest to praise her.

"She didn't swallow his blood, did she?" Devon's concern turned to fear as he spoke the words.

"You'd have to ask her," Grey replied. "I was kind of busy."

She reached through the fog clogging up her memory. It had all happened so quickly. She'd bitten down hard as she could, but it wasn't onto bare skin. Layers of clothing had been between her and the damn vampire. She shook her head, and the movement tugged at the bandages Devon had just applied. Tape ripped at her hair just at the root, and she groaned. Everything she did brought on new levels of pain.

"Scrappy little fighter, aren't ya?" Devon laid the praise on a little thicker than she'd ever heard. A testament to his relief at seeing her on the mend. "I told you not to go messing with vampires."

Her voice failed when she tried to speak. She was awake, but that was mostly due to pain. With the right meds, she'd be happy enough to drift off into unconsciousness.

"We stirred the hornet's nest pretty good, white flag or not," Grey said.

Devon stroked his chin. "I still don't understand Ava's motivation for sending you."

"It's well known she hates me." Grey sounded on the edge of pure exhaustion. "But she also knows I have ties to the covens. Friends in low places. I'm less threatening than the typical ASSET agent. And newbie over here is practically wearing a neon sign advertising her inexperience. It was clear we weren't coming for a fight."

"You don't waste good men on fool's errands." Devon didn't sound convinced by Grey's easy explanation. "And whether you were there to fight, they had already shown their willingness to pick one."

"I don't know then." Grey sighed and paced around the room, moving in and out of Sage's field of vision. "Ava's not a great general like you. Too many years spent pushing pencils. I bet she hasn't seen action in more than a hundred years."

Sage took a deep breath and called up whatever remained of her strength. She hated listening on the sidelines when she should be part of the conversation. She rolled onto her side and propped herself up on her elbow.

"Careful now," Grey called out, rushing to her.

She swung her feet off the edge of the table and used the momentum to help her lift up to a seated position.

Grey was at her side, ready to catch her if she fell, but Sage managed to find her balance.

"I'm not going to go dark, am I?" She struggled to push the words past her chapped lips.

Devon shook his head. "I don't think so. But you might want to take things slowly. You're as white as a ghost. You must have lost quite a bit of blood." He walked away for a moment, disappearing into his office. When he returned, he had a small box of coconut water in hand. "Drink this. It will help."

"Do I have to? That stuff tastes horrible." She grimaced. Matt had forced her to drink it on many occasions. *That and a little B12 will cure what ails you,* he'd say.

"Nature's electrolytes. A perfect drink to help speed you into recovery." Devon twisted a small cap and handed her the box.

Why does everything healthy have to taste like crap? She'd almost rather take the bitter medicine again than endure a full bottle of coconut water. "Don't blame me if I gag."

"Don't you dare!" Devon threatened her with a look.

She took a sip, holding her breath as she swallowed. It wasn't as bad as she remembered, or maybe she was just that thirsty. A sip turned into a chug before she wiped her mouth clean. Her mind suddenly flashed back to Zack, swiping his finger across her bloody neck and whispering in her ear. "Why didn't Zack try to kill us?" she blurted out with disgust.

Grey shrugged. "He's an opportunist. Probably didn't serve his needs."

"But won't his people be in an uproar if they saw him let us go?" She asked.

Again, Grey shrugged. "Not our problem. If they kill him for being a traitor, so be it. If they don't, he'll continue to inform to whoever pays his price."

"Slimy little worm." Sage choked down another gulp and grimaced.

"We all have our parts to play," Grey said.

"And when you report their attack on you," Devon stroked his bare chin, "then ASSET will be obligated to respond."

"Vegas might be vampire-free by the end of the week." Grey waggled an eyebrow at the prospect.

"Sounds a lot like war to me. Someone's orchestrated it, and we're all playing into their game," Devon suggested. "Ava might not be a general, but someone out there is using us all as pawns."

"So you don't think I should report the attack?" Grey asked.

Devon's brow furrowed in deep thought. Minutes went by and he still had no answer.

"The first thing they'll ask is if I was in danger. Then if I got any information," Grey said.

"And I'm guessing you didn't?" Devon asked.

Grey shook his head.

But they had gotten something out of that trip. Sage struggled to push away the fog. Her memory was still sketchy. Zack had said something. He'd whispered it. "We did get something."

Both pairs of eyes were on her the moment she spoke, but the memory hadn't finished playing out. Zack had licked her wound. No. He'd run a finger through her wound. And said… No. It was before he tasted her blood. "Glamour," she whispered.

"Is something we can see through," Grey sighed with annoyance.

"No. He said a glamour of ink." Sage struggled to remember his exact wording. "Not magic!"

"So then a disguise." Devon filled in the blanks.

"Yes." She nodded. "Whoever attacked only looked like a Terra. Wore the mark. That's what he said."

"And the only true identifying mark of a Terra is on your wrist," Devon added. "So someone is walking around with a tattoo."

They sat in silence again. Sage could almost hear the wheels working as the machinery of their brains went into overdrive. She sipped her drink, gagging as she forced it down. She wasn't quite up to speed just yet, but already gaining strength. She sat a little straighter. Their kind was supposed to heal quickly. At least, that was what she'd been told. She had to have been made of tough stuff to have held up for as long as she had against Snaggle-tooth's attack.

She hadn't seen Grey fight, but he'd taken out three vampires all on his own and finished off her fourth. She owed him thanks for that. In lieu of praise, she might give him her trust. That was the crux of it all. Who could she be certain of in this whole new world of violence she'd been ushered into? "Who is trustworthy and who isn't?" Sage spoke aloud as her mind worked out the problem.

"If we knew the answer to that, our problems would be solved," Devon snorted.

"Ava?" she asked.

"Has made questionable leadership choices lately," Devon answered matter-of-factly, but not condemning her outright.

"She's been around a good long time," Grey added.

"But is she someone you trust?" Sage asked, hoping for a straight answer.

"Why?" Grey looked at her curiously.

One of these days, that man was going to give her a simple yes or no. Clearly, this was not that day. Sage ground her teeth, frustrated at having to qualify everything. "You say she got onto you for being nosey when the weapon came through Vegas. Punished you, right?" Sage asked. "Made you babysit me."

Grey's eyes narrowed, but he didn't respond. Like a confused puppy, he looked at her curiously, as if needing more clarification.

Talking was hard enough as it was. Why did he have to make her work for answers? "Okay," she sighed. "What if Ava's just using your best gifts?"

"I'm not sure if I should be insulted." Grey looked even more like a confused puppy dog. "Are you saying my best gift is babysitting?"

Devon slapped a hand over his mouth, muting his laughter. If he understood her line of questioning, he could offer to help. Sniggering certainly wasn't doing any good.

Sage took another chug of her drink and tried to streamline the chaos of her tired mind to deliver her point clearly. "What have you done since meeting me? Traded secrets with vampires, shades, elementals, and ethereals, right? You've gathered information on the weapon everyone is searching for, right? And all this time, you've worked pretty independently from the standard operating procedures of ASSET. Right?"

A glimmer of understanding flickered to life in Grey's eyes. "You think she's armchair quarterbacking me?"

"I think you're her best agent right now. You're abrasive, rude, and you don't seem to care for rules—"

"Careful now," Grey warned. "I did just save your newbie ass."

"Let her finish. I'd like to see how many ways she can insult you before you blow your top." Devon snorted, not bothering to hiding his amusement, and wiped tears from his eyes.

"What I mean is," Sage continued, "you're the best kind of undercover agent. The disillusioned castoff."

Grey's brow furrowed even deeper now. "You're not saying I'm—"

"Much as I'd like to hate you, and distrust you, and punch you in your arrogant face, you've always had my back. I hope I'm not wrong in saying I trust you to do what's right. Ava might trust you as well, to make your reports on everything you've seen as my babysitter."

"Oh, now you think you're the chosen one?" It was Grey's turn to laugh.

"I was close to Mark. Mark was close to Miranda. My mother. One of the last few people to have been with the weapon before it went missing." That should have been obvious, but it wasn't until she'd said the last word that everyone in the room got the point. She thanked the gods for that. Trying to get them to follow her train of thought had given her a massive headache.

"But you don't know anything about the seed, do you?" Devon asked, but the look he gave her begged Sage to say no. "How could you?"

"I don't," Sage lied quickly. "But Ava doesn't know that. She wouldn't trust me to answer her honestly, if she asked, anyway. Trust is earned."

"So she's using me to get you to open up and reveal your secrets and connections?"

"It's one possibility." Sage shrugged. "My question, though, is, do you trust her?"

Both men looked at each other. Neither one appeared willing to offer judgment. That didn't bode well. They had more experience with Ava, years more. Sage had been rubbed the wrong way by her the moment she'd met Ava, but first impressions weren't always accurate. Ava could very well have been cracking under the stress of upper management who were putting pressure on her to find the missing weapon. Or she could have been the one to order its use. And after it had been lost in the scuffle, she might be worried for her safety.

"There's one way to find out for certain," Devon offered. "We feed her information and see what she does with it."

THIRTY

The ride back to ASSET didn't leave enough time for Sage to mentally prepare herself. She hadn't fully committed to the idea of Ava being on the wrong side, but being short of a decent list of suspects left them grasping at any shadows. "I don't like this idea."

"Losing your nerve?" Grey joked, but even he had a worried edge to his words.

Sage fixed her hair after pulling off the helmet. "If we're wrong, we look like idiots." *If we're right, it could be even worse.* She wouldn't say that aloud. Gods forbid it to be true.

"But isn't that what's expected of us?" Clearly practiced at the art of deception, Grey wore the mask of indifference well. "We're ASSET's flunkies."

"You're the flunky. I'm a newbie," Sage said defensively.

"With the battle scars to prove it." Grey pointed at her bandaged neck. "You might want to wear a scarf or something."

She reached a hand up, gently grazing the massive bandage covering her wounds. How was she going to hide it? No one wore scarves in the middle of the summer. Leaving her hair down wasn't an option. She could hardly stand clothes sticking to her with the heat. Thousands of strands of hair?

Nope. That would be unbearable. There was no hiding it. She'd just have to wear the bandage proudly and deal with the fallout. "Matt is going to kill me when he sees this."

"What's your deal with him, anyway?"

"Why? You interested?" She giggled, hoping to get a rise out of him.

"Not my type."

"Is anyone?"

"No," Grey replied flatly, slicking his hair back and putting the stupid fedora back on his head.

"Touchy about that, are we? Relationship troubles?" Was that stony exterior cracking a bit? Could there be a little humanity beneath the assholish exterior? If not, she could at least enjoy some fun time poking the bear. "Lonely? Broken-hearted? Either one explains your—"

"Don't."

Not exactly what she'd been aiming for, but her offhand remark had reached Grey's soft underbelly, and it was definitely raw. "Okay, sorry. I was just—"

"No. You weren't 'just'… anything. I'm not your friend. I'm your partner. That goes as far as our mission. Not personal lives."

"But you just asked me about Matt." So much for a little friendly ribbing.

"You live with him. He could cause trouble for ASSET because he cares about you, romantically or otherwise." Grey's words were matter-of-fact, but she saw through them. If he didn't want to talk about it, fine, but she wasn't buying his pretense of being all about the mission.

Sage adopted his grim tone. "Matt won't be a problem."

"See that he's not."

They entered the elevator and rode it all the way to the top in silence. Rina was there, sitting at the reception desk, smiling when she saw Sage emerge. "They moved me out of the dungeon!" she said and then caught sight of the bandage on Sage's neck. "Oh, hell, what happened to you?" Rina rounded the corner and was at Sage's side in a flash, inspecting her bandages. "Are you okay?"

"I'm good. It's all good." Sage shied away from Rina, feeling uncomfortable having someone so eager to invade her space. "We've got news… to report… for Ava… Director Masters. Where is she?"

"Are you sure? I think you should be checked out in the infirmary." Rina took her by the hand, reeling her in for further inspection. "Just want to make sure it's not still bleeding."

"No. I'm fine." Sage twisted away, breaking free of Rina's grip. "We really need to talk to Ava."

"Battle scars, Rina. You'd know all about them if you'd do some field work." Grey's comment worked to pull the attention away from Sage, who used the distraction to make him the middleman and avoid being pulled in again.

"I *have* been out in the field, remember?" Rina's tone soured.

Grey shrugged.

Rina lifted her shirt. Through a thin layer of gauze, a wound—red, raw, and recently stitched—ran across her belly, still swollen and puckering where the skin was working to heal. Her chest was bound tight with a medical wrap. "Fresh enough wounds for ya?" she sneered at him. "I'm not meant for field work. But I have tried."

"You should be proud to have battle scars. We all earn them. Want to see mine?" He winked. Grey was a terrible flirt—if that was actually flirting. It almost seemed as if he were playing at it, a caricature of what he thought flirting should look like.

Rina didn't seem to be buying it either. She rolled her eyes and retook her position behind the desk. "You're going to have to wait a bit. Ava's on a major conference call."

With the desk as a barrier, Sage felt safe closing in to talk. "You know what it's about?"

Rina might not have reacted well to Grey, but she perked right up when Sage spoke to her. She cupped her hands around her mouth and whispered, "Assistants know everything."

"Really?" Sage wondered aloud.

"Well, we have to. I mean, how can the boss do her job without adequate help? So many details to remember and schedules to keep." She bristled with pride and aimed her cocky gaze at Grey. He didn't seem to care what Rina was saying. His attention remained locked on the office door, as if willing it to open. "Ava might be hard to work for, but the things she handles are so important." Rina might not have done much fieldwork, but Sage had no doubts she had battle scars from dealing with the director, as many weapons as that woman kept in her office.

"It's a good thing she has you, then." Sage said politely, realizing that her question had gone unanswered. She might know things, like whom Ava was talking to behind those closed doors, but that didn't make her a blabbermouth.

"Doing my part for the cause." Rina shrugged bashfully.

"Us too."

"I can't believe you went out to see those vampires." Rina sounded horrified again.

Sage's hand found her bandages again. She cringed at the memory.

"They're so dangerous." Rina looked pitifully at Sage. "Does it hurt much?"

She must look like a weakling, babying her wounds. Sage took a steadying breath and let her hand fall back to her hip. "I'll be fine."

"What happened?" Rina asked.

"They didn't want to talk. Still mad at us, I guess." Sage shrugged.

Rina's expression turned to sadness. "I'll bet. So many attacks. People dying. It's horrible."

She sounded as if her father had died all over again. Sage could see tears in Rina's eyes. She wasn't much of a hugger, but at that moment, it was all she could do to avoid looking at the poor girl suffering in front of her.

Rina accepted the hug willingly, wrapping her arms around Sage's neck.

Sage winced with pain and pulled back, her wounds tender even with the bandage.

Before Rina could apologize, Ava's door opened and the queen mother herself glared from the doorway. "Report!"

Sage breathed a heavy sigh, steeling her resolve to deal with the director and hold her tongue.

Grey filed in, with Sage close behind. She gave a passing nod of solidarity to Rina before closing the door behind her.

Ava strolled around to her desk and as she sat, she folded the screen of her laptop down. Sage remembered Zack's words and looked for the mark of the tree on Ava's wrist. It was there, surrounded by the lacework tattoos like gloves covering her hands and arms, just as she expected. But below it, she noted another marking.

"Well?" Ava demanded.

"What does that mark mean?" Sage asked, staring down at the strange design. Was it letters? Numbers?

"Runes, dear," she replied impatiently. "It's the mark of my position and age. Have you not seen similar ones on Mr. Sorenson?"

"In truth, no. Mark always wore a watch on his wrist with a big fat strap."

"Yes. That would help to avoid stupid questions, I guess." She snorted, and the first real smile cracked her lips—amusement at Sage's expense. "But I want to know about the vampires. I hear they weren't very friendly."

"What was your first clue?" Sage mumbled under her breath.

Grey cleared his throat. "The major covens are pretty mad we assaulted them."

"As was evident by their attack on us." Ava waved her hand around as if to say, *Get to the good part.*

"But we think we know why." Grey let his words hang.

The Director's eyes glittered with interest. "Go on!"

"The artifact that came through a little while back. Apparently, some kind of weapon was employed—and then lost."

"You've mentioned it before to me." Ava's eyebrow lifted sharply. "Have you finally learned what it is?"

"Yes. And I know where it will be." He slid a paper across the desk. "They tried to kill us, so I thought it only fair to return the favor. When the dust settled, I spotted a little note. They had found it and were hoping to learn a way to use it against us."

"Ava scrutinized the small scrap of paper. "This is where it is?"

"Where it will be," Grey corrected. "I have one of our friends retrieving it."

"If you know what it is, then you know it's dangerous." Ava's tone turned cautiously optimistic.

"Sage here has been doing her research." Grey nudged her shoulder.

"Touching the object is the danger. So long as it's encased in something, preferably silver, it's harmless." Sage met the Director's eyes, adding weight to her words.

Ava crumpled the paper in her hands. "Who else knows about this?"

Grey shook his head. "Only the four of us."

"Four?" Ava asked. "Who is this fourth friend?"

"Didn't you see the address? Someone we all trust," Grey replied. "I'm having him hold on to it for a few days until the vampire's rage dies down. Then we can move it again."

"I knew I sent the right agent on this job." Ava nodded at Grey approvingly.

"With all due respect…" Grey's jaw tightened. Ava's approval had clearly failed to give him the same pride it did Rina. "You sent us on a suicide mission."

"No one knows the vampires better than you. With all due respect." Queen bitch came back strong as ever. So much for her feigned approval. "You should have been better prepared to deal with them."

"The way things are headed, we're on the brink of war," Grey replied.

"We fight wars on battlefields." Ava locked eyes with him. "This is a test of wills."

As angry as he looked, Grey maintained his monotone. "Where lives are at stake."

"When are lives not at stake?" Her tone sharpened. The vein in her head made itself known, throbbing with the speed of her anger. "What do you think our job is here? No one appreciates the law until they need the law."

"According to them, it's we who need to be policed," Grey answered grudgingly.

"Are those your girlfriend's words or yours?" Ava shot back at him.

Sage's mouth dropped open. Grey had a girlfriend? And if she'd followed that conversation correctly, a vampire girlfriend… That explained a lot. She filed that under questions to ask later, when they had more time for her to annoy him until he told her his story.

"If she were alive to speak them, yes, I believe they would have been her words." Grey's voice warbled slightly, the strain of trying to maintain his calm voice apparently cracking his resolve.

"She'd be right." Ava's lips tightened. If only Sage had a window into that woman's mind to see what she was thinking. One moment she was a royal bitch, and then a moment later, she came across as a competent leader. There was just no accurate way to measure whether she was genuine.

"We have much to correct in our operation. Most importantly, we need to retrieve what has been misappropriated."

"All in good time," Grey said. The calm returning to his tone.

"Is that wise?" Ava asked. "I'd prefer it here under ASSET protection."

"We've already come under attack. The vampires are all riled up. They'll expect us to bring it home when they notice it's gone missing. This is safer until we neutralize the threat," Grey assured her. "And while we lie in wait, you must be seen operating business as usual."

"Yes. To that extent, I have to agree with you." Ava's eye twitched. Boss lady clearly disliked being ordered around. "The more people who know about this, the more of a danger it becomes." Ava's tone might have been all business, but there was an underlying edge of strain there. "That item should have never been tampered with from the start. When you have deemed it secure enough to return, it must be brought in under the utmost secrecy."

Grey nodded. "Our mutual friend has always been a trusted extension of the team."

"Which makes him a liability." Ava's resolve wavered. She tapped her tattooed fingers nervously on the desk. "He's very well known. Well connected. That changes things a little."

"You can order me to bring it in now," Grey dared her. "But I know the vampires are planning another run at us. Look how easily they came at us the last time, throwing our own people at us. Our mutual friend might be well connected, but he's also extremely capable of defense."

Ava sighed deeply, the vein in her head still throbbing furiously. *Stress kills. But does it kill Terras?* Was Ava really a Terra?

"You, Miss Cynwrig, are you okay?" Ava sounded almost genuinely curious about her health.

"I'm good." She shrugged. "Nothing I won't recover from after a day of rest."

"Go home. Take your rest," Ava ordered. "And Grey, until further notice, you are her shadow. Stay with her."

Grey nodded.

"I'll let you know my decision regarding our mutual friend shortly." Ava waved them off like pesky flies and re-opened her laptop. "Dismissed."

THIRTY-ONE

Delivering the message had been surprisingly easy. Sage had expected much more pushback from Ava. People in control often struggled with not having it. All the more reason for her to be a suspect. Ava would make sure she got her hands on that stone before anyone else knew about it. And if she were secretly something other than Terra, they'd have her!

The hard part would be waiting—holding her breath until those suspicions could be confirmed.

Sage needed a distraction, or she'd drive herself crazy. "Are we going to talk about the elephant in the room?" she asked Grey as they left Ava's office.

Grey took the lead, putting his back to her, walking like a man on a mission to avoid any conversation. "Nope."

"A vampire? Really?" she whispered, still trying to process the shock of that information.

"We're not doing this." Grey passed Rina at the reception desk as he headed toward the elevator. "We're going to take you home to collect your belongings."

"But I don't want to move in here." Sage made a good show of pouting angrily, realizing what Grey was doing to aid in their quick getaway. "I have a home already."

"Listen up, newbie. That bandage on your neck is proof you can't be left alone. And I'm not going to babysit your ass out in the open any longer." Grey pressed the button for the elevator and took hold of Sage's arm with his free hand. If she didn't know better, she might have taken his overwhelming act of dominance seriously. Her knee itched to give him a taste of just how capable she was of defending brutes like him, but that would be taking things a bit too far.

"Be nice to her." Rina came trotting up, looking equally ready to start a fight. "Being new sucks sometimes."

"At least *she* understands," Sage grumbled.

Grey all but rolled his eyes. "You'll thank me when you're older."

"It won't be so bad." Rina tried to look hopeful as she reached a hand to pat Sage's shoulder. "When you get back, I'll hang with you."

That small gesture of solidarity almost made Sage feel bad for her deception. Rina had been nothing but nice. She was probably the only person at ASSET who hadn't tried to manipulate her or talk down to her. They even shared a common grief, both having recently lost a parent. But since Sage and Grey had agreed that everyone within ASSET was a potential suspect, even Rina had to be kept completely in the dark.

The elevator doors opened, and Grey shoved Sage inside. She gave Rina a silent look of sorrow before the doors closed. Grey didn't say another word until they reached his motorcycle. "I hope we did the right thing?"

Definitely not what she expected to come from his usually arrogant mouth. Mr. Asshole suddenly going soft? "You getting cold feet now?" she asked.

"No!" he scoffed, but she saw straight through his pride. Grey avoided eye contact as he retrieved his helmet. "I'm hoping we were wrong to suspect—"

"We're not wrong to seek the truth." She cut him off, annoyed by his wavering tone. "Remember, that weapon is a danger in the wrong hands. And if those hands are inside this building, we're all screwed."

"This isn't a damn game, you know!" Grey shot back at her. "We're playing with real people and real lives. Ava is the director of this facility."

"Was my mother playing a game when she was destroyed? Believe me, if I could just roll the dice and resurrect her, I would."

"I'm sorry for what happened to her."

"All the more reason we need to find out if Ava can be trusted." Sage fisted a hand at her side to give her strength. "Ava controls everything here. That kind of power can be used for good or evil."

"We still don't know where the weapon is." Grey's tone lacked confidence. "Ava's alliance is moot if it's in the wrong hands right now."

If only he knew the truth! But Sage wasn't about to reveal that little nugget of information just yet. Ava might be the primary suspect, but anyone attached to ASSET could still be a mole. She hoped that the small amount of trust she'd given Grey was not misplaced, but until all was revealed, her lips would be sealed on that subject. "That's why we have to know who to trust in the organization. If Ava's as good as her word, she won't let on to anyone where the weapon is. We can explain ourselves after we're certain she can be trusted. But, if she so much as sets foot in Devon's gym, then we know ASSET is compromised at the highest level, and it is best we don't have the weapon at that point."

***

They rode fast, making it back to the gym in record time. Nyx, sporting a calming shade of lavender, flitted around Devon's office, casting her magic in every corner of the room.

Deadly as she'd learned the pixie could be, Sage still stood in awe as she watched the explosions of color knitting themselves into a tight webbing that encased the room.

A small part of her wished that she could use magic—pull whatever she wanted from the very air and bring it to life. During her dungeon raids, she would often be the one casting healing magic, but occasionally she enjoyed a good damage blast. Her imagination would conjure up lightning bolts or green fog. But the glittering specks that Nyx tossed around were far more beautiful than anything she had envisioned. If she could not use it herself, at least she was able to watch.

Devon came out from the back of the gym, clipboard in hand, and immediately began doling out instructions. "Make sure the doorway isn't blocked. We want our burglar to enter and feel they've made it through our defenses without a problem. Once they break the seal of my office, that's when they need to be blocked. I want them trapped there." Devon gave a quick nod to Sage as he continued on to an electrical panel by the door.

Quarn had a bag of tools and sat clipping wires and running cables from an outlet to a small box he'd fixed to the wall outside Devon's office.

"Looks like you've been busy since we left." Sage admired the new security system being installed.

"To keep the illusion, we're rigging some alarm boxes and a new key code lock for my door." Devon handed the clipboard to Quarn. "Key code."

Quarn nodded and tapped some numbers from the page Devon had just given him.

"What do you need us to do?" Grey asked.

"Go make yourself comfortable in the back. I've set out some cots and stocked the fridge back there. We might be in for a long haul."

The work Devon had put in was impressive. The place definitely looked more secure, though she wondered exactly how much was needed for this hoax.

Devon held a silver ring box in his hands. "A decoy for our thief." Inside it even held a small garnet gem. He'd gone to great lengths to make it all appear believable. All they needed now was to see if Ava would take the bait.

"What do you want me to do?" Sage asked.

"Nothing. We have it all in hand. Go home. Tend to your wounds," Devon replied, pocketing the little silver box.

"Licking them," she scoffed. No way in hell was she going to be benched for this. It had been her idea from the start. "I've come this far. I'm not turning back now."

"Can't blame me for trying." Devon smirked. "But one day you'll learn to heed warnings."

"Today is not *that* day."

"If you end up dead—"

"As long as we're not facing vampires again…" Her hand moved to the patch on her neck. The look on Devon's stole the sound from her voice. Her heart nearly came to a screeching halt. No one said anything about involving those jerks! She'd made that comment as a joke. Why had no one thought to let her in on that part of the plan?

They were only supposed to find out who was after the stone. Bringing the bloodsuckers in meant retaliation. *If the vampire covens got involved in this*…. Sage sucked in a breath. The image of her mother gone dark again flashed in her memory. Her instinct was to plead for Devon to change his mind. Send the vampires away. But just as she wouldn't allow herself to be sent away, she knew begging Devon would be futile.

"Why vampires?" Sage groaned.

THIRTY-TWO

Zack was the last person she hoped to run into, but he was far better than another Twisted Sister reunion. When he arrived to represent the vampire covens, Sage found herself a little relieved, though she wouldn't admit it aloud. She'd seen what vampires were capable of. Tough as she pretended to be, Sage still had a lot of learning to do if she hoped to hold her own in another fight. Zack, however, had a reputation for being the least lethal of his kind, though he had an amazing level of overconfidence and those dangerously hypnotizing eyes.

Night wore into day and back into night again, with not so much as a solicitor coming to call at Devon's gym. Waiting was the worst kind of hell. Bingeing on reruns and old movies would be the best way to pass the time, but Devon didn't have a television. She tried reading, but as close as mythology came to epic fantasy, the plot just couldn't hold her interest, and definitely needed more dragons.

She regretted not returning home when her wounds began to itch. The tape at her neck caught on her hair every time she moved. Between the boredom, discomfort, and severe lack of sleep, Sage was ready to snap. She couldn't remember the last time she'd had a nice hot shower, either. Showers always made the world more bearable.

Hours blended together, and she worried if their plan would actually work. She'd been uncertain about Ava's position and if she was a person who could be trusted. Surely having not attempted to take the weapon herself was a credit to her worthiness. But how long would they wait before giving up and coming clean?

Scratching at her neck again, Sage remembered to send a message to Matt. Not knowing when she'd return home, she kept her words vague, making sure he understood she was safe. Vampires might be scary, but nothing topped her roommate when his claws came out.

Zack's eyes wandered in her direction as she tugged at her bandage.

"Don't even think about it," she threatened the hungry-looking vampire.

"As you wish." His lips drew back, not quite a snarl, but still an obvious attempt to put his teeth on display. "You seem afraid."

Sage glared at him. "Not of you."

"Is that wise, I wonder?" He mocked her openly.

"How do I kill him again?" Sage threw the question to Devon. He'd been pacing the lounge like a caged animal for the better part of the afternoon. The wait was putting a strain on everyone. More than once, she'd caught Devon muttering to himself, discussing backup plans and fail-safes, as if confirming items on a checklist.

"Play nice, you two." Devon glared at Zack angrily.

"I'm not playing." Sage rolled her eyes. "He's sitting here looking at me like I'm his next meal."

Zack leaned in close and whispered, "You are most certainly an acquired taste."

That sent a shiver down her spine. Goosebumps erupted all across her skin. She remembered his finger tracing through her bloody wound just before he licked it clean. *Disgusting!*

The smile blooming across the vampire's face turned her fear into anger. He was screwing with her head, and it was working.

Two could play at that game. Sage put every ounce of aggression into her face as she replied in a deadly whisper, "Say something like that to me again, and you'll be drinking your next meal through a hole in your neck!"

"Will you two shut up?" Grey groaned loud enough to stop Sage from adding more to her threat. Grey had been lying with his legs stretched across an old pleather futon, his fedora covering his eyes.

Zack responded before Sage could summon a good comeback. "I remember thinking the same thing about your last girlfriend."

Grey's hat fell as he sprang to his feet, machete in hand, ready to strike.

Sage ducked out of the way as Devon jumped in between the two men. "Is this how it ends? We all fight each other until there's no one left to fight the true threat?"

Devon was right, of course, but she wondered who might win between the two of them. Zack had been called a pushover more than once, but like everything else she'd been told, the truth didn't always match up. Grey was quick, but she had a feeling Zack might surprise them all.

Grey sheathed his machete, but the look on his face said he'd rather put it somewhere else.

Zack folded his arms, turning his annoyance toward Devon. "Waiting. Waiting. Waiting. This is pointless. We know the weapon came from ASSET. Why are we trying to get them to come here?"

Devon returned to his pacing, offering no response to Zack's petulance. The lounge, just behind the gym, wasn't large enough for much more than a few strides in either direction, but it had all the necessities to keep them safe and close while they waited to see if anyone took the bait. After the hours of waiting, though, the walls felt like they were closing in on them. Any longer and they really would come to blows.

"Your people attacked ASSET already," Grey reminded Zack. His tone was no less angry, but he no longer held his blade, ready to strike.

"Not my coven. Not me. You of all people should know that my kind are very much independent," Zack replied as if insulted.

"But you were the one to offer us information," Sage added. "Little as that has been."

"At great personal cost!" Zack rounded on her. "The only reason I'm here is to get back into their good graces."

"How exactly?" Sage asked.

"Honey, there are things you should not know." His tone turned deadly. His cold eyes came within an inch of hers before she had time to register his movement. A viper masquerading as a worm—he'd had them all fooled by his personality, which allowed them to take him for granted. She had his number now, and would not soon forget the lesson he'd just given her. His warning meant death for whoever it was that dared come after the bait they'd laid.

Although she was standing so close she could feel his frigid breath on her skin, Zack's eyes were not on hers. He stared at the bandage. A thin barrier between him and the fresh wound. Could he smell the blood there? She gulped down the knot blocking her throat.

"Still wearing your silver necklace?" Zack jabbed a finger toward her chest.

Her hand flew up to her neck, fingers seeking the chain. "You don't like silver, do you?"

Zack scoffed, backing away slowly. "Silver doesn't bother me as much as that tree."

"Terras aren't your enemy." The words flew from Sage's mouth on instinct.

"Your murderer is not Terra." Zack said the words to Sage, but his tone was loud enough to be a reminder for the entire room. "They're pretending to be one, though. And they know the secret to the weapon that can destroy magic."

"That it must touch its victim?" Sage replied, trying to hold back the trembling notes of fear. "So, how did it wipe out a whole coven?"

"One painful death at a time, as far as I was informed." Zack resumed his pacing. "And that is exactly how they will be paid back."

That was not something she wanted to see. Death. More death. Too much for one lifetime, and yet, there would be more. All the angst and pacing in the room only made the tension thicker. They needed to take their minds off revenge and murder, at least for a few moments, or they would end up killing each other from sheer boredom. She struggled for something to say to change the subject, maybe bring a little lighter tone to the conversation, but she came up empty.

Devon returned to his muttering. Grey pulled out a whetstone and sat on the futon, sharpening his machete, and Zack paced round and round, eyeing everyone like a hungry cat.

An unspoken truce of avoidance. Not entirely comfortable, but safe.

The lights went out, sending them all into shocking darkness. Sage's heart skipped a beat.

Had Ava really fallen for the bait?

With the power gone, the alarm systems were rendered silent, but they had magic on their side, too. Nyx had long since left, but her barrier remained strong. The office was a magical rattrap waiting to be sprung by anyone not of Terra lineage.

Patiently they waited in the lounge just behind the gym, listening at the walls for the intruder to go to work. The door unlocked and opened with barely a sound. Whoever it was had skill. Next came the office door—Sage heard small scraping sounds as the lock was carefully picked.

As tempting as it was to jump out and stop them, the group remained silent, waiting for the trap to be sprung. The true test was whether the interloper could pass in and out of the barrier. The one who had used the weapon was not a Terra.

Sage's heart ticked double-time as if racing the clock. Seconds felt like hours, an eternity trapped in the bubble of a few precious minutes.

A woman groaned loudly—her voice angry and afraid at the same time—followed by the hard slam of a fist against walls.

Devon, Zack, Grey, and Sage rushed for the door, as if there were a prize for the one who learned the intruder's identity first.

The front door had been propped open for a quick escape. The office door was gaping as well. Inside, the woman's grunts and groans of frustration quickly turned to demanding shrieks. "Let me out!"

Sage emerged the winner, first to the office door, her eagerness having superseded her judgment. This was the person responsible for the death of her mother, the one who had started the violence that had them all teetering on the brink of war.

Her eyes met with a haughty glare, condemning as much as they were pleading for Sage to let her go. "You can't do this. Let me out of here!"

THIRTY-THREE

"Rina?" Sage gasped the name in horrified shock. Ava was supposed to have sprung the trap—the woman who'd been nothing but a bitch who'd placed them in danger with seemingly no concern for their wellbeing. Not Rina—she'd been so kind. This had to be a trick.

"It's not what you think," Rina pleaded. Her fist banged against the shimmering barrier Nyx had created.

"How… Why?" Sage could hardly put two words together. Rina had been a cheerleader for ASSET. She had tried to convince Sage to stay and see the good they did. How could she not be one of them?

She wasn't Terra. That was about the only thing clear to Sage.

"You betrayed us all," Sage whispered, as she watched Rina continue to test the barrier, pounding on it with her fist, and then palming it in places, as if searching blindly for a way through. She couldn't see it, nor could she get through it. "Why?"

"You don't understand." Rina's eyes widened as they lifted over Sage's head to the others behind her. "They're murderers. The vampires killed my father. And your mother, too."

A low blow, well struck. The pain of Miranda's loss was still fresh in Sage's mind. But not revenge. Rina, however, looked as if she'd strike at Zack if the barrier weren't in the way. Either her hatred was that strong or she was something stronger. But that didn't make sense. Only Terras were immune to the magic of the seed.

"How is she not one of us?" Sage turned to Grey, hoping he'd have some answers.

"Her father was." Grey shrugged. He didn't look as shocked as Sage felt, but confusion pulled at his brow, creating lines that gave his ageless face a little history. "She had the mark."

"I don't understand." Sage's eyes fell to the leather strap on Rina's wrist. Beneath it, the round canopy of leaves peeked out from the edges of the blue leather. But Zack had said it was false. Ink. Like the tattoos all over her arms. "Why tattoo yourself with our mark?"

"I wanted to be like him." Rina dropped the silver box as her shoulders slumped. "My dad was the most amazing guy. He was the best. An agent. Like your mom, Sage."

Every time someone mentioned Miranda, Sage's heart ached. Pain that passed sadness as it twisted into anger. Her mother wouldn't have died if she'd been able to finish her mission. She'd suspected the stone had been tampered with. She'd given her life to protect it. "Don't you dare mention my mother," Sage snarled.

"I'm sorry. I know it hurts. I miss my dad, too." Rina sounded so genuine. But how could she be?

"Did you know what he was?" Sage's mother had never said a word about being Terra. Her work had been a secret. Sage would have never known of her magical lineage if not for Grey ruining her happy existence with the truth. "Your father was a Terra."

"Dad always told the best stories. And I suspected there was more truth to them than he let on." Rina stared straight at Sage, her eyes pleading for understanding. She spoke as if they were the only two in the room. "He made up the best stories about the great tree." She pointed to her bracelet. "I loved Dad's tattoo. The nobility it represented. The nobility *he* represented by wearing it." Rina sniffled and wiped away the tears forming at the corners of her eyes.

Rina might as well have been telling Sage's story. It rang with so much truth. She had tears welling in her eyes, too. Miranda had often told great bedtime stories about fantastic creatures and dangerous battles between good and evil. Magic was always woven into her tales. And when Sage had whined about the deformity of her birthmark, her mother had tried to make Sage feel that same pride Rina spoke of.

"But those were just fairy tales. Did you actually know what he was?" Sage demanded.

"Not exactly. But I suspected." Rina cleared her throat. "I was always good at drawing, so I made a template of his marking, and had the tattoo done while Dad was away on assignment."

Sage had spent her entire life wanting to wipe away the deformity, covering it up with clothes or makeup. And here Rina was claiming to have proudly added it to her body.

"Dad was furious and made me cover it up. He gave me this." Rina held out her bracelet, the one Sage had thought was a brilliant idea. "He never thought it would cause me any trouble. And he never thought he would get hurt, I guess. But then one day he didn't come back. When they came for me, to tell me about his death, they saw I too bore the mark of the Terras."

Sage watched as Rina wiped the tears from her eyes. She'd seen them before, but hadn't truly paid attention. They weren't turquoise like everyone else's. Hers were more milky and pale, but still a shade of blue. She couldn't have truly been the child of a Terra. Magic passed through their line, just as the mark had passed down from Miranda to Sage. Rina had been adopted, most likely. Maybe even lied to her whole life. The more she learned about Rina, the more sympathy she had. Secrets were the true tragedy, and the reason for nearly all the bad deeds that had been done. Sage nearly opened her mouth to say as much, but Zack spoke before she could.

"A sad story, truly, but none of this makes you any less guilty of mass-murder." Zack's tone held no sympathy.

"How can you stand here and call me a murderer?" Rina demanded. "How many lives have you ended, vampire?"

"None that have brought me as much pleasure as yours will, I can assure you." Zack slammed a fist against the magical barrier. Just as it stopped Rina from escaping, it also prevented anyone else from reaching her. "Remove the magic. I will take my justice now."

"She's not yours yet," Devon's voice boomed with authority. His eyes were on the move, scanning the room, focusing on the doors, and taking extra time at the corners and shadowy places. "Who's with you?"

"Just me," Rina replied, slowly backing away from the edge of the magical barrier.

Zack eyed her like a lion, ready to pounce on its kill. The fangs were out, proving just how deadly his intent was.

But he couldn't take his justice yet. Not that Sage considered murder justice by any stretch of the imagination. There was still a piece of the puzzle missing. They'd given the address to Ava. They'd never spoken aloud where they would be or who their special friend was.

"Why did you come here? Why not go after the vampires again?" Sage asked.

A collective hush fell over the group, as each one of them seemed to be holding their breaths in expectation of what Rina might say next.

"You know as well as I do the weapon had gone missing." Rina took a deep breath, as if steadying her nerves. "Ava had you searching for the stone. When you didn't return after your last meeting with her, I knew you'd found it and were most likely hiding it for safekeeping."

"No one was supposed to know the details about my mission," Grey growled defensively.

Rina ignored him, keeping her eyes on Sage as she spoke. "I told you—assistants know everything."

"And what do you think you know, little girl?" Zack narrowed his eyes, turning that deadly gaze back on his prey.

"I know how the weapon kills vampires," she spat at him.

She would have been dead if not for the barrier protecting her. Zack slammed against it so hard it shook the walls of Devon's office. "You've heard her admit it. She's guilty!"

"She's stupid. That's all I've heard her admit so far," Devon responded with casual curiosity. "So what? Were you hoping to collect an 'atta girl' for retrieving the weapon?"

"It would definitely put me in Ava's good graces if I found it." Rina's tone wavered as her eyes flitted between Zack's feral rage and Devon's calm. "I've been searching ever since I lost it. I saw you pull up Miranda's records in the database. I knew you were on the trail. And then... there was this address in her trash."

"Where does Ava think you are?" Grey asked. "She's on the alert for all her charges these days."

"I'm off duty right now." Rina shrugged. "No one pays attention to my comings and goings."

"You think yourself pretty smart, don't you? I remember a girl who showed little potential when I assessed her for combat," Devon said, scrutinizing Rina's face as if trying to see past another glamour. "Clearly, I was deceived. That doesn't often happen."

"I'm not a fighter," Rina agreed.

"And yet you managed to massacre a vampire coven, how?" Devon asked, coming as close to the magical barrier as he could without touching it.

"The weapon." She gulped, those milky blue eyes widening with fear. Between the vampire threatening her death and the ogre who could pummel her into oblivion, she had to know how dangerous a position she was in. "I was able to hold it." Her voice trembled, but she continued. "But anyone I showed it to became very weak. I knew immediately that it could be used to avenge my father."

"You took it into a vampire den." Zack's muscles twitched as if wanting to reach out and throttle her, but his hands remained at his side.

"Before I learned about the seed, I had begged Ava to let me go on a mission. I didn't know I wasn't truly one of you guys at that point. I was so eager to do my part for ASSET—fight the good fight, as my father had always done. The mission was supposed to be a show of force to stop one of the covens from killing and leaving their," she nearly retched as she said the word, "victims."

"We don't judge," Grey said. "We do what is necessary to protect the magical community."

"Those vampires are the reason my father was killed. He was a victim once." Her voice soured as she found the strength to rise above the sorrow she'd given into moments before. "I thought we were going to stop them. But no! We were negotiating terms with them. After that meeting, I was disgusted. But what could I do?" She huffed and lifted her hand, holding the tiny garnet between her fingers. "Keeping peace with killers and protecting magical law trumped the life of my father, just as it trumps the lives of countless people who die because of those stinking leeches."

"You idiot." Grey shouted. "If that's what you truly believe, you've failed to understand our place in the world. Every day we lay down our lives to keep the peace. It's not simple, nor is it pretty, but we do what we must to avoid another magical war from erupting."

"Vampires kill people! How can we let that happen?" Rina shot back at him just as angrily.

Zack clucked his tongue. The quiet disapproval pulled more interest to him than any shouting he might have added to the already raised voices. "When your diet consists of only one thing, how can you call someone evil for sustaining themselves?"

"Murder is evil!" Rina replied.

"When you eat meat, is that not murder?" Zack scoffed. "Perspective is necessary when dealing with those who are different than you."

"My father wasn't a cow." Rina's anger did not abate.

"If your father had been turned dark, I can assure you it was because he was doing things that fell outside the realm of ASSET's rules." Zack's voice had a deadly edge to the deceptively calm tone. "Those negotiations you hate so much, mean a lot to my people. We don't act against ASSET unless provoked."

"I don't believe that for a second." Rina's voice sharpened. "My father was a hero. He deserved to be avenged. And then the weapon came through our office. And once I saw what happened to Hukkel… I knew it could be used to stop the vampires from killing."

"That's murder!" Zack whipped his finger at her.

"No. That's justice." She glared at him accusingly. "I was told Terras were noble and proud—the Mother's answer to the horrors brought on by magic."

"You have yet to see the horror magic can bring," Zack threatened.

"Enough!" Devon silenced the vampire with his booming voice. "Where is the weapon now?"

"When I got back, I thought I had put everything away without being seen, but then the next day, the seed went missing. Records were locked. And... the vampires retaliated. Agents were sent out and never came back. It's been going on ever since." Rina crumpled to the ground. "I never meant for that."

"You started a chain reaction of events that could have brought back the wars of old," Grey snarled. "All because you wanted revenge."

"I wanted to be one of you." Disappointment echoed in Rina's voice.

Sage understood better than anyone else in the room how dubious the nature of ASSET was. Human law and magical law being held to different standards. If given the opportunity, Sage would have avenged her mother's death. But revenge wasn't the answer. Rina's need for vengeance had already racked up a sizeable death count from both innocent and guilty parties alike, her mother included.

"You're not Terra!" Grey shot back at Rina.

"No, I'm not, thank the gods. You people are nothing like the stories say. You don't fight against atrocities of magic. You only throw a cloak over the ugly parts, so people are left unaware." Rina found her feet again. Her eyes were bloodshot from crying. She held up the garnet Devon had set as bait.

"And if this were real, I'd use it to remove the magic from all of you."

"Magic is not evil," Sage found herself saying, before she'd even committed to the thought.

"Really?" Rina's eyes narrowed on Sage. "You have been wronged by every person in this room. Your own mother, I bet, didn't even tell you what you were. Secrecy is wrong. Condemning you to a life you did not choose is wrong."

"She didn't condemn me to anything," Sage said. "She died fighting a battle you started."

Rina's contempt didn't falter. "He tricked you." She pointed at Grey. "He drank your blood." Her finger moved to Zack. "He filled your head with false prophecy." Her finger landed on Devon. "Everyone in this room has wronged you…"

"Including you." Sage finished the sentence for her.

"Magic has wronged us all, Sage. I was trying to fix the wrong done to me. The wrong done to innocent people who are murdered at the hands of those vampires. Like my father." She had no more tears. Her voice cracked as she spoke. "I believed in what my father did. I believed all the stories. My father was the knight in shining armor, the great defender of peace between the races of magic." She sniffled and wiped her face. "But the truth is, he wasn't even my father, and he did little more than turn a blind eye to murder. And what did he get for his trouble? Death."

"I've heard enough." Zack's hungry eyes were locked on Rina's puffy face. "She's admitted her crimes. I claim justice."

"She's not Terra!" Devon said loudly.

"She'll bleed just the same." Zack licked his lips before sending a smirking glance at Grey. "I'll make sure her body is properly disposed of, so as to not cause any more problems with ASSET regulations."

This wasn't how it needed to end. As angry as she was at Rina, death at the fangs of a vampire didn't feel right. Sage cringed, remembering how painful those teeth could be, and searched for something to say to stop it from happening. "We don't have jurisdiction." Whether it was true or not didn't matter, her words stopped Zack and Devon from coming to blows.

A knock at the open door added further distraction.

Ava Masters stood in the threshold, suited up and ready for action. "Oh good, I'd hoped to see everyone here." Her domineering tone bordered on cocky.

"You shouldn't be here," Devon replied to her.

"You think you have the market cornered on deception?" Ava shot back at him. Hands on her hips, she stared at them like naughty little children. "Grey, your information was an easy lie to uncover, but I commend you for the effort. Did you really suspect me?"

Grey shrugged. "If not you, someone in your inner circle."

"Yes," she scoffed, her eyes moving from one face to another. "I've been looking into that myself. When I saw little Rina here sneaking away, I hoped my suspicions were unfounded. But look where I found her." Ava pushed past the group and came face to face with her assistant, who was crying again. "It's time she came in for questioning."

"She's already admitted her guilt," Sage offered.

"Signed, sealed, and delivered. Excellent work. I have three agents and a transport vehicle waiting in the parking lot." Ava cracked a wicked smile. "And as for you lot"—her gaze turned to Sage—"let it be known the weapon has been retrieved." She spoke the words louder than was necessary. Sage wondered if her intent was to ensure that anyone lurking in the shadows might hear her, too. "It is currently under armed transport to its final destination in Germany. So we can be done with all the posturing and threats."

Sage's hand nearly flew to the necklace, but she stopped herself from revealing even through body language that Ava was lying.

"I wasn't told this," Zack growled angrily. He'd been so close to a meal, only to be denied at the last second. Sage was all too glad to not have to witness it. "I'm here as the representative for my people," he said furiously. "I demand justice."

"It will be given. Publicly," Ava countered, with just as much domination in her voice. "I've called for an emergency meeting of the magical councils in this city, and Rina will be placed on trial for her crimes, with punishment to be doled out at their discretion."

"More tricks to protect your people's mistakes. We have the guilty party. Justice will be dealt with now." Zack had never looked so deadly.

Ava rose up to her full height and stared him down like an alpha wolf. "It must be done publicly. That is the only way we can return to peace. This war must not happen. You all know the cost is too high for any of us to pay."

Devon picked up a wrapped bundle made of dried leaves and twine, and lit the end of it. As it began to smoke, Sage watched the magical barrier shimmer. As if burning its magic out, it grew brighter until it shattered into a glittering shower.

Rina stood for a moment as if she had seen what happened, although being human, she couldn't have. Sage scrutinized her expression and then turned back to Devon.

"If that is the will of ASSET, we can do nothing but allow this to happen," Devon agreed respectfully. He made one final pass with the smoking stick and then snuffed it out in a bowl on the desk next to Rina.

Zack looked murderous. He'd been eager for revenge, and in one fell swoop, Ava had robbed him of it. But to his credit, he did not make a move toward Rina as Devon worked to unravel the magic imprisoning her.

Grey wasn't taking any chances. His eyes were riveted on the vampire as he gripped the handle of his machete, ready to strike.

Moment of truth time. If Zack wanted to, he could have Rina's throat in a heartbeat. But he'd be stupid to try. Either Grey or Devon would end him with little more than a nod from Ava. Bloodshed was the last thing Sage wanted to see. As angry as she was at Rina, vengeance was what had started this. Only justice would bring peace.

Her heart thrummed as she watched Zack, hoping he'd let them take Rina into custody. It was better to slink away and lick his wounds than to die a pointless death demanding his satisfaction.

A hand slithered down Sage's leg. Before she could react, Rina had lifted one of the knives from her belt, and the blade found her neck.

The sharp edge stung her neck, opening up a hairline slit in her skin as she gulped.

"I will not be murdered to please your bloodlust!" Rina found her voice loud and clear. She had both arms wrapped around Sage's neck, hugging her, making the knife press even deeper against Sage's skin.

"You don't want to do this, Rina," Devon cautioned.

"You're planning to murder me. What's my play here?" Rina shrieked like a madwoman, clearly at the end of her rope. "Everyone better back away nice and slowly, or Sage here will be the last of her line."

For a moment, no one moved. They stared at the pair, their eyes moving from Sage to Rina and back again, as if judging whether they should cooperate. Ava's eyes didn't quite meet Sage's. She looked at her, but her gaze was lower, as if searching for something beyond the knife at her throat.

Devon was the first to hold his hands up and take a non-threatening step away from Rina. "You want to be a hero?" he asked. "You gotta earn that cape."

"I tried being a hero," Rina spat back at him.

But he hadn't been talking to her. Sage remembered Devon's promise to make her a cape when she'd proven herself. She needed to remember all the training sessions and find a way to get the knife away from her throat.

"You see what happens when you deny swift justice?" Zack gnashed his teeth and turned to Ava. "How many more innocent deaths will be on your head?"

Ava's scrutinizing gaze remained on Sage, perhaps calculating the cost of another life to bring her assistant in for trial. Sage prayed she'd not have to pay that price, but between Rina's grip and the bite of the blade at her neck, the situation seemed grim.

Zack backed away, following Devon's lead. "My people will be told what happened here tonight."

"See that they are well informed. This isn't over," Ava agreed. "Your people will have justice." She inched back one-step at a time, her eyes still locked on the pair. "Grey, come on. Let Rina have some space."

Grey was the last to move, looking more reluctant that the rest. He was the only one to look Rina in the eyes as he backed away. "You had other options. Why take this one?"

"You left me only one choice." The tremble in her arms proved Rina wasn't a fighter. But desperation made people do crazy things, and all it would take was a flick of her wrist to open Sage's throat.

"Not killing me would be a very good option," Sage said as calmly as she could, though her heart was thundering loud enough to echo in her ears.

"We do what we have to do," Rina said, but rather than loosen her grip when the room cleared, she pressed even harder. "It's not personal."

"Never *is* personal." Her throat burned as the knife's blade ripped at her neck. There would be no talking sense into the girl. All hopes for a peaceful way to avoid death trickled down her neck in a warm stream of blood. Sage sighed, knowing what she had to do. She moved quickly, lifting her hands up before Rina could react. Both her hands tightly gripped Rina's forearm and pulled sharply away from her neck. She tilted her shoulder hard at the same time, creating enough of a window between the weapon arm and her body to slip her head away.

Rina struggled to keep a hold of the knife, but Sage refused to let go of her forearm. She twisted free and let the tension of Rina's arm do the rest of the job.

As sharp as it was, the knife sliced through her skin like butter. A moment of silence passed between them as realization struck a split second before the gasp of pain. Blood bloomed out from Rina's chest.

This wasn't how it was meant to end. Sage reached out to steady her, but she was too slow. Rina crumpled to the ground with a silent moan. Blood stained her shirt as she futilely pawed at the dagger sheathed three inches into her chest. It was buried so deeply there would be no removing it. And doing so would only kill her quicker.

Sage fell to her knees next to Rina. "You left me no choice."

Rina gathered her breath and replied, "Better I die… this way than fall victim to… a vampire."

Sage should have felt satisfied. She'd avenged her mother, but as she held Rina dying in her arms, all she could do was weep. She could neither hate her nor love Rina for what she had done. Secrets and manipulation had twisted noble intentions into evil deeds. If not Rina, someone else might have taken up arms, feeling they were working for justice. How many more *Rinas* were out there? Sage could have easily fallen into the same trap. Thankfully, she was a true Terra, and the weapon that had started it all was useless in her hands. She vowed then and there to never let it out of her sight. She'd take the secret of its location to her grave. No one should wield such power, no matter their intentions.

THIRTY-FOUR

Ava gave orders to her agents to remove the body. She spoke with Grey, commending him for keeping a close eye on Sage. She even sounded kindly when discussing the upcoming meeting with Zack. Sage had never seen the diplomatic side of Ava. She was scary good at it.

One by one, people were talked to and sent away. When only Sage remained, Ava zeroed in on her with all the swiftness of a predator. Confidence sparkled in her eyes. Something else too, but Sage wouldn't go as far as to say pride. Though they had pulled victory from the jaws of defeat. "You and I share a secret now."

Sage looked around the empty office, making sure that they were alone before answering. "I don't know what—"

Ava clucked her tongue at Sage and waggled her finger. "Mark assured me you were smarter than that."

She knew. Sage's eyes widened as she sucked in a breath. *How long has she known?* The question burned on her lips, but she didn't ask it.

Ava pointed her waggling finger at Sage's chest. "The price of peace is often higher than we are willing to pay. But it must be paid. For that, I am truly sorry."

Miranda had sacrificed too much for peace. Sage wasn't sure she had it in her to pay the same price. "My mother—"

"Was truly a noble woman," Ava added with a note of reverence. "She may not ever have a plaque to commemorate her courage, but those of us who keep the truth will always honor her memory. She was the best of us."

"Thank you for saying that." Sage fought the tears. She'd cried too much already.

"No matter what you decide to do with your future, you must always bear the burden of that secret." Ava's tone turned serious. "I need your word on that."

Sage reached for her mother's necklace. Buried beneath her shirt, the silver had warmed to the temperature of her skin. She fingered the outline of the tree pendant. "My Mom told me to keep this close and I would always feel her presence."

"Of that, I have no doubt. And I will take that as your solemn oath."

Sage nodded. She would keep it close and guard its secret. In her hands, it was little more than a trinket, its power neutralized. And with no one the wiser about its location, it was safe from the destructive forces of its tempting justice.

"You have a choice now, one I feel you need some time to consider." Ava placed a hand on Sage's shoulder. She took a breath, pausing as if struggling with the right words. For a woman who wore her power like a second skin and strutted around with unchecked confidence, Ava's hesitation spoke more truth than the words coming from her mouth. "Go home. Think about your future. And if you feel I have earned your trust, come back, become an agent, and work with me at ASSET."

"It's hard to know who to trust, with all the lies and manipulation I've dealt with so far," Sage said calmly. The offer sounded genuine, and she would go home and think.

"You'll learn. Trust comes from actions, not ass kissing. Those you can truly trust might anger you at times, but they'll always have your back, no matter the cost." Ava's hand fell from Sage's shoulder as Sage remembered her mother's final words.

When the time comes, you'll understand why I had to remain silent. But know that I have never once left you vulnerable, and even in my absence, I have thought of your protection.

Her mother had surrounded her with the best ASSET had to offer. Mark understood what needed to be done. He had sent her to Ava, who ordered Grey to be her shadow. And despite all her efforts to shake him, Grey had not left her side. Faithful to his mission, despite his obvious dislike of Sage. Even placed in the path of Zack and Devon, Sage had been surrounded by people who would not harm her. It had been manipulation of the worst kind, but done out of respect for the sacrifice her mother had made.

Sage wasn't sure how long she'd been standing there stupidly staring off into space. When she blinked back to reality, she found Ava staring at her—arms crossed—as if waiting for a reply.

"Thank you," Sage mumbled, still not able to make the commitment Ava clearly wanted.

"When you're ready to take the oath, I'll see you in my office." Ava wore the satisfied grin of a woman who'd just gotten what she wanted. "Until then…. Dismissed."

About the Author

Katie Salidas is a best-selling author known for her unique genre-bending style.

Host of the Indie YouTube Talk show, Spilling Ink, nerd, Doctor Who fangirl, Las Vegas Native, and SuperMom to three awesome kids, Katie gives new meaning to the term sleep-deprived.

Since 2010, she's penned many bestselling book series including: the Immortalis, Olde Town Pack, Little Werewolf, Agents of A.S.S.E.T., and the RONE award-winning Chronicles of the Uprising. And as her not-so-secret alter ego, Rozlyn Sparks, she is a USA Today bestselling author of romance with a naughty side.

Facebook
http.//www.facebook.com/pages/Katie-Salidas-Author/214780936916

Web
http.//www.katiesalidas.com/

Spilling Ink
https.//www.youtube.com/c/spillinginkshow

Rising Sign Books
https://www.risingsignbooks.com/

Find My Books
https://books2read.com/ap/RJj4GR/Katie-Salidas

OTHER TITLES BY KATIE SALIDAS

Chronicles of the Uprising
Dissension
Complication
Revolution
Transition
Retribution
Annihilation

Little Werewolf
Pretty Little Werewolf
Curious Little Werewolf
Fearless Little Werewolf

Immortalis
Carpe Noctem
Hunters & Prey
Pandora's Box
Soustone
Dark Salvation

Olde Town Pack
Moonlight
Mated
Being Alpha

Running From the Devil
Beneath
Between
Beyond

Non Fiction
Go Publish Yourself!
Write (and Edit) the Damn Book
Acknowledge & Heal (A Woman's Guide to PTSD)

Your Opinion Matters!

When people first look at a book, beyond the description and the cover, they pay close attention to what others **like you** have to say.

If the book is getting overwhelmingly good or bad reviews, it can weigh heavily on that reader's decision whether or not to click that purchase button.

It does not have to be a book report.
It does not have to be five stars. I would never ask for any special favoritism.

A book review is simply sharing what you thought of the book. It answers two very simple questions.

Did you like it?
Would you recommend it to someone else?

That's it. Your opinion matters. Most importantly to me, because I want to be sure you are enjoying the books I write. But beyond my hope for your satisfaction, the review you write caries great weight in the publishing realm as well. It can quite literally make or break a book.

So, here I am, groveling at your feet.
If you have read one (or more) of my books, would you do me the greatest of honors and leave a review?

www.ingramcontent.com/pod-product-compliance
Lightning Source LLC
Chambersburg PA
CBHW031647100726
47898CB00006B/2012